Kate Alexander is the pseudonym of a highly successful author of romantic novels and short stories published on both sides of the Atlantic. Born and educated in Surrey, she trained as a secretary and worked overseas for the World Health Organisation in Geneva as well as for a foundation for the preservation of the history of Western Canada. Currently she is employed as a personnel officer in London.

Her hobbies are long-distance walking, the theatre, and archaeology – in which she takes what she calls an ignorant but keen interest. She is presently at work on another novel.

Kate Alexander

Fields of Battle

Futura
Macdonald & Co
London & Sydney

A Futura Book

First published in Great Britain in 1981 by
Macdonald & Co (Publishers) Ltd,
London & Sydney

First Futura edition 1982

ISBN 0 7088 2154 5

Reproduced, printed and bound in Great Britain by
Hazell Watson & Viney Ltd, Aylesbury, Bucks

Futura Publications
A Division of
Macdonald & Co (Publishers) Ltd
Maxwell House
74 Worship Street
London EC2A 2EN

Chapter 1

On a bleak day at the beginning of December 1939 a small group of people waited in the church of St. Luke's, Barbury, to witness the marriage of Rilla Gray to Barnaby Wainwright. Even at two o'clock in the afternoon the church was cold and full of shadows. The footsteps of two newcomers echoed as they walked down the aisle; the whispered greeting of the bride's aunt to her sister, the bride's mother, rasped into the silence. There was no organ, no choir, no flowers to decorate the bare walls. It was a very quiet wedding.

The bride's mother merely nodded without speaking as her sister settled down into the pew behind her. She was a woman in her early forties, grown not so much stout as shapeless with the passing years, her body confined by a strong corset, her feet crammed into shoes which were already beginning to hurt, her brown hair, streaked with grey, arranged in rigid waves under a new hat which had been an extravagance at three shillings and eleven pence. Her electric-blue marocain dress was not really warm enough for a winter's day, but it had only been worn twice before and, what with a war on and all the expense of a new outfit for Rilla, Edith Gray had not felt justified in spending any extra money on herself. She sat staring straight ahead, her face flushed, her lips compressed, her hands clasped tightly together in her lap, and her second daughter, Joyce, sitting next to her, glanced at her and thought to herself that Mum was in a proper state about this wedding.

Joyce was a thin, bony girl of thirteen, who had not been taken into anyone's confidence about the reasons for her sister's hurried marriage, but who nevertheless was fully aware of the necessity for haste. She rubbed one cold hand over the other and wondered whether she should put her gloves back on, but they were knitted gloves of brown wool and not very smart, so she just pulled the sleeves of her coat down further over her wrists. She was beginning to grow out of that coat. She had suddenly begun to get tall and she wondered hopefully whether she would also become good-looking, like Rilla. She caught the vicar's eye and gave him a tentative smile and he smiled back, vaguely aware that he knew her. One of the Gray girls had been a Girl Guide, and it must be this one in the pew. His acquaintance with the family was slight, since the Grays were not regular church-goers, but he knew enough about them to be just a little surprised that one of the daughters should be marrying a young man so obviously of a different social standing.

On the other side of the aisle the bridegroom, Barney Wainwright, sat with his brother, Daniel, the best man. A fine-looking young man, tall, dark-haired and dark-eyed, and he wore the uniform of a second lieutenant with a dashing air. He had called on the vicar to make arrangements for the wedding ceremony and Mr Lovelace had been struck by his easy, unconscious arrogance, as well as by his considerable good looks. A touch of bravado about him on that occasion perhaps, had roused the vicar's suspicions about this hurried marriage by special licence and today, looking at the empty church and observing the lack of communication between the two sides of the aisle, he knew his guess had been correct. He sighed inwardly. The war was only three months old and this was not the last such match he would solemnize before it was over.

Barnaby Wainwright seemed more subdued today, sitting with his dark head bent, looking down at his clasped hands, and the vicar had few illusions about the nature of his thoughts. His brother had picked up the Book of Common Prayer from the ledge in front of him and was turning over the pages. Barney glanced at him and then looked away again. The brother appeared to be some years older than the young army officer. He, too, was tall and dark, but he was thinner than Barney and something about his face made the vicar look at him more closely. A look of suffering, resolutely borne. An interesting man, with an air of distinction about him. A person he would like to know better.

The little bride, when she arrived, clinging to her father's arm, looked terrified. They hesitated in the open doorway and the candle flames on the altar flickered in the sudden draught. The vicar stepped forward. The bridegroom had to be nudged to get him to his feet.

Len Gray, in his best navy-blue suit, with a white carnation and a spray of maidenhair fern pinned to his lapel, gave Rilla's arm a squeeze, but he was too inarticulate to do more than ask in a low voice: 'All right, pet?'

She nodded without looking at him and they started down the aisle.

Rilla was having one of her plain days. Sleepless nights and anxious tears had taken their toll. Even her eyes, always her best feature, were spoilt by a suspicious puffiness. She cast a piteous look at Barney as she reached his side, but he was looking straight ahead and did not see it. It was only when he took her hand in his and found it icy cold that he turned his head to look at her and saw her distress. A faint warmth showed on his face and he made his responses in a firm voice which seemed to reassure her a little. Nothing about him at that moment betrayed his feeling of disbelief that this could possibly be happening to him.

Up to this point in his life Barnaby Wainwright had been a singularly fortunate young man. He was noticeably good-looking, although there was still a touch of immaturity about his face; he would be even more striking in a year or two when age and experience had fined him down. He was dark, with thick brown hair which he had difficulty in keeping under control, and eyes which could sparkle like the brown waters of a trout stream in sunlight when he was interested or amused or excited, but which could darken menacingly if his mood changed. One of the few faults in his features were his eyebrows, which were a little too heavy for his face. This could give him a threatening look when he was displeased—'Barney peering out from under a thundercloud' was how one of his irreverent school friends had described it.

He excelled at all sports, and took it for granted that he should do so, which had called down the caustic comment from his former sports master that just because he was good there was no reason why he should not be better, if only he would put in the proper practice. It was breath wasted; Barney trained to a sufficient pitch to remain on top of the opposition and refused to interest himself in taking his skill any further, on the grounds that he only played games and ran and swam because he enjoyed the sport and he had no intention of becoming 'a damned professional.' It was generally felt to be unfair that he should also be intelligent. Again there were regretful sighs because he would not apply himself seriously, but when he dropped rowing in his final year at Cambridge and concentrated on his books he succeeded in taking a respectable degree.

He had felt he deserved a holiday after this and had accepted an invitation to join some friends in the south of France for the whole of the summer, until it had suddenly been borne in on them that while they had been lazing the golden days away the war which had been hanging over their heads for so long was about to start. In a fever of enthusiasm, Barney had returned to England, offered himself to the county regiment in which his father had once served, had been accepted, rushed into uniform, and then disconcertingly discovered that the battle for which he was champing at the bit showed no signs of commencing.

It was something new for Barney to find himself living in conditions which were neither comfortable nor congenial. He had endured the trials of communal life while he was at school, but at Cambridge he had contrived to make himself very comfortable, while his friends' villa in the south of France had been the height of civilized luxury. He laughed at himself for becoming soft, but that did not stop him finding the restrictions on his freedom and the spartan living conditions irksome in the extreme, lacking the incentive of danger to justify the hardship.

His colonel, who had known his father, cast an aloof but knowing eye over his new young officers and summed him up accurately.

'A resty youngster, high-spirited, high-bred; needs a firm hand on the reins, which I think he's lacked, having lost his father at an early age. Reminds me of a racehorse I once had a share in. Splendid creature; went like the wind over the gallops; trouble was, once we got him to the racecourse there was no holding him. Sound of the crowd, sight of the starting gate, and he went plunging all over the place, mad with excitement, fretting to be away—wore himself out before the off. Same with young Wainwright. Got the scent of gunpowder in his nostrils, wants to get into the fight. No use telling him he's still got a lot to learn, thinks he knows it all. Sit on him, sit on him hard. Keep him busy. Don't leave him with too much time to *think*. He's got more brains than most of our new intake; could end up being quite useful.'

The iron discipline that resulted from this advice bore hard on Barney, who considered himself a responsible adult able to make decisions for himself. He accepted it as a part of army life, without fully believing in the necessity for instant obedience rather than reasoned argument, and gritted his teeth when he was told that he would see things differently when he had actually been in action, feeling that he was being patronized by his more experienced colleagues.

He was missing, too, the attentions of the delightful Frenchwoman who had acquired him as a lover within a day or two of his arrival on the Côte d'Azur. Barney had believed himself to be adequate in this, as in all other aspects of his life, but Yvette Gallimard had completed his education and he had taken whole-hearted advantage of the situation, while secretly considering her a little old. He was not entirely sorry to have had an excuse to make a graceful departure. She had shown signs of becoming demanding. Barney did not like possessive women, and disposed of them with a ruthlessness that was masked by his undoubted charm.

His mother was partly to blame for his dislike of being tied down. She had indulged him as a child and continued to do so as he grew older, but in return she had expected a devotion which was not quite reasonable. Barney's father had died when he was fifteen and this had caused Winifred Wainwright to cling to her younger son. His older brother had been on the other side of the world and impossible to reach at the time of his father's death. It had been Barney, with unexpected maturity, who had supported his mother through the last difficult days of his father's illness. By the time Dan was located, the funeral was over.

It was something Mrs Wainwright could not forget, Barney had always been her favourite child, while Dan, who had shown an obstinate independence at an early age, was far more sympathetically attuned to his father. After her husband's death, with the management of her affairs in her own hands, Winifred Wainwright had not hesitated to grant favours to Barney which Dan had been forced to earn for himself. She boasted how close they were, unaware that Barney no longer considered himself her little boy, until she suddenly realized that Barney, while still appearing to fall in with her wishes, had quietly severed the apron strings and was going his own way. His departure for the south of France, when she had wanted him to accompany her to Cornwall, had been a case in point. His decision to join the army, when she had wanted him to wait to be mobilized, was another. She put a good face on it, but she had not reconciled herself to his independence and each time he reached a decision which was not in accordance with her wishes she experienced a tiny, but very unpleasant, shock.

It was amazing, people said, that he was not completely spoilt. Only his brother Dan's eyebrows rose slightly when he heard this comment made, but then Dan was one of the few people who could see any fault in Barney. He was ten years older and had survived some hard knocks in his own life. His belief was that young Barney would be all the better for a few setbacks and disappointments. It was true that Barney did not appear conceited, that he deprecated his successes with a pleasing modesty, that he had good manners and could charm the birds off the trees, but Dan had an uneasy feeling that all this arose from an inward belief in his own superiority, so deeply rooted that he himself was unaware of it. It was just a fact of his life: he was better at most things than other people; what he wanted he could have, because he was Barney Wainwright and it had always been that way. Dan had applauded his decision to go straight into the army, but not only out of patriotism; in Dan's opinion, the army might be the making of Barney.

For all that, he could not help reflecting as he watched his brother marrying Rilla Gray that this was not the method he would have chosen for improving his brother's character. What on earth had Barney found to attract him in this unhappy little elf? He got a partial answer as Barney slipped the ring over Rilla's finger. She lifted her head and smiled for the first time and Dan blinked at the transformation caused by this sudden radiance. For just one moment she had been beautiful; not pretty, but beautiful. Perhaps there was more to her than was apparent at first sight.

Barnaby Wainwright and Rilla Gray had met in September 1939, only three weeks after German troops had marched into Czechoslovakia and Britain and France had declared war. Since the air raids everyone had predicted had not, in fact, materialized, places of amusement were beginning to open their doors again and Rilla had been preparing for a visit to one of the local cinemas with her friend, Dinah Gloster, at about the same time as Barney had allowed one of his fellow officers to talk him into driving into Barbury in search of amusement. He was not sure that he wanted to go, not sure that he particularly wanted to spend an evening with Martin Marshall, but neither was he sure what else he would do if he did not go with Martin. And so, bored and restless, he got out his car and went along to see what Barbury could provide in the way of entertainment.

Rilla took time over her preparations for the evening out, not for any particular reason, except that Dinah always looked smart and she knew that she did not shine by comparison. She had been considered a plain child, always a little too thin, no matter how many milk puddings her mother forced her to eat, with eyes that were too big for her face and hair that was inclined to straggle. But once she had entered her eighteenth year she had begun to improve in appearance. Her angular body had rounded into a beautifully proportioned young figure; her skin was creamy instead of sallow, with a delicate flush of pink on her high cheek bones; and her hair, anxiously tended as soon as she had realized that she was no longer the scrawny little girl who was such a poor advertisement for Mrs Gray's good cooking, had begun to take on a shine that reminded Rilla of her mother's mahogany sideboard. She still did not admire her looks, but she was humbly grateful that she was no longer quite such an ugly duckling. In fact, there were times when Rilla dared to believe that she was almost pretty. Her eyes were her best feature, enormous, dark grey, fringed with long silky lashes, and unusually expressive. Rilla's eyes betrayed her every thought. They had overshadowed her face in childhood, but now that she had 'plumped out a bit,' as her mother put it, they no longer seemed disproportionately large, although she could still disconcert people by the wounded look they could assume at the hint of an unkind word. She was too sensitive, according to Mrs Gray. The truth was, she found it difficult to fathom Rilla. The child had always been the quiet one of the family, reserved where her younger sister was an extrovert, and 'finicky in her ways,' said Mrs Gray, torn between pride at her elder daughter's refinement and exasperation because she did not entirely understand it.

As Rilla stood in front of the looking glass that September evening, dreamily combing her hair, her father's newspaper rustled ominously from the far side of the kitchen.

'How much longer you going to stand there?' Len Gray demanded. 'It beats me why you girls can't do your hair upstairs.'

'The light's better here,' Rilla said.

'It may be better for you, but I can't see to read the paper,' Len grumbled. 'Hairs all over the kitchen, too, it's not right.'

It was an old argument and they went through the ritual of protest and reply more as a matter of form than conviction, but Edith Gray, coming in from the scullery where she had been doing the washing up, said, 'That's enough, Rilla. You're as beautiful as you're ever going to be, no matter how long you comb your hair. Get out of your Dad's light.'

'You ought to have a perm,' Joyce Gray said, looking up from the homework she was doing on the end of the kitchen table.

'I don't like the feel of my hair when it's been permed,' Rilla said. 'And it only goes fuzzy. My hair's too fine.'

'Rilla's got very pretty hair and as long as she's got that bit of a wave in it there's no sense in her paying to have it mucked up with a lot of chemicals,' Mrs Gray said.

She looked fondly but critically at her elder daughter. The blue and white flowered cotton frock she and Rilla had made between them had been a success, and she was pleased with it. It was surprising how much Rilla had improved lately. Nearly eighteen. Spreading her wings. Edith's thoughts hovered for a moment over the dangers and temptations open to a pretty young girl.

'Where're you off to this evening?' she asked.

'Going to the pictures with Dinah,' Rilla answered. 'The Adelphi, I think.'

Mrs Gray sniffed. 'She's a fast piece, that Dinah. Don't go letting her lead you into any mischief.'

'Oh, Mum!'

Len looked up from the racing results. 'You be home by ten or I'll want to know the reason why.'

'But Dad, we may have to queue, and the big picture doesn't end till ten.'

'Half past ten,' Len conceded. 'If you're not home by then you won't go out again for a week. I don't like you girls walking about the streets in the black-out.'

'If she gets picked up in the black-out, he'll drop her under the first lamp,' Joyce remarked.

'That's enough from you, miss,' Edith put in quickly. 'Get on with your homework.'

'It's daft, doing homework when the school's closed,' Joyce grumbled.

'Daft or not, you'll do it and take it round to the school like you've been told. That'll mean you won't be quite so far behind when the schools are opened again. And when you've finished your homework I've left the tea things on the draining board for you to wipe up.' She turned back to Rilla. 'Have you got your torch?'

'Yes.'

'And your gas mask?'

'Oh, Mum, do I have to take that?'

'Yes, you do.'

'It's so ugly,' Rilla murmured, picking up the square cardboard box and eyeing it distastefully.

'Buy yourself a cover for it. They've got some nice ones in Wanford's.'

'If you go round to Dinah's without it, Mr Gloster will only send you back,' Joyce pointed out. 'He's ever so strict since he's been made an air raid warden.'

Len Gray's paper rustled again. 'Bill Gloster!' he said. 'His little armband's gone to his head, if you ask me. Gawd 'elp us if he's the only warden around when the air raids start.'

'I don't think they're going to start,' Rilla said indifferently. 'It's been three weeks now and nothing's happened. They're saying at work Hitler's got cold feet, he never really expected us to go to war. Do you think I ought to take my cardigan, Mum?'

'I would if I was you, you'll feel it chilly by the time you come out, after the stuffy atmosphere inside.'

Rilla ran up the stairs to fetch the blue woollen cardigan she had knitted herself to match her frock, and Edith said to Len: 'Are you going out this evening?'

'Might walk down to the Crown. Coming with me?'

'If I do it'll be one pint and then home. I'm not sitting in the pub all evening and I'm not waiting for hours while you finish a game of darts.'

'What about Joyce?'

Edith waited until Rilla came clattering downstairs again and then she said, 'Dad and I are going out for an hour. If I give you the money will you take Joyce to the pictures with you?'

Out in the scullery, Joyce paused with an unwiped plate and the teacloth in her hand to listen for the answer. When she sensed her sister's hesitation she called out, 'They won't want me, I bet. Prob'ly got a couple of boys waiting for them up the road.'

Len looked up again. 'Is that right? Because if it is . . .'

'No, it isn't!' Rilla interrupted him, her face a furious pink. 'And even if it was, what harm would there be? I'm nearly eighteen, Dad.'

'I'm sure I'd be pleased if you found a nice boy-friend,' Edith said. 'And so would your Dad. I just hope it would be someone who'd call for you in a proper fashion, not meet you in the street.'

'I don't want to go to the pictures,' Joyce said. 'When you go for Dinah, ask Norma if she'll come round and listen to the wireless with me. That's O.K., isn't it, Mum?'

'Just so long as you're not left on your own,' her mother agreed.

Rilla draped her cardigan over her arm, slung her gas mask over her shoulder, picked up her handbag and escaped.

The Glosters lived only three doors away. Rilla went round to the back door, knocked on the glass panel, then opened the door and walked in. It was a larger house than the Grays', and needed to be, since Dinah was the eldest of a family of eight. Rilla glanced round the kitchen and, not for the first time, compared it unfavourably with her own home. They might comb their hair in the kitchen, but Edith Gray was a better housekeeper than her neighbour, and even if she had been saddled with eight children would never have allowed herself to slide into a state that came dangerously near to squalor.

Mrs Gloster was seated in a low chair, suckling the latest of her brood. Rilla averted her eyes from the large pale breast she exposed.

'Good evening, Mrs Gloster,' she said. 'Is Dinah ready?'

'She's still upstairs. I'd go and hurry her up if I was you, duck.'

Thankfully, Rilla edged past the dirty nappy steaming gently on the floor and went up to the bedroom Dinah shared with two of her sisters, both of whom were sitting on one of the beds watching Dinah get ready to go out. She was a few months older than Rilla and had been working for much longer, having gone into training with a hairdresser as soon as she was fourteen. Rilla had gone on to a commercial school and had only been employed, as a very junior shorthand typist in an insurance company, for the last six months. Dinah considered herself infinitely more sophisticated than Rilla and the two girls remained 'friends' more out of habit than because of any real affinity between them. Rilla was conscious that Dinah thought her slow while she herself shrank from a certain coarseness in the other girl, even while she followed her lead. The truth was, and deep down inside herself Rilla knew it, that she went about with Dinah because of her ability to attract male attention, which was something Rilla had not been very successful at doing on her own. Her quiet, understated looks were not the sort to stand out in a crowd and she had none of the obvious appeal that radiated from Dinah Gloster.

Dinah's hair had been a mousy brown when she had been at school with Rilla, but after a few weeks at Maison Julie she had become a radiant peroxide blonde. Her shoes sported higher heels than Rilla's white sandals, her black barathea skirt was tight over her round little bottom, her frilly white blouse was transparent enough to show her shoulder straps and the line of her petticoat underneath and, ultimate sophistication, she wore bright red lipstick and had painted her nails to match. This was what was causing the delay. She blew on her nails and waved her fingers in the air.

'My varnish isn't dry,' she explained. 'Tell you what, Rill, you carry my handbag and gas mask and I'll keep my hands spread out till it's stopped being tacky.'

Rilla delivered Joyce's message to Dinah's younger sister, Norma, and the two girls left, Dinah walking with her hands extended in front of her, admiring her red nails, and Rilla cluttered by two handbags, two gas masks, her cardigan and a jacket Dinah decided to add at the last moment.

They walked up the road, under the railway bridge, past the gas works, and into the better part of Sudbury Road. In the distance, far above them, barrage balloons glinted silver where they were caught in the slanting rays of the evening sunshine, turning ponderously on their cables like a school of airborne whales.

'I don't understand what they're supposed to do,' Rilla said, with her eyes on the strange, finned objects.

'The Jerry planes will fly into them and get tangled up in

the cables and crash,' Dinah said with the assurance of complete ignorance. She paused at the street corner. 'Where are you going?'

'Aren't you going through the churchyard?'

'No! Up the High Street, then we can look in the shops. There's a frock in Esme's window, ever so nice, just my style. I want to have another look at it.'

'If it's in Esme's it'll cost more than you can afford,' Rilla pointed out.

'Nothing to stop me looking, is there?'

They took the side turning into the High Street, almost deserted now that the shops were shut, and stopped to look in the windows of the town's most expensive dress shop, peering through the strips of cellophane which had been pasted over the plate glass windows to reduce the danger from splintering glass.

'My Dad says they all ought to be boarded up, really, or else sandbagged,' Dinah remarked. 'Look, that's the dress I fancy.'

Rilla studied it doubtfully. It was an elegant gown in black *crêpe de Chine*, scattered with a design of bright pink cherries.

'It's very smart,' she admitted. 'But when would you wear it? And I don't think that *crêpe* washes.'

'Oh, you are a wet blanket! I can just see myself in that frock and being black it wouldn't need cleaning often.'

'There's no price on it,' Rilla pointed out.

'No.' Dinah's attention had wandered. She glanced across the road, put up her hand to her hair and then ostentatiously turned her back again and said in a hissing whisper: 'I think those two boys in the car are looking at us. Don't look round!'

She was too late. Rilla had turned startled eyes to the far side of the road, where a red two-seater sports car had drawn up. The two young men in it were certainly looking across the road towards them. With heightened colour, she followed Dinah's example and turned back towards the shop window, staring blindly at the expensive gowns it displayed. She heard the sound of an engine starting up.

'Oh, blow! They've gone!' Dinah said in frank disappointment.

Rilla tried not to feel relieved. 'Come on,' she said. 'We'll miss the beginning of the first picture.'

'There's no great hurry,' Dinah said, peering down the road. 'Rilla, I think they're turning round!'

'Oh, come on!' Rilla began walking away and Dinah reluctantly followed.

'I wonder who they are,' she said. 'No one I've ever seen before.'

'You don't know everyone who lives in Barbury,' Rilla said. She glanced nervously over her shoulder. The little red car was coming back up the hill. She began to walk more quickly. The car passed them and stopped. Dinah gave a gasp and an excited giggle and then deliberately slowed down to a provocative saunter. The passenger in the car got out and stood, leaning against the bonnet and obviously waiting for them to draw level. He was in his early twenties, a pleasant-looking boy with straight, straw-coloured hair and an open, cheerful face, dressed with studied carelessness in sports jacket and grey flannels with a spotted scarf tucked in the open neck of his shirt.

'Hello,' he said.

Dinah tossed her head in a way that unconsciously betrayed her pleased excitement. Rilla shrank back, tongue-tied and nervous, and only too willing to allow her more forthcoming friend to deal with the situation.

'Are you talking to us?' Dinah asked.

'Yes, I am, if you don't mind.'

'It's a free country, you can talk to who you please. That's not to say you'll get an answer though.' She was pleased with this bit of repartee.

Barney Wainwright, who had not left his place in the driver's seat, looked at her with glazed boredom. If he had realized that Martin's idea of entertainment for the evening was to pick up a couple of shop-girls, he would certainly not have driven him into Barbury; that was not Barney's style at all. He

/15

looked past the giggling Dinah to Rilla, hanging back in an agony of embarrassment, and his expression softened. Rather a pretty little kid, very different from the knowing piece Martin was chatting up. He caught her eye and smiled. The colour in her face changed to an even deeper pink, but all he got in response was the tremulous hint of a smile.

The banter between Martin and Dinah was progressing. 'The thing is, we're strangers here,' Martin was explaining. 'It's Saturday evening and we are at a loose end. I'm sure two pretty girls like you must know what amusements there are in Barbury. Where can we go for the evening?'

'There's a dance hall over at Callaford,' Dinah said, pretending to consider.

'Is that where you're going?'

'Actually, me and my friend were on our way to the pictures—when we got waylaid, as you might say.'

'The pictures, that's not a bad idea. Can you direct us to the cinema?'

'There's two, actually. If you go up to the crossroads at the top of the High Street and turn either right or left you'll find one on either side.'

'Which one are you going to?'

'I'm sure it's nothing to do with you! We're going to the Adelphi, the one on the left. They've got *Gunga Din* on there, with Cary Grant in it.'

'We may see you up there, then. Unless we can offer you a lift?'

'In a two-seater car?'

'It's a bit of a squash, but it can be done. I don't mind a squash myself, in the right company.'

Dinah might have allowed herself to be persuaded, but Rilla put a hand on her arm and gave it a surreptitious tug. 'No, thank you,' she said with determination. 'We'll walk.'

Martin Marshall raised his hand in a casual salute, climbed back in the car and they roared away.

'Cheeky thing,' Dinah said. 'You know what, I think they

must be from the army camp. I wonder if they're officers? I bet they are. He talked ever so nice, didn't he, and they've got that sort of nerve.'

'I thought you were going to get in the car with them,' Rilla said, allowing herself to enjoy in retrospect the excitement of an encounter which had filled her with alarm while it was in progress.

'Not me, I'm too fly for that! They might have been white slavers for all we knew.'

Rilla remembered the dark eyes and warm smile of the driver of the car. 'I think they were just what they said they were: two boys looking for somewhere to go for the evening.'

They hurried up the hill and round the corner. Outside the cinema the two young men were waiting for them.

'There you are!' Martin said. 'We've got the tickets.'

'What do you mean, you've got the tickets?' Dinah demanded, deeply pleased by this development.

Martin held up the strip of tickets. 'Four seats in the balcony; now don't say you're going to disappoint us?'

'We don't even know your names!'

'Martin Marshall, at your service, and this is Barney Wainwright.' He waited expectantly.

'Well, I don't know, I'm sure! You've got a nerve!' It was no more than a token protest. 'My name's Dinah Gloster and my friend's called Rilla Gray.'

Martin wasted no more than a passing glance on the frightened rabbit called Rilla: let Barney cope with her. Dinah was his cup of tea.

'There's nothing on but the news and a cartoon for half an hour,' he said. 'Barney and I thought we'd pop across the road for a drink. How about it?'

He pretended not to hear Rilla's agonized whisper: 'Dinah, Dad'll kill me if he finds out!' nor Dinah's fierce reply: 'Don't be so soft, I'm going if you're not!'

They crossed the road to the Golden Lion and went into the saloon. Barney held back the heavy red serge curtain which would guard the black-out later in the evening and Rilla looked up with the same shy half-smile she had already given him. Her agitation had brought a flush to her cheeks and her great eyes were full of light. For one moment, in the swift upward glance, she was quite lovely and this curious flash of beauty surprised Barney and intrigued him.

Rilla looked round swiftly as they entered the bar. It was extremely unlikely that any of her father's cronies would be in the Golden Lion, particularly in the saloon, and if she kept in the background she would probably not attract any notice. She would die of embarrassment if anyone challenged her for being under age in a public house.

'What are you going to have, girls?'

'Gin and orange, please,' Dinah said, with all the aplomb of her greater experience.

'One gin and orange, one double whisky for me.' Martin glanced at Rilla and Barney enquiringly. Barney waited politely for Rilla to say what she would drink, caught her look of agonized indecision, and said easily, 'I'm too thirsty to drink spirits. I'm going to have a shandy. Why don't you join me?'

'Oh, yes, thank you, that would be lovely,' Rilla said in a breathless rush, quite unaware that her thankful acceptance of this innocuous suggestion was perfectly apparent to him.

She sipped carefully at the half-pint mug that was handed to her. She had had shandy before and had quite liked it, in spite of the beery smell, which had put her off at first.

'What do you boys do for a living?' Dinah asked.

'Haven't you guessed?' Martin replied. 'We're in the army.'

'I thought you might be. Are you officers?'

'Yes, actually we are. Second lieutenants, the lowest of the low.'

'Why aren't you in uniform?'

'Have a heart! We wear the beastly khaki on duty. We like to forget it occasionally.'

'I expect you look ever so smart.'

'Not half as smart as you do. What do you girls do, apart from breaking hearts?'

Dinah gave a delighted squeal. 'I haven't broken any hearts that I know of! I'm a hair stylist and my friend is a secretary.'

Rilla blinked at this description of her status. She looked up and caught Barney's eye and he gave her a slow, sympathetic grin. It was the first intimation she had had that he was not taken in by Dinah's pretensions. She returned his smile and the small conspiracy created a warmth between them.

'Have you always lived in Barbury?' he asked. He had a lovely voice, deep and quiet.

'Yes, I was born here,' Rilla said. 'What about you?'

'My home is in the West Country.'

'I expect you miss it.'

He grimaced. 'Yes, I do.'

'What made you volunteer for the army?'

'I'd been in the O.T.C. at school and then the Territorials. It seemed the natural thing to do.'

Rilla was not sure what the O.T.C. was. She wondered whether she should confess her ignorance. Dad always said if you didn't know it was best to ask. 'What is the O.T.C.?' she enquired.

'The Officers' Training Corps.'

He didn't seem to mind that she had not known. Emboldened by finding him easier to talk to than she had feared, she asked, 'What were you studying at college?'

'I was reading law. I just managed to get my degree before war was declared. I was hoping to be called to the bar eventually, but it hardly seemed worth going into chambers when I knew that I would be called up at any moment, so I volunteered. If I'd known it was going to be so boring I might have thought again.'

'Aren't you doing anything interesting?'

'Square-bashing and playing with dummy rifles. Not quite what I had anticipated.'

She considered this carefully. She had an oddly endearing habit of catching her lower lip between her teeth while she was thinking, so that two small white teeth showed against her soft pink mouth. No make-up, that was rather nice. An unsophisticated little rabbit, except that no rabbit ever had eyes like hers.

'Nothing much seems to be happening anywhere, does it?' Rilla ventured. 'It's not like being at war at all.'

'The Americans are calling it the "phony war," but I think there's a lot more going on behind the scenes than we realize.'

'Will you be sent to France?'

'I expect so.'

'Anyone ready for a second drink?' Martin asked.

'I think we ought to be going,' Barney said. He drained his glass and then glanced thoughtfully at Rilla's half-consumed shandy. Unostentatiously, he put his own mug down in front of her, picked up her drink and swallowed it down, and then stood up. Her startled, grateful look amused him.

Rilla followed him out of the pub and into the cinema in a daze of delight. He was nice, really nice, and terribly good-looking, taller than his friend Martin, with a leisurely way of moving that made it curiously difficult to stop watching him.

She was more than ever grateful that he had fallen to her as a partner when they were installed in their expensive balcony seats. Martin immediately draped his arm round Dinah and they went into a huddle which seemed to promise that they would see little of the picture. Rilla felt herself stiffening. If Barney expected the same treatment from her, she was not at all sure she would know how to cope with it. It was a tremendous relief when he felt for her hand, took it in a firm, warm clasp and watched the film with every appearance of concentration. She felt contented and at ease. At one point, towards the end of the picture, his fingers moved and tickled the palm of her hand. It made her want to giggle. She felt effervescent, as if little bubbles of happiness were rising up inside her. She half-turned her head and looked up at him and saw in the dim light that he was smiling. He leaned towards her and kissed her lightly on the ear. Rilla made a little noise, somewhere between a snort and a giggle. Funny creature, Barney thought. She was really very sweet; thank goodness he had not been landed with the other ghastly specimen.

They left the cinema a little after ten o'clock, the time when most performances finished, now that the war had started. In the foyer they stood undecided for a few moments. Dinah was clinging tightly to Martin's arm. She looked dazed and sticky, her hair dishevelled and her lipstick smudged.

'Are we all going to pile into the car?' Martin asked.

'No, I don't want any trouble with the police for over-crowding,' Barney said. 'We'll walk the girls home and then come back for the car.'

'We live quite close to one another,' Rilla said, but al-though they started out together down the High Street she was not sorry when the squeals from Dinah, as she stumbled along in the black-out, faded away. She glanced back, but there was nothing to be seen and no sound of any footsteps following them. Dinah and Martin had stopped in a conveniently dark shop doorway.

Now that she was alone with Barney, Rilla felt her tire-some shyness returning. 'Shall we . . . shall we go through the churchyard?' she asked. 'I've got my torch.'

'Anything you say,' Barney agreed lazily.

Rilla found her torch, carefully pasted over with brown paper so that it showed only a slit of light, and shone it on the ground as they turned into the deserted churchyard.

'I like coming this way,' she said. "Dinah doesn't, she says it gives her the willies, but to me it seems just peaceful, and the church looks as though it's always been there and always will be.'

Barney looked up at the solid Norman tower, silhouetted against the night sky. 'Fine old church, as far as one can judge in the darkness.'

'My Mum and Dad were married there and me and my sister were both christened there too. Just about here somewhere is the tombstone I'm named after.'

'You can't be named after a *tombstone*,' Barney protested, startled.

'After the person who's buried there,' Rilla conceded. 'My Mum used to walk through here and see this tombstone. She thought it was a pretty name and if she ever had a daughter she'd call her Amarilla, and so she did, only for me it usually gets shortened to Rilla.'

'Amarilla!' Barney murmured. 'It's certainly unusual. Yes, it is rather pretty.'

'Here it is: Amarilla Hunter.'

'Shine the torch so that I can see.'

He squatted down and by the light of Rilla's torch read aloud: ' "Sacred to the memory of Amarilla Louisa Hunter, beloved wife of James Elias Hunter. Born 2nd May 1843. Died 28th July 1880"—I say, she was only thirty-seven, poor thing —"A model of rectitude, A pattern of virtue, Deeply mourned on Earth, Received with rejoicing in Heaven." ' He stood up. 'Don't you find that a little difficult to live up to, Amarilla number two? Are you a model of rectitude?'

'No, I don't think so,' Rilla admitted.

They resumed their walk once more.

'Dad doesn't like my name much. Mum let him choose my sister's name.'

'Have you got just one sister?'

'Yes, Joyce. She's younger than me. Have you got any brothers or sisters?'

'One older brother.'

'Is he in the army too?'

'No. Dan is going to have to stick this war out at home.' He hesitated and then he said: 'He's had his share of adventure. Possibly you may have heard of him. Daniel Wainwright.'

Rilla was so excited that the light of her torch wavered upwards and she stumbled on an uneven patch of gravel. 'Didn't he write a book, about exploring in South America?' she demanded.

'Yes, he did.'

'I've read it! Fancy you being Daniel Wainwright's brother!'

Her tone was so reverent that Barney gave a smothered laugh. 'I shall have to write and tell him he's got a fan in Barbury.'

'Why can't he go into the army? I would have thought he'd be just the sort of person they want.'

'He is. Unfortunately, he got himself smashed up climbing in the Himalayas. He has a stiff leg and a collapsed lung as a result. Not a chance of any of the forces taking him on. He's staying at home to run . . .' He was going to say 'the estate,' but it sounded pretentious, and so he changed it to '. . . the farm.'

'At least he's doing something useful,' Rilla said consolingly.

She guided him out of the churchyard and into Sudbury Road. 'We have to go right down to the other end, I'm afraid.'

'Don't worry, I'm enjoying the walk, even though it is along a street. Is there anywhere you know of nearby for a real country walk? I might be able to get away tomorrow afternoon.'

'Maggs Hill is one of our favourite places. It isn't far from where you're stationed. There are beech trees on top and a lovely view.' She hesitated, trying to get up her courage, but all she could bring herself to say was: 'I like walking, too.'

She waited, hoping that he would suggest they should meet, but Barney was looking up at the sky, lost in his own thoughts, and did not respond.

'There's one thing to be said about the black-out, you do see the stars better,' Rilla ventured.

'I was thinking the same thing. I used to walk on the hills near my home at night sometimes and the sky was like this, pitch black and full of stars.'

He tilted his face up to look at the sky and in the darkness Rilla did not see that he was smiling as he remembered that he had not always been alone on those dark nights in the Gloucestershire hills, remembering the quick, hot tumbles on the damp grass, the smell of the earth and the way the stars seemed to wheel round above him. Without thinking what he was doing he reached out and put an arm round Rilla's shoulders, pulling her close against him. Very tentatively, she slipped her own arm round his waist and their walk slowed to a stroll. Rilla's heart was beating so fast that she did not feel able to attempt further conversation. Her throat felt dry. It was almost a relief when they reached Number 62.

'This is where I live,' she said, pausing with her hand on the gate. The black-out curtains at the windows were too efficient for her to be able to tell whether there were still any lights on, but in any case it was unthinkable to ask him in. 'Thank you very much for . . . for everything,' she said breathlessly.

'Thank *you*. I enjoyed it very much,' Barney said with mechanical politeness. It had hardly been a scintillating evening, but it could have been worse, and little Rilla Gray was rather a poppet. He tilted her head up with one hand under her chin and kissed her. She kissed him back, a fervent, childish kiss with her mouth tightly closed and her lips slightly puckered. When he released her Barney was smiling.

'Goodnight, little Rilla,' he said.

To Rilla, every nerve willing him to suggest another meeting, it did not seem possible that he should be turning away.

'Shall I see you again?' she asked desperately.

Barney hesitated. 'It's difficult to know when I shall be free,' he said. 'Are you . . .' He glanced at the small terraced house; no, it was unlikely that they were on the telephone. 'Can I ring you? At your office, perhaps?'

'Oh, yes!'

'Give me the number. Hold the torch so that I can write it down.'

He scribbled the number in his address book, but he had no real intention of following up this chance meeting.

Rilla was restless and absent-minded the next day. She never mentioned Barney, but her mind was full of him. By the afternoon she had decided that there would be no harm in going for a walk, and the walk would be to Maggs Hill. She often did go there on a Sunday afternoon and in any case, they might not even see one another. He had not said for certain that he would go there.

'I think I'll go out,' she said. 'It's such a lovely day and goodness knows how long this weather will last.'

Her mother glanced out at the cloudless sky. 'It's unbelievable,' she agreed. 'Are you going too, Joyce?'

Rilla held her breath.

'Not me,' Joyce said. 'I'm playing tennis over the Rec this afternoon.'

'I'll go and see Aunt Debbie,' Rilla said. 'I'll take the bus to High Combe and walk up over Maggs Hill.'

'Good idea,' Edith replied and Rilla had a momentary pang of guilt at her mother's unsuspecting acceptance of her plan. 'I've got a knitting pattern she wants and you can take it for me.'

Edith's sister, Debbie, lived in a place Edith referred to as being 'right out in the wilds,' which meant that she had a twenty minute walk to the nearest shops and there was only one bus an hour. The bus from Barbury only went part of the way, but there was a footpath up the hill, through a wood, along a path which skirted a golf course and down the other side. It was a favourite walk for a Sunday afternoon.

Barney, approaching from a different direction, thought it suburban and a poor substitute for the peacefulness of his Gloucestershire home.

They met among the beeches on the crown of the hill. Rilla, caught scuffling her feet through the fallen leaves like a schoolgirl, blushed vividly. She thought for a moment that Barney had not seen her, but suddenly his gaze focused, as if he had just realized that the girl in blue was someone he knew. She was wearing her blue and white cotton dress again. 'Dirty it out,' Edith had said. 'And I'll put it in the washtub for you tomorrow.' She looked familiar and friendly, and Barney was surprised how pleased he was to see her. She was a nice young-ster, but not really his kind of girl. He had followed Martin's lead the night before out of boredom and restlessness, but he had no desire to get involved. Martin, he knew, would lead a girl, any girl, up the garden path as far as she was willing to go, and he had a shrewd suspicion that Dinah was prepared to go quite a long way. Barney considered himself more discriminat-ing and if he wanted a woman he could do better than that.

Nevertheless, the sight of Rilla, pink-faced and smiling, right there in his path, drew an answering smile from him. They agreed it was a remarkable coincidence that they should meet again like this.

'May I walk with you?' Barney asked. 'I wasn't sure which way to go once I'd reached the top of the hill.'

Rilla could ask for nothing better. 'What would you be doing if you were at home?' she asked.

'Playing cricket probably. About the last match of the season, I suppose.'

As he spoke he was seized by a terrible nostalgia for his home. He could smell the newly-cut grass, hear the click of the ball on his cricket bat, feel the satisfaction of opening up his shoulders, hear the ripple of polite applause. He saw the line of the hills above the valley, saw the mellow golden stone of Appleyard and the tumble of pink roses climbing up the wall —his mother was always saying they ought to be cut back—and the old cedar tree he had climbed as a child. It was ridiculous, this homesickness. He had been away before, to school and to Cambridge, but never before had he thought of it with such yearning, as if he would never see it again.

'I miss my dog when I'm out walking like this,' he said abruptly. 'I usually have him with me. I even took him to Cambridge.'

'What kind of a dog is he?'

'He's a black cocker spaniel called Fluke.'

'Fluke?'

Barney grinned. 'Yes. It's a daft name, I know, but his

mother was an old bitch who was supposed to be past having any more pups. Everyone was stunned when she produced a fresh litter. One of them was given to me and I called him Fluke.'

Barney would have been incredulous if he had seen Rilla blink at his use of the word 'bitch.' To Rilla a dog was a dog, and an old bitch was something that a coarsely-spoken woman might call another one of her kind.

'It's pleasant up here,' he said, still trying to shake off his unaccountable depression.

'I love the beech trees,' Rilla agreed. 'It's lovely in the spring when the new leaves come out, that shining green, and there are bluebells underneath.'

They came out of the belt of trees and on to the golf course, skirting it by the edge of the silver birches, with the crisp short turf under their feet. A skylark was singing overhead, flinging himself into the air until Barney, trying to follow his flight, grew dizzy with watching him.

'Sometimes I think we are being given these wonderful autumn days to make sure we understand what we are losing,' he said. 'Look your last on all things lovely, Rilla; this is the end of peace.'

She was puzzled by the underlying bitterness in his voice. 'You think the war will start properly soon?' she asked.

'I'm sure of it. What are you going to do?'

'Do? For war work, do you mean? I shall just go on doing my job, I suppose. I'm starting first aid classes next week.'

'No plans for going into one of the forces?'

'Oh, no!' Obviously the idea had never occurred to her. 'I'll go if they want me, of course, but I think I'll wait and see what happens.'

The path began to wind downhill. 'Is there any sort of café or tea place around here?' Barney asked.

Rilla hesitated. Her aunt was a kind, hospitable person who was bound to have a good tea ready for Sunday afternoon, even though she was not expecting a visit from her niece. What was more, she had a placid, unquestioning mind and she would accept Barney as a friend of Rilla's without asking awkward questions. Rilla had the vague feeling that it would be a good thing to effect an introduction of Barney to her family by this slightly back-door means and so she said, 'I'm going to visit my Aunt Debbie. She'd be ever so pleased to give you a cup of tea if you'd like to come with me.'

It was not quite what Barney wanted, but he could not see any way of refusing this invitation. Rilla was a funny little creature. It was a bit like having Fluke along, walking with her. She was just as soft and silky and anxious to please and she had the same warm, trusting light in her big grey eyes. It would be a pity to hurt her.

The visit passed off successfully. Edith's sister accepted Barney unquestioningly as Rilla's friend and thought him a very nice boy. Barney, consuming home-made scones and strawberry jam with relish, was reminded of farmhouse teas he had eaten as a schoolboy, and Aunt Debbie had something of the monumental calm of the farmers' wives who had made him welcome at their tables.

'I can't stay very long,' Rilla said regretfully. 'I promised Mum I'd catch the six o'clock bus home.'

'I started my walk from this side of the hill, and I left my car only about half a mile down the road,' Barney said. 'I'll go and fetch it and run you home. I may as well make use of it while I can still get the petrol.'

It seemed to him the least he could do, a very slight gesture, but to Rilla it was one more proof of his special quality, that he should be prepared to go to this trouble just for her.

Something of her silent bliss communicated itself to Barney. He felt indulgent towards her and flattered by her shy admiration. On an impulse he said as they drove along, 'There's a dance in aid of the local hospital next Saturday and we've been asked to support it. Would you like to go?'

So much for his good intentions of steering clear of little Rilla Gray. Her acceptance was ecstatic. He was touched, a little bewildered at being the recipient of so much gratitude. As for Rilla, she was floating on air when she entered her front door.

It was as well that she had something to armour her against the hostile reception that was waiting for her. Edith barely allowed her time to get inside.

'What's this I hear about you, miss?' she demanded. 'Picked up by a couple of army officers in the High Street, I'm told, and not a word about it when you came home. Dinah told her mother all about it and Mrs Gloster told me. Fine goings on, I must say! I thought I'd taught you better than that.'

'Mum, it wasn't like that!' Rilla protested, but without conviction because, of course, it had been exactly like that. She tried to explain. 'It was the other one, Martin, who did all the talking and I suppose you could say, in a way, he picked Dinah up, but I just went along because I was with Dinah, and it was the same with his friend. His name's Barney and he's ever so nice, really he is.'

Edith's expression relaxed slightly. It was not difficult for her to believe that her quiet Rilla had merely tagged along behind the enterprising Dinah. Seeing this softening in her mother, Rilla rushed on: 'I met him again this afternoon — completely by accident, honestly—and I took him to tea at Aunt Debbie's.'

'Oh, did you! A fine thing, eating your aunt out of house and home when there's a war on. What did she think of him?'

'She liked him,' Rilla said with conviction. It was impossible for her to imagine anyone not liking Barney.

'I don't know why you had to take up with an officer,' Len remarked from behind the *News of the World*. 'Can't you find a nice boy of your own kind?'

'Barney is my kind,' Rilla said. 'He's not stuck up, not a bit. He was studying to be a lawyer when the war broke out, and his brother's a farmer.'

It sounded all right. 'I suppose there's no harm in it,' Edith said cautiously.

'He misses his home. He's lonely,' Rilla said, pressing her advantage.

'So are thousands of others and some of them are further away from home than what he is,' Len pointed out.

'He's asked me to go to a dance with him next Saturday.'

Rilla held her breath. Nothing was going to stop her going to that dance and not for the world would she have admitted that it was necessary for her to have permission to go, but it would be awkward if her father or mother refused to agree to it.

There was a brief silence. Since it did not seem too disapproving, Rilla said, 'I'll have to wear a long frock. I thought perhaps I could wear my bridesmaid's dress.'

'I suppose you could,' Edith said, and with that grudging agreement Rilla knew that opposition had been withdrawn.

'I think I'll try it on straightaway,' she said. 'Just to make sure it still fits.'

'Your cousin's wedding was only in the spring,' Edith pointed out, but Rilla had already disappeared upstairs to try on her only long dress.

She reappeared looking anxious. 'Do you think it's too kiddish?' she asked.

Edith looked the blue taffeta dress over judiciously. Perhaps the puff sleeves and Peter Pan collar did look a bit young, now that Rilla had suddenly matured to such a surprising extent.

'I'll cut the neckline down for you, if you like,' she offered. 'Take it off and I'll make a start on it this evening, while I'm in the mood.'

'I suppose I'll have to wear my ordinary coat over the top,' Rilla said.

'Your Aunt Debbie will lend you her fur coat, I dare say, if I ask her. I'll drop her a quick line and ask her to bring it over when she comes shopping on Saturday. It'll be a bit on the big side for you, but the length won't matter over a long frock and you can wrap it round you so that it won't look too wide.'

Barney called for Rilla on the night of the dance and realized he was being given a searching inspection by the other members of the Gray family. It was an awkward few minutes, particularly since none of them found much to say to him, and he was relieved that Rilla did not keep him waiting. He had been regretting his impulsive invitation all the week and it would not have taken a great deal to have made him take the coward's way out and fail to turn up, but when Rilla appeared in her altered bridesmaid's dress and borrowed fur coat, so obviously intended for a larger woman, there was something about these makeshift arrangements, and about her starry-eyed anticipation of the dance, that gave him a curious, almost painful, stab of compunction for her.

As for Rilla, it was the first time she had seen Barney in uniform. She thought he looked terribly smart, but somewhat remote. She really preferred him dressed casually, with his dark hair ruffled by the breeze, as she had seen him in the beechwood on Sunday. The shyness she had lost with him returned and she was tongue-tied and awkward during their brief trip to the local hotel where the dance was to be held. She scolded herself for it when she went to the cloakroom to leave her coat and to peer anxiously at her reflection in the mirror. It was stupid not to be able to talk to him; he would think her feeble-minded. With her head held high and a resolution to appear as easy as Dinah, if not quite so forthcoming, Rilla descended the stairs.

But Rilla, even if she was not a fluent talker, possessed a means of communication which was all the more potent for being instinctive and wordless: she danced like a wood nymph on the slopes of Olympus. She had all the talents of a born dancer: a sense of rhythm, a musical ear and perfect control over her body. Barney had never had a partner like her. Small and light and boneless as a kitten, she moved in his arms like an extension of himself, every muscle perfectly co-ordinated, every nerve attuned to his slightest whim. The lack of assurance which rendered her inarticulate dropped away at the sound of music. If she could not talk, she could express herself in movement and she did so in a trance of thoughtless happiness; careless and, indeed, with a total lack of understanding of the effect her uninhibited response to the throb of the dance-band drums might have on a young man to whom she was demonstrating with every movement that she was in love.

For dance after dance they took the floor together. Once or twice Barney paused to introduce her to his colleagues and she danced politely with them, faceless men to her, innocuous and unimportant because they were not Barney, but as soon as possible she and Barney moved back together again—'like a magnet and a needle, you can almost hear the click,' Martin Marshall remarked, half-derisively, half-enviously. They were more generally remarked than Rilla knew or cared, the slim, demurely-dressed girl, her brown hair swinging from her head as she tilted it back to look up at the young man who bent towards her, her great eyes fixed on his, with a dazed, blind look in them, her face flushed, her lips slightly parted; and Barney, tall and carelessly good-looking, with the unconscious arrogance of his privileged background, intent only on an experience which had no parallel in his previous knowledge of women.

They stayed to the end, standing to attention but still surreptitiously holding hands, as the band played the national anthem, and then escaped into the darkness and solitude for which Barney, at least, by that time had a burning need.

Rilla was still in her trance of delight as they drove away and when Barney pulled up in the first possible secluded spot she went into his arms with the utmost readiness. He drew back after only a moment or two.

'Darling Amarilla,' he protested, amused and a little exasperated, 'Must you kiss me with your teeth clenched? Relax, my sweet, I shan't eat you.'

Rilla was not so sure about that. To her it seemed as if he was swallowing her up. She moved her head in surprise as his tongue delicately touched her own.

'It's not nice, to do that,' she protested.

'Oh, yes, it is,' Barney retorted. 'It's very, very nice indeed.'

Still laughing, he found his way through the voluminous folds of Aunt Debbie's fur coat until he could feel the soft warmth of Rilla herself through the thin silk of her dress. His arms tightened and he kissed her again, trying to extract from her the same response she had shown on the dance floor, and Rilla wound her arms round his neck and kissed him back with all the fervour of her romantic love for him.

His mouth moved down over her throat. 'Take your coat off, darling,' he ordered. 'I'm getting mouthfuls of fur.'

Obediently, she slipped her arms out of the coat and he arranged it loosely round her shoulders so that she should not get cold. He tried to pull back the neckline of her dress to kiss her shoulders, but the puff sleeves defeated him.

'Oh, why haven't I got an enormous limousine with a large back seat?' Barney groaned, with his head buried against Rilla's neck. 'I suppose it's no use suggesting we should get out of the car and disappear into the woods for a while?'

Rilla did not take this seriously. She shook her head, regretful but determined.

Barney accepted the rebuff without demur. It was no more than he had expected. They began kissing again, and Rilla gave herself up to the same mindless ecstasy she had experienced when she and Barney had danced together. The only coherent thought that came to her was that they were perfectly suited to one another—'made for one another' was the phrase that ran through her mind—and the slight differences of class and upbringing which had troubled her were no longer of the slightest importance. The significance of the delicate movements of Barney's hands over the buttons which closed the back of her dress were completely lost on her until the silky fabric began to slide away from her shoulders. He felt the little shock that went through her and began to make soothing noises.

'Sh, darling, keep still; don't worry, I won't hurt you.'

'I can't . . . you mustn't . . .' Rilla whispered desperately, but she had neither the power nor the desire to stop him as he freed her small, perfect breasts and bent his head to them. A long shudder ran through her, she arched her body and stroked the back of his head. It was she who heard the sound of another car coming along the road behind them and drew back. Barney raised his head.

'Damn,' he said. He sat up as the other car went past.

Rilla had moved away from him and was trying with shaking hands to fasten the back of her dress. Regretfully, Barney began to help her, and his fingers were not much steadier than her own. He held her coat so that she could slip her arms back in the sleeves and then they sat for a few minutes, arms loosely round one another, just sitting without saying anything.

'I suppose we'd better go,' Barney said at last.

They drove the rest of the way to Rilla's home in almost unbroken silence. When they arrived, Barney helped her out of the car and kissed her lightly. 'If I start again I shall shock the neighbours,' he said, trying to make a joke of the emotion which filled him with elation and dismay. 'I'll see you again soon, shan't I, Rilla? Darling Amarilla, lovely Amarilla.' In spite of what he had just said, he pulled her against him and kissed her hard once more. 'I'll ring you at your office one day in the week,' he promised.

His decision to see no more of little Rilla Gray was wholly forgotten now, lost in the primitive urge which drove him beyond prudence or kindness. He wanted her fiercely, and what Barney wanted, Barney had.

Chapter 2

It took several more sessions of insistent love-making and impassioned pleading to break down Rilla's defences. As he had expected, the first time Barney whispered: 'Let me love you, Rilla,' she drew back in alarm and shook her head in mute but vehement refusal. It took all the tact and gentleness of which he was capable to woo her back into his arms again, even though he knew that she was ripe and ready for his love. His own patience surprised him. It was not Barney's custom to waste his time on unwilling girls, but Rilla was something special and his desire for her was beyond all reason.

He was not helped by a break in the glorious weather, which kept them confined to the unaccommodating space of his small car, while the rain streamed down the windows and drummed on the hood.

'It's lovely, being shut up in here with the nasty weather only just outside,' Rilla said dreamily.

'I can think of better places to be,' Barney said, but he understood what she meant and even agreed with her. There was something exciting and special to them about the small dark space they inhabited, warmed by the heat of their bodies, the windows misted over by their breath, an enchanted oasis in the cold night. To Barney there seemed to be a similarity between their situation and that of their country, still safe, still undisturbed, in a world that seemed to grow increasingly menacing day by day. At the back of his mind was the realization that at any time he might be sent off to France, and before he went he must make love to Rilla. Her reluctance made him the more determined. He even began to be superstitious about it. If Rilla would give herself to him then it would be a good omen; he would not be wounded, he would survive.

Their relationship had reached a critical point of frustration when the opportunity Barney was seeking was handed to him on a plate. His mother wrote asking him to visit a friend of hers in a hospital only a few miles from Barbury.

> Barney, darling, I know it will be a terrible bore for you, but Dora Somers is such an old friend. Major Somers was whisked off to France at a moment's notice and Dora is completely incapacitated by a very bad broken leg. She is in traction and everything and is likely to be in hospital for weeks yet. Take her a bunch of flowers from me, and give her my fondest love.

Barney grimaced at this encroachment on his scanty free time, but he went along to the hospital and made polite conversation with a middle-aged woman whom he vaguely remembered as a visitor at Appleyard. It was a painstaking effort and it brought its own reward.

Towards the end of his visit he asked if there was anything he could do for Mrs Somers, trusting that the answer would be in the negative.

'Just one thing,' she said. 'And only if you can get away

for an hour or so. I fell down the stairs just after Bob had gone away. One of my neighbours went in to make sure everything in the house was locked up, but she's an elderly woman and I don't feel at all happy about it. I lie here having terrible visions of water cascading down the stairs or burglars breaking in through an unfastened window. It would set my mind at rest if you would go over and make sure that everything really is secure.'

Barney took the keys she offered him. 'I don't suppose I could have a bath, could I?' he asked. 'Arrangements at the camp are not very adequate.'

'My dear boy, of course you can! Treat the house as if it were your own home. Have a game of tennis if you feel like it, take your friends over. I'd rather no one went there without you, but I trust you completely and it will be a relief to know that the house looks as if it's being lived in.'

The phrase 'take your friends over' put the idea into Barney's head. He could take Rilla there. A house to themselves, secret, comfortable, with every amenity, it seemed too good to be true.

It was not difficult to persuade Rilla to accompany him. She was a little awed by the size of the house, but her practical streak perfectly understood Mrs Somer's concern about leaving such a fine place empty at a moment's notice. It was she, not Barney, who went round the house with a seeing eye, looking at windows and trying taps. It was she who inspected and cleared the larder.

'The gas, water and electricity must be turned off at the mains,' she said seriously.

'Not much point if I'm going to be popping in and out,' Barney said. 'Would you like a drink?'

'Do you think we should?' Rilla asked. 'It doesn't seem right, taking people's drink when they aren't here to offer it.'

'Mrs Somers said I was to treat the house like my own home. To me that means helping myself to anything I want.'

What Barney wanted at that moment was a stiff whisky;

what he prepared for Rilla was a strong gin. He did not want to get her drunk, but the dear girl must be brought to realize that her hesitation was slightly ridiculous when they had this heaven-sent opportunity to be alone together. Her last remaining inhibitions had to be broken down somehow. She was disturbing him too much. Something must be done to get her out of his system and restore his peace of mind.

He pulled her down beside him on the sofa and began to make love to her and she responded with a sweet, wild abandon that intoxicated him far more than any alcohol. Her skin had a silvery sheen to it. Seen like this, at such close quarters, the details of her face were astonishingly beautiful. It was a warm day and the lovely hollow where her neck and shoulder joined tasted of salt. He could have taken her there, on the wide sofa, but it would be even better if he could get her to go upstairs with him. His only fear was that such a move might change her mood and she would once more draw back, which in his present state would send him out of his mind.

He was braced for a protest, but Rilla followed him blindly when he drew her to her feet and guided her with an arm round her waist towards the stairs. She stumbled slightly, but it was not the half-consumed drink which affected her.

With a flash of tact Barney did not take her into the Somers' bedroom, but into one of the spare rooms. Her silence worried him, and the fact that she trembled as he undressed her. When he stepped back to look at her her head drooped, and something about this classical attitude of maidenly modesty touched him to tenderness.

'Let me see you,' he said, not quite steadily. 'No, don't hide yourself from me.'

He took hold of the hands she had crossed over her breasts and opened her arms out wide so that he could look down at her.

'You're beautiful, really beautiful, just as I knew you would be. Darling Rilla.'

He put one hand under her chin and lifted her face to kiss

her and then he led her over to the bed. It was covered by an embroidered counterpane, which Barney tossed aside. Underneath, the bed was not made up, but the mattress was covered by an undersheet and there were pillows with white cotton covers.

He began to undress, throwing his clothes carelessly on one side. While his back was turned Rilla could look at him, at his long straight legs and the way the muscles in his back moved as he stooped down to take off his shoes. His skin was smooth and brown from his holiday in France, except for a triangular patch of white skin over his buttocks, where he had worn abbreviated bathing trunks. When he turned she looked away quickly and the breath caught in her throat in momentary panic.

It was easier when he was lying by her side with his arms round her kissing her in the way that was already familiar to her. She slid her arms over his bare brown shoulders and stretched herself against him. His hands moved over her and Rilla, with nothing to guide her but her untaught instinct, shuddered with delight and touched him tentatively in a way that made Barney laugh softly and then begin to kiss her with a passion that swept them both away. There was just one moment when Rilla still felt afraid—when she realized that there could be no possibility of turning back, that Barney was oblivious to everything but the fierce demands of his own body—and then she put the tiny stab of fear away from her and gave herself up to him, following blindly where he led, her eyes tightly closed, her hands digging into his back, her body moving with his.

It worried Barney to discover afterwards that her face was wet with tears. He propped himself up on his elbow and looked down at her.

'Why are you crying, darling?' he asked. 'Did I hurt you, my poor sweet?'

'A bit. It isn't that. I don't know why I'm crying, except that I'm so happy.'

It occurred to him that she was the first virgin he had ever had and he gave a fleeting thought to the idea that he might perhaps have been a little hard on her. He got up and found his handkerchief and then came back to her side, bending over her to dry her eyes. She smiled at him shakily and he was reassured.

'I didn't know what to expect,' she excused herself. 'Oh, Barney, it was wonderful! I didn't know it would be like that. Was it . . . did it seem the same to you?'

'It was perfect, and you are perfect, and everything is perfect, except this blasted war!'

He felt around over the side of the bed and found the discarded coverlet and pulled it over them and they lay for a long time with their arms wrapped round one another, reluctant to move.

He started to tease her with his hands, laughing when she squirmed against him in protest. It was extraordinary, never before had he had quite this feeling of triumphant well-being, not even with Yvette at her most talented.

'Lovely Rilla,' he said lazily. 'You're something special, did you know that?'

He pulled back the counterpane, ignoring her murmur of protest. 'You're like a beautiful statue, except that you're too warm and soft to be made of marble.' He cupped her breast in his hand, touching the small pink nipple with one finger. 'So small and sweet and perfect.'

He bent his head to take her nipple between his lips and she pressed his head to her, stroking his dark hair, weak with love. He raised his head and they began to kiss again, lazily at first, lips scarcely moving, and then more urgently.

She clung to him, mutely acquiescing. There was nothing she would not agree to, nothing she would not give him.

'No crying this time?' he asked when at last he lay quietly by her side, too spent for further love-making, replete and satisfied.

Rilla shook her head slowly from side to side on the pillow, unable for the moment to make any other response. Her heavy eyelids closed and she nuzzled her face down against his shoulder.

'My love, we mustn't go to sleep,' Barney said. He flung back the crumpled coverlet. 'Come on, let's take a bath.'

It amused him to find that Rilla was shocked by the idea of bathing with him. She hung back, but he coaxed her into the bathtub, splashing her with water and demanding that she should soap his back.

There was a towel on the rack, pale blue and soft, the biggest bath towel Rilla had ever seen. Barney wrapped it right round the pair of them and they clung together, their skin still warm and damp.

'Shall I hug you dry? No, perhaps I'd better not!'

He bent his head to savour once more the hollow that he loved where her neck and shoulder joined. 'Hell's teeth, I wish we could stay all night! But I've got to get back.'

He watched indulgently as she mopped up the water which had swamped over the floor and then wandered back into the adjoining bedroom to take a surreptitious look at his watch.

'We haven't got much time left,' he said.

He had nothing in mind but the need to get back to his depot, but to Rilla his words struck a more ominous note. She shivered, clutching the damp towel to her.

'At least we've had this,' she said.

'Yes. Are you happy, Rilla?'

'Very happy.' She spoke steadily, but already there was a little line of pain between her finely arched eyebrows as she watched him, perfectly confident in his nakedness, as he began to collect together the clothes he had scattered over the floor.

'You don't have to worry, you know. It was perfectly safe,' Barney said as a belated afterthought, and she smiled at him with perfect trust.

Barney had hoped that once he had persuaded Rilla to let him make love to her he would have got her out of his system, but to his dismay the cure did not work. On the contrary, he found his mind turning towards her at the most inconvenient moments. This was an unexpected and unwelcome outcome of what he had intended to be no more than a passing episode. It was not only that she had proved to be a wonderful sexual partner either. There was something about the trusting light in her eyes, the way her face lit up as she smiled at him, that woke him up in the middle of the night to toss and turn with the uneasy realization that she had taken the whole thing far more seriously than he had.

In the hope of introducing a lighter note into their relationship he made their next meeting a foursome, joining up with Martin Marshall and a girl called Cynthia, yet another of Martin's acquisitions.

All very well, but he did not bargain on Cynthia's insisting on going somewhere where they could dance, nor on the effect holding Rilla in his arms would have on him, still less on what a couple of glasses of wine and a brandy would do to Rilla.

They left the Red Pine Road House a little after eleven o'clock because Rilla had to be home by midnight.

'Mum thinks it's all right if I'm with you, but Dad cuts up rough,' she said apologetically.

The other two decided to stay on, so Rilla and Barney were alone. It was a beautiful autumn night with a full moon. The Red Pine Road House, which had only recently reopened and was doing unexpectedly good business in this curious period of war and no war, was set in a large garden with lawns that sloped down to an artificial lake. The restaurant was blacked out, but they could still hear the music from the band inside. Rilla hummed the tune beneath her breath. She stepped on to the grass and pirouetted lightly, her arms uplifted.

'Oh, I do love to dance!' she said. 'Come and dance with me, Barney.'

He reached out a hand towards her, but on a sudden teasing impulse she evaded him and began to run away from him towards the lake. She was a flying shadow, maddeningly difficult to catch. She knew that she was annoying him, but she also sensed that he was excited by this pursuit of an elusive quarry over a moonlit lawn, and she enjoyed the feeling of power it gave her until at last Barney lost patience and pinned her to the ground with a flying tackle. It was Barney's turn to laugh triumphantly. He wrapped his long arms and legs round her and they began to roll over and over down the slope until they met the rhododendron bushes that overhung the lake and lay there, laughing helplessly.

'We m . . . might have landed in the lake!' Rilla said when she had got her breath back.

'Shall we go for a midnight swim, little mermaid?'

'No, too cold!'

She freed her arms so that she could put them round his neck. They exchanged a long kiss. Barney shifted himself into a more comfortable position. They kissed again and then Rilla said in an uncertain voice, 'We ought to go.'

'No.'

'But Barney, I must get home. Barney, no! We can't . . . not here!'

She got no answer from Barney. The moon slid away, down the sky, the shadowy bushes concealed them, there were no sounds except the lapping of the water at the edge of the lake, a thread of music from the house on the hill, an occasional voice and the slam of a car door, Barney's quickened breathing and the sledge-hammer of her own heart.

Barney was kept particularly busy in the days that followed the night at the Red Pine Road House and he and Rilla were unable to meet. At the back of his mind he was vaguely uneasy, ashamed of his lack of control, knowing that he had been careless with a girl who was not capable of looking after herself. As for Rilla, she remembered Barney's assurance that their love-making was perfectly safe and she believed him.

It was more than a week later that she began to feel afraid. She told herself that it was not possible for anything to have gone wrong. Barney had said it would be all right. She waited day by day and nothing happened. The following week she felt compelled to tell him what she was beginning to fear.

He could find nothing to say in response to her stumbling words. All he could think of was his own sick dismay. His silence struck her coldly and she turned her head away so that he should not see that her eyes had filled with tears.

'I'm sorry,' she said.

Barney pulled himself together. 'I'm the one who should say I'm sorry,' he said. 'Rilla, isn't it a bit soon to be sure? Couldn't you possibly be mistaken?'

'It could still come to nothing,' she admitted. 'But I've always been so regular . . .' Her face reddened and she could not go on.

'I see. Then I suppose we have to take it that you really might be pregnant.' He was reluctant to touch her, but he steeled himself to put a comforting arm around her shoulders. 'Don't worry, Rilla. I'll see that you are looked after. Do your parents know?'

'No, I haven't dared tell them, but Mum will guess soon. Oh, Barney, what am I going to do?'

'Leave it to me,' he answered mechanically, without the slightest idea of how to answer such a question. 'I . . . I need time to think. One thing you can rely on, Rilla, I won't run out on you, I promise you that. I'll meet you again on Thursday and we'll talk it over properly.'

She looked up at him with her enormous, trusting eyes and he felt a pang of real compunction. He had been a selfish swine and Rilla, dear little rabbit, was the one who was going to suffer. His guilty feelings made him gentle and she went home almost happy.

Barney, racking his brains for a solution to his predicament, decided he needed to talk to someone. He thought of Martin Marshall, who certainly knew all the answers, and dismissed the idea with distaste. Only one other possibility occurred to him. His brother Dan was a knowing old devil who had knocked about the world and, although he had sometimes made a caustic comment or two about Barney's extravagances, he could be depended on to stand firm in a crisis. Barney put through a telephone call to his home.

The one remaining old servant, Agnes, answered the telephone and, recognizing his voice, had to be given patient answers to her enquiries about his health before she would go and find Dan. When Dan finally came to the telephone Barney wasted no time.

'I'm in trouble,' he said abruptly.

'What sort of trouble?' Dan sounded more resigned than surprised.

'A girl.' Barney stopped. It was more difficult than he had anticipated to tell Dan why he had called him.

Since he showed no signs of going on, Dan said drily, 'I take it that what you actually mean is that the girl's in trouble?'

'Yes.'

'Damned young fool. What are you going to do about it?'

'That's what I'm ringing you about. Dan, there must be somewhere I can take her. Some doctor who's safe. I thought you might know . . .'

'Just a minute,' Dan interrupted him. 'Are you asking me to help the girl have an illegal operation?'

'Yes,' Barney said miserably.

'Well, I won't do it. It's risky and it's against the law. Quite apart from that, it can be damned expensive. Did the girl put you up to this?'

'Good Lord, no! I don't suppose the idea has even entered her head. She's . . . she's not like you might think, Dan. She's a bit shy and terribly young.'

'How old?'

'She won't be eighteen until next week.'

'My God, I should think her father will be loading up his shotgun! I suppose you're sure the child is yours?'

'She was a virgin,' Barney said simply.

There was a dismayed silence at the other end of the line.

At last Dan said slowly, 'Is there any good reason why you shouldn't marry her?'

'No,' Barney said with brutal frankness. 'Except that I don't want to.'

'Is she what Ma would call presentable?'

'Ma wouldn't think so. Her father's a plumber. Rilla is a typist. She's a sweet kid and she got under my skin. I just don't want to get married, that's all.'

This time there was no mistaking the coldness in Dan's voice. 'You've asked me for help and I've refused to give it to you in the form you suggest. If you change your mind and marry this girl I'll give you all the support I can. If you don't marry her then I'll help you out with money for the child. But I do implore you not to put it into her head to go to a back street abortionist. There's no need to add murder to your sins.'

It was hardly a satisfactory conversation and it did not solve Barney's problem. He muttered a word of thanks for his brother's offer of assistance and put down the telephone. At the other end of the line Dan did the same. Neither of them heard the telltale click as Winifred Wainwright replaced the receiver on the extension in her bedroom.

She was utterly astounded by this development in her son's life, but she was not a woman to sit down under misfortune. As a result of her intervention Barney endured an interview with his colonel the following day, which did nothing to enhance his self-esteem.

Colonel Franklyn was annoyed, and he had no scruples about taking it out on a fledgling second lieutenant who couldn't keep his flies buttoned.

'Had your mother on the telephone,' he said. 'You'd better sit down. This is a private talk, not a service matter. Winifred wants me to get you posted—I don't know who she thinks I am! Something about some girl you've got pregnant. True, is it?'

'Yes, sir.'

'Did you have to go running to mother with the story?'

'I didn't. I told my brother.'

'Hm. Well, Winifred seems to think her boy's life is going to be ruined if he isn't sent abroad post haste. Doesn't seem to have occurred to her you might get killed. What's going to happen to the girl then, hm?'

'I don't know, sir.'

'You don't know. You've got no damned business to knock up a decent girl and then say you "don't know" what's going to become of her. Not the sort of thing I expect to have to deal with. Sort of thing that crops up in the ranks. Fine officer you'll be, sending one of your platoon off with a flea in his ear to marry his girl, and you with a little bastard of your own in Barbury.'

'Yes, sir.'

'Don't sit there saying "Yes, sir," go and sort it out. *I've* got no power to make you marry the girl, nor to stop you either, and I'm not getting you posted. It's your mess, you clear it up.'

Barney departed, outwardly composed, for which Colonel Franklyn gave him one good mark at least. Inwardly he was writhing with shame, furiously angry that Dan should have given him away to his mother, even more angry that she should have gone over his head to an officer so senior in rank. He lost no time in ringing his brother again.

'I didn't tell Ma,' Dan said wearily. 'When you rang me the other day Agnes told her Mr Barney was on the phone. Ma ran up to her bedroom and picked up the extension, intending to have a happy three-way chat. She got a shock she's hardly recovered from yet. She seems to be under the impression that your little girl seduced you, not the other way round. Have you decided what you're going to do?'

'I'm still thinking about it,' Barney said.

'Don't think too long. These things can't be kept hidden, you know.'

He was right.

The next day Mrs Gray said to her daughter: 'Rilla, are you feeling all right?'

'Yes.'

'You're looking very peaky and you've been sitting around

with a face like a wet week. I suppose that boy of yours has dropped you. Well, you can't say you weren't warned. I never expected it to last. No use moping about it.'

Rilla turned her head away, but not before Edith had caught sight of the tears that were running down her face. She sat down heavily and stared in dismay at her daughter's averted head.

'Now I come to think of it, you're overdue, aren't you? Rilla, you haven't done anything silly, have you?'

Rilla did not reply.

'Rilla, answer me! Don't pretend you don't know what I'm talking about.'

Still there was no reply. Edith's own mouth began to work. She sat pleating the edge of her apron between her fingers.

'Oh, you little fool! How could you have been so stupid! I could kill him. He must have known you weren't one of the knowing ones. Why couldn't he have taken care of you, and him an officer, too?'

There was no need to mention Barney's name. They both knew there was only one man in Rilla's life. Edith's mind worked busily, turning over such remedies as she knew for an unwanted pregnancy. It was early days yet, they might work. On the other hand, there might be something to be said for finding out first what Barney intended to do.

'Does he know?' she asked.

'Yes.'

'Has he said he'll marry you?'

'No.' The idea had always seemed so unlikely to Rilla that she had scarcely dared to hope for it.

'We'll have to see about that. He knows you're a girl who's been decently brought up—though God knows you've not shown much sign of it over this business! I'd better get your Dad to speak to him.'

'Oh, no!'

'Don't be a fool! He'll have to know and a good talking to

by an older man is just what Mr Second Lieutenant Wainwright needs.'

'Dad'll be so angry with me.'

'He'll be upset, yes, but you should have thought of that a bit sooner. He always said no good would come of taking up with an officer and it seems he was right. I never thought you'd disgrace us like this, Rilla.'

Rilla's tears turned into sobs, partly out of distress and partly from relief that her mother knew about it and was taking it rather better than Rilla had expected.

'I'm sorry, Mum,' she whispered. 'You won't turn against me, will you?'

'You'll be sorrier yet, my girl. No, it's been a shock, but your own's your own, no matter what they do, so there's no need to sit there crying, that won't help.'

She looked with frustrated affection at her weeping daughter, then she reached out and pulled Rilla's head down against her shoulder, holding her tightly and stroking her hair.

'There, there, no need to take on so. Bloody men. You think I don't know? You're not the first to get caught and I don't suppose you'll be the last, especially with a war on. You're seeing him again, I hope?'

'Yes, tomorrow night.'

'Thank goodness for that. He might have run out on you once he'd got what he wanted. Come to that, he still might.'

'He won't,' Rilla said. 'He loves me.'

Edith said nothing in reply to that. If Rilla was to be disillusioned let it be by the young man himself. In the meantime, Edith would keep her gin and hot baths in reserve in case her husband's interview with young Barney turned out to be unsatisfactory.

It was not an interview that Barney anticipated with anything but dread when Rilla broke it to him that the news was out and her father wanted to talk to him. He had no idea what he was going to say to Len Gray. He hardly knew the man. He saw that Rilla was watching him anxiously. She was looking pale and tired to the point of exhaustion. She noticed that he was watching her and she straightened her back and lifted her head, even managing to smile. It touched him, her brave attempt to hide her anxiety.

Len was waiting for them when they returned to 62 Sudbury Road. He nodded briefly to his daughter, avoiding her eyes. To Barney he said, 'I'll talk to you in the front room.'

He waited until the door had closed behind them and then he said, with a pugnaciousness that masked his worry and his acute embarrassment, 'So you've got my girl into trouble, I hear?'

Barney nodded miserably. At that moment speech was beyond him, but when the silence continued unbroken he managed to say, 'I'm sorry.'

'Being sorry won't do her much good now. What are you going to do about it?'

'Naturally, I will help to support the child,' Barney said with a touch of hauteur which did nothing to endear him to Len Gray.

'That's not good enough,' he said. 'There's a war on. No doubt you'd do your duty as you saw it as long as you were able to, but what's to happen to Rilla and the baby if you get yourself killed? There'll be nothing for them then. You'll have to marry her.'

'I don't think you quite understand my position, sir,' Barney said desperately. "I'm not able to support a wife. I took my degree before war broke out, but I have not yet started earning. My father left everything except the entailed estate to my mother and I'm entirely dependent on her.'

'You're in the army, aren't you?' Len sounded surprised. 'As your wife, Rilla would draw a regular allowance. If you were killed—which God forbid, but it's a thing we have to think about—she'd have a widow's pension, and an officer's widow's pension at that.'

There was truth in this and it was almost a relief for

Barney to find one person who was quite sure what the right course was. Dan and Colonel Franklyn had both refused to be definite, his mother's only solution had been to ignore the problem and send him away, Barney himself wavered between his repugnance at being tied and his inability to find another solution. To Len Gray the matter was clear-cut black and white: Barney had got his girl with child and now he must assume responsibility for it and that, to Len, meant the firm reassurance of a legal tie. Barney considered explaining that his brother would continue to help Rilla if anything happened to him, but he could not help seeing that this solution was scarcely fair to Dan and would certainly meet with opposition from his mother. She had already behaved atrociously. The memory of her interference made a fresh spurt of anger shoot through Barney. To hell with his family, he would manage his life without them and if he chose to give his name to little Rilla Gray they would just have to put up with it. It could be only a matter of weeks before he was sent overseas; perhaps it would be months, or even years, before he returned. The marriage would be little more than a matter of form, a temporary solution to a problem that could be shelved until peace came, and in the meantime it need hardly affect his way of life.

'All right,' he said abruptly. 'We'll get married as soon as possible.'

Len Gray relaxed. The interview had been easier than he had expected and he felt a twinge of admiration for Edith's long-headedness. She had said they might make a wedding out of it if Len didn't lose his temper. He was not the sort of son-in-law Len had ever contemplated having, but perhaps he was not such a bad young chap.

'You'd better talk to Rilla,' he said. 'She's feeling pretty low. It'll make her feel better if you—you know—ask her yourself.'

It was an awkward, unexpected flash of delicacy that made Barney feel even more guilty. The decent thing would have been to propose to Rilla immediately after she had broken the news to him. He had fallen short of that high standard, but now that a wedding seemed inevitable he was prepared to put a good face on it. As far as the world was concerned, and that included his mother, he was marrying Rilla Gray of his own free will and in spite of opposition.

But still he could not really believe that this was happening to him.

The feeling of unreality was still with him when Len went out of the room to send Rilla in, but at least the brief moment on his own gave him time to compose a suitable speech before she appeared.

'I have asked your father to consent to our marriage at the earliest possible date,' he said steadily. 'And he has said yes.'

Rilla raised her strained eyes and studied his face carefully. 'You don't really want to marry me, do you?' she asked.

'Yes, I do. The question is, do you want to marry me?'

Rilla put both her hands on his shoulders and looked up at him. 'What I want doesn't matter,' she said. 'I won't have you pushed into marrying me. It was my fault as much as yours. Don't take any notice of what Dad says. There's no need to marry me if you're unwilling.'

Looking down into her worried face, having to endure the scrutiny of those great, candid eyes, it occurred to Barney that the one person who had uttered no reproach was Rilla herself. She was even willing to take the blame for what had happened. Her words filled him with shame. She was so defenceless and so valiant. Barney took a deep breath.

'You must marry me,' he said. 'Do you really think I could have a moment's peace once I'd gone overseas, not knowing what had happened to you and the baby, not being in a position to make provision for you in the future? We'll get married as soon as we possibly can.'

To his own ears, it did not ring entirely true, but he was speaking to someone who was only too ready to be convinced. Rilla dissolved into thankful tears and took Barney through to the kitchen to break the good news to the rest of the family.

Barney rang his brother the following day. He ought, he knew, to speak to his mother, but for the moment it was more than he could bring himself to do. Let Dan break it to her.

'When's the wedding to be?' Dan asked.

'In ten days' time. I've got forty-eight hours leave that weekend. I want to bring Rilla to Appleyard.'

'Is that wise?' Dan said, a little startled.

'There may not be another opportunity for me to get home and I want to do that before . . . before anything happens. I can't very well marry Rilla that weekend and then leave her behind.'

'I see.'

So things were moving at last. Barney was likely to be sent overseas in the very near future. Dan made no comment on this, but merely enquired, 'Where's the wedding to be? The Registrar's Office?'

'No, Mrs Gray won't hear of that. It'll be at the local church—St Luke's—by special licence.'

'You'll need a best man then, you'd better have me.'

It was more than Barney had expected and Rilla, when he told her about it, was even more grateful, feeling that it gave an air of respectability to a ceremony which was too hurried to be innocent.

'Fancy you getting married before me,' Dinah said enviously. 'And to an officer, too. I think he's ever so nice, Rill, honest I do. How did you get him to ask you to marry him?' Her eyes flickered over Rilla's slim figure. 'I didn't think you'd got it in you. Though if you didn't before, I suppose you have now!'

'We love one another," Rilla said in a subdued but dignified voice. Her condition remained unchanged and there could be no doubt now that she really was pregnant, but not for the world would she make such an admission to Dinah. It had not needed her mother's warning to stop her doing that.

'There's no need to spread it all down the street,' Edith said. 'Keep a still tongue in your head, Rilla, and above all don't let it out to any of the Glosters. As well hire a town crier to shout our disgrace up and down the High Street.'

Rilla winced at her mother's reference to disgrace, but in truth Edith was secretly elated at her daughter's advantageous marriage. She entered with zest into such arrangements as wartime conditions and the limited time at their disposal would allow, even digging into her meagre savings for a new outfit for Rilla to wear to church.

'Well, it's more practical than white, you have to admit that,' Mrs Gloster remarked when she called in to find out what she could and was shown the wedding dress. 'And, of course, it'll come in very well for her later on, with that loose jacket, won't it?'

'Loose jackets are being worn this autumn, the girl in Esme's told us so,' Mrs Gray riposted. 'Of course, not everyone could wear that skirt cut on the cross, but my Rilla's got such a neat little figure she can carry it off lovely.'

Mrs Gloster retired, defeated and respectful. Not for one moment did she doubt that the Gray's Rilla had fallen for a baby, but she had to admire Edith's high-handed way of carrying it off—and, of course, it was a very nice marriage for the girl.

And so Rilla went to her wedding in the church where her own parents had been married, where she and Joyce had been christened, wearing a jacket dress in dusty pink moss *crêpe* and a little straw hat decorated with an artificial rose which clashed slightly with the colour of her outfit. She looked sick with fright and scarcely raised her voice above a whisper, but in something under half an hour she emerged as Mrs Barnaby Wainwright, clutching Barney's arm as they posed for Joyce to take a photograph with her box camera and blushing into sudden radiance when Dan claimed his right as best man to kiss the bride.

There were two unexpected witnesses to the marriage. The ceremony had just started when two late arrivals were heard entering the church. Neither Barney nor Rilla looked round, but Len looked cautiously over his shoulder and blinked at the sight of a lieutenant colonel in a pew half-way down the church, while Edith's eyes were riveted on the Paris hat the woman accompanying him was wearing. She hoped that it might be Barney's mother—it seemed funny, her not coming to her own son's wedding—but this was not the case.

Barney introduced them as they stood outside the church when it was all over. 'Colonel and Mrs Franklyn. It was good of you to come, sir.'

'Thought we'd just pop in and wish you well. Knew your father, after all. Went to *his* wedding, 'smatter of fact. Good to see Dan here. Winifred didn't come?'

'No.'

'Ah, well. Pretty little girl you've got. Can I give her a kiss?'

He removed his hat, bent down and planted a kiss on Rilla's cheek, which reduced her to speechless embarrassment. There were handshakes all round, Mrs Franklyn refused with fluent regret Edith's suggestion that they should come back to the house to drink the health of the happy couple, and they departed.

'What do you think?' Colonel Franklyn asked his wife. 'Good-looking little thing in a quiet way, isn't she?'

'Not at all bad,' Mrs Franklyn agreed. 'One could make something of her. I shall ring Winifred and tell her to stop being a fool. Young Barney, of course, is *devastatingly* attractive. I wonder whether it will last?'

'It'll last the war out, I dare say. I shall be shot of young Wainwright after that. Not my business any more. Thank you for coming along, my dear. Stupid young idiot, but he is one of ours, temporarily at any rate. Now perhaps we can put it out of our minds and start fighting the war!'

Thanks to Mrs Franklyn's telephone call, Dan found when he arrived home that his mother was at least prepared to receive Rilla. Previously she had threatened to walk out of the house the minute 'that girl' entered it.

He had sacrificed more of his precious petrol than he could really spare in order to drive to Barbury the previous day. Stupid, perhaps, but he had not been able to contemplate the possibility of having to stand for hours in an over-crowded train. As it was, his bad leg ached abominably, and he felt tired to death. Barney and Rilla were following on behind in Barney's smaller car, which he planned to lay up at home for the duration of the war.

He was glad that he had managed to arrive a little ahead of the newly-weds when his mother pounced on him as soon as he entered the house.

'Tell me the worst,' she said with a jarring laugh. 'It's done, I suppose? The little bitch didn't have a miscarriage on the church steps?'

'They are married,' Dan said. 'And it's by no means as bad as you might think. Rilla strikes me as being a very sweet girl. Her parents are respectable, honest people, trying to do their best for their daughter. Barney could have done a lot worse.'

'And a lot better,' Winifred retorted. 'What about Candida?'

'There was nothing between Barney and Candida but a boy and girl affair, if that. They played tennis together. You can't build a great romance out of that.'

He hoped this was true. He was just a little uneasy in his mind about young Barney's relations with Candida Blewett, but Barney had not so much as mentioned her, so presumably there were no regrets on his side. It was only natural that his mother should be disappointed that a flourishing friendship with the daughter of an exceedingly rich man had not progressed into marriage, but in any case Candida was away, training to be a nurse, and as far as Dan knew there had been no contact between her and Barney in recent months.

He limped across the hall and into the drawing-room, the stiffness in his leg accentuated by the fatigue of his journey.

'Let's sit down with a drink,' he suggested. 'They'll be here within the next hour, I suppose. Gin?'

'Whisky. Don't make it too strong, I've had one already. Tell me truly, Dan, is she really not so dreadful?'

'Not dreadful at all,' Dan said steadily, pouring their drinks. 'You ought to know Barney better than that. He's an irresponsible young beggar, but he's got an eye for quality. The sort of common little gold-digger you obviously have in mind would never have attracted him in the first place. As far as appearance is concerned, Rilla is perfectly acceptable.'

He sat down with a sigh of satisfaction in his favourite armchair and took a long pull at his drink.

'I've had Barbara Franklyn on the phone telling me much the same thing,' Winifred admitted.

'She and Colonel Franklyn came to the wedding. They've made it plain that they give it their approval. I think you'll have to do the same.'

'When I heard Barney with my own ears saying that he didn't want to marry her?' Winifred asked bitterly.

'He's got over that. He's really very fond of Rilla, and you'll find he's surprisingly protective towards her. He'll take it badly if you criticize her, and he doesn't need you to tell him he's made a hash of things. He's perfectly well aware of that already. If you force him to defend what he's done you'll only antagonize him. Rilla is a sweet, shy, unhappy little girl. Be kind to her and you'll keep Barney; treat her roughly and he might storm out in a rage—and you don't want that, I'm sure.'

'There's something in what you say,' Winifred admitted grudgingly. 'Very well, I'll try to be civil to the girl. At least it's only going to be for a couple days. I ought to be able to bear that.'

Dan hesitated, but now, when his mother seemed to be in a slightly more conciliatory state of mind, might be the best time to bring up the plan he had in mind.

'I would like to make it rather longer than that,' he said. 'I think Barney's baby should be born here and, until he can come home and make other arrangements, Rilla and the child should make their home at Appleyard.'

'Oh, no! That's asking too much! I won't have her here in my house.'

'It's my house,' Dan said quietly.

Winifred Wainwright gasped. She could not have been more shocked if he had thrown cold water over her. It was, of course, perfectly true. Appleyard belonged to Dan. It was something she had grown to overlook in her long, undisturbed tenure of the house to which her late husband had brought her as a bride.

'Perhaps you'd like me to leave?' she asked, her voice shaking.

'By no means. Without you Appleyard would just be a house, not a home. I need you, love, and Appleyard needs you, but if this child of Barney's is a boy then he may inherit the place one day. I think he ought to be given the chance to grow up in it, just as Barney and I did.'

'You'll marry, have children of your own,' Winifred said, but she sounded uncertain.

'Possibly. In the meantime, Barney is my heir, and Barney, my dear, is about to become a fighting soldier.'

'Nothing will happen to him,' Winifred said quickly. 'The war will probably be over soon . . .'

'No, it will be a long war, and a hard one. I hope and pray that Barney will come through it safely. I feel that the least I can do, sitting at home like an old crock, is to look after his wife and child while he's away.'

It was the most recent of many battles Winifred had fought with her elder son—fought and lost. Once Dan got that implacable note in his voice there was no arguing with him. She eyed him surreptitiously. It was absurd that he had not married, though that, too, would have meant her leaving Appleyard. One had to admit that there was something in what he said. She ought to keep the child at Appleyard and see that he was properly brought up. If she were free, the tiresome little girl Barney had got entangled with might go off and do war work.

It was a thought that enabled Winifred Wainwright to

meet Rilla with some degree of complacency and she was forced to admit to herself that the picture she had previously formed of the girl was wrong. This was no hard, designing minx with an eye to the main chance. On the contrary, as Daniel had said, she was patently terrified at meeting Barney's mother and overwhelmed by the unexpected magnificence of his home.

Appleyard was by any standards a beautiful house. To someone coming to it from Sudbury Road and expecting something along the lines of a four-bedroom suburban villa, it was breath-taking. It was two hundred years old, built of golden Cotswold stone. It stood on the crest of a low hill, protected by rising ground at the back, with a fine view of the village in the valley below. Additions had been made to it, so that the original symmetry of the design had been lost, but for all its size there was something homely about the way it rambled around corners and tumbled down a step or two to accommodate the sloping site. It was a house with charm, lovingly tended by generations of Wainwrights, a little shabby in places, but full of light and warmth.

'Unfortunately, we no longer have it to ourselves,' Winifred Wainwright said as she showed Rilla upstairs. Rilla had cast a piteous look at Barney when his mother had made a stiff suggestion about showing her to her room, but Barney avoided meeting her eye and stayed downstairs with his brother.

'The whole of the west wing has been taken over to accommodate civil servants who are working nearby,' Mrs Wainwright went on. 'Not very convenient, but at least we can let them have it to themselves, and I suppose it's better than hordes of children all over the place.'

Rilla, following her up the wide oak staircase, her eyes on the full-length portrait of Barney's grandfather that hung on the first half-landing, agreed automatically, not really hearing what was said to her.

'We've managed to keep the family portraits,' Winifred said, seeing the direction of her fixed regard. 'Some of the other pictures have had to go, to meet death duties and other expenses, but I've always felt it was important to keep the pictorial record of the family together.'

'Yes,' Rilla said. Incongruously, her mind turned to the photograph album which was one of Edith Gray's most treasured possessions. It hardly seemed the moment to mention it.

She tried to explain her feelings about Appleyard to Barney when they were at last alone together that night after an evening which had reduced Winifred's nerves to shreds. She had at last suggested that Rilla must be tired and Rilla had seized thankfully on this excuse to retire to the bedroom, which seemed the last word in luxury to her. By the time Barney joined her, she was already in bed, wearing a new white nightdress and beginning to feel a little anxious about his non-appearance. He was, although she did not realize it, embarrassed by their situation, so much so, that it had been impossible for him to go up the stairs and enter Rilla's bedroom until after his mother was safely out of the way.

'You didn't tell me your home was so grand,' Rilla said reproachfully, sitting up against the pillows and watching him potter about the room.

'Grand? I wouldn't call it that.'

'It's enormous! And it's old and historical and you've got ancestors' portraits all over the place. You didn't tell me any of that.'

'Would it have made any difference?'

'No, perhaps not, except that I would have been even more frightened,' Rilla admitted.

She looked very young in her frilly nightdress. It was ridiculous to feel reluctant to undress in front of her when they had already seen one another naked. He turned his back and began throwing off his clothes.

'You're terribly untidy,' Rilla said, shocked by his carelessness.

'You can tidy up for me while I'm in the bathroom,' he said. He touched her cheek lightly with his hand as he went past. It amused him to find that when he returned all his clothes were neatly folded and hung. 'I ought to take you with me as my batman,' he said.

'I wish you could.'

It was an exchange which brought the imminence of their parting out into the open and it had a depressing effect on both of them. Barney slid into bed without touching her. He was not at all sure that he wanted to make love to her and yet that, presumably, was what she was expecting.

'Is it all right, our sleeping together?' he asked tentatively. 'I mean, it won't hurt the baby or be bad for you?'

'I don't think so.'

She moved close against him, like a young animal seeking warmth, and his reluctance began to subside. There were as yet no signs of the child she was carrying. She was as slim and lithe and firm-fleshed as ever. He kissed her and was startled by her response, not knowing that Rilla saw this as the only way she could show her burning gratitude to him for having married her. The first time they had been together she had been tentative and unsure of herself, the second time had been uncomfortable, brief and stormy, but now she believed she knew what it was all about and, what was more, it was perfectly right and proper and they had been blessed in church for just this purpose. Barney's scruples and inhibitions were discarded as if they had never been; he became ardent, demanding and a little selfish because at the back of his mind he knew that this would probably be the last opportunity he would have to make love to the girl who had become his wife. The last opportunity for a long time, he hurriedly amended, and then drove the thought away with renewed kissing and the delight of Rilla's response.

Rilla woke up late the next day. Barney had slipped out of bed and dressed in the bathroom so as not to disturb her. He had paused and looked down with a reminiscent smile at the hunched shoulder and spread of dark hair, which was all that was visible of his young wife. Marriage to Rilla might have its problems, but it certainly also brought its rewards.

She got up and dressed quickly, worried by her lateness.

Before she screwed up her courage to go downstairs on her own she pulled back the bedroom curtains and looked down into the garden. She was surprised for a moment to see a group of young women walking down the drive and then she remembered the evacuated civil servants. As she watched, Barney appeared from among the trees to one side. He was dressed for riding, which suited him and looked romantic to Rilla, and as he crossed the grass every female head turned to look at him.

It came to Rilla with something of a shock that she was not the only woman to find her young husband singularly attractive. His height and build were bound to catch the eye, but there was more to it than that. Everything about him, from his deceptively casual grace to his teasing, lazy smile, even the hint of sulkiness about his face when he was not getting his own way, carried an aura of sexual promise. She had found him irresistible, and other women would feel the same. She sank down on the window seat, her face troubled, her eyes still fixed on Barney's unconscious figure, and for the first time thought about the future beyond the time when the baby would be born. It was going to be difficult, far more difficult than she had realized before she saw his magnificent home, to turn herself into a proper wife for Barney.

Chapter 3

Towards the end of February 1940 Rilla packed her maternity smocks, made from outgrown cotton frocks, her knitting wool, unravelled from old jumpers, and her special green ration card for expectant mothers, and went to live at Appleyard. It had not been an easy decision to make, nor had it been easy to explain to her parents. Edith, in particular, who thought a girl had a right to be near her own mother when she was expecting her first baby, was hurt and did not scruple to show it. She was only slightly mollified by Rilla's explanation.

'I don't want to go,' Rilla admitted. 'I'd much rather stay here with you, but if you'd seen Barney's home I think you'd understand. The size of it, Mum!'

'Grander than anything we can offer you, no doubt, but your home's been good enough for you up till now.'

'It isn't that. Mum, it's all very well, Barney having married me for the sake of the baby, and while he's away it's easy for me to stay with you and everything to go on as before, but what about when he comes home? I've got to be able to join him in the life he's been used to. I was lost when I went to Appleyard, I didn't know how to go on. They have wine with their meals every day—at least, they did when I was there, though I don't suppose they'll be able to carry on like that much longer. They've got their own tennis court and horses in a stable— Barney went out riding when I was there. He brought a girl back with him that he'd met while he was out and she was all togged up in Jodhpurs. That's the sort of girl he's used to, Mum, and I've got to try to learn to be a bit more like her.'

'You're going to end up thinking yourself too good for the likes of us.'

'Not that, never that! Mum, I don't *want* to go. I'm scared stiff of being without you when the baby comes, but it's good of Mrs Wainwright to ask me and it's a big step on her part. I don't feel I can turn her down. Besides . . . I write to Barney every week, regular as clockwork, but it's difficult to find things to write to him about, things that interest him, I mean. If I'm in his own home I can tell him what's happening there. He'd like that.'

The invitation from Barney's mother had taken her by surprise, but Rilla had had both the time and the courage to think very deeply about her relationship with Barney and in the end she had decided to go to Appleyard, for all the reasons she had given her mother, reinforced by a fear she did not want to put into words.

She had spoken of the girl Barney had met while out riding on the Sunday morning of their visit to Appleyard, but she took care not to betray how strongly she had been struck by Candida Blewett's obvious rightness for such a setting. Candida had all the assurance Rilla lacked and Rilla had not needed telling that here was one of the girls who would have been capable of making Barney the sort of wife Mrs Wainwright thought suitable for him.

He had brought her back for a prelunch drink—reluctantly, if the rest of his family had but known it—and had found his mother, Dan, and Rilla in the drawing-room. Rilla had looked with awe at Candida—tall, slim and elegant in her silk shirt and beautifully cut Jodhpurs, her fair hair dragged back from her face and tied with a narrow black ribbon at the back of her head—and had been able to do nothing but blush painfully when Candida offered congratulations.

'Although I believe one is not supposed to congratulate the bride, but only the bridegroom!' Candida said, with a note in her voice that made Dan look at her with closer attention. 'When I met Barney just now and he told me he was married I nearly fell off my horse! Really, the things one's friends do in wartime! Yes, I will have a drink—I feel I need it!'

'It was a surprise to us,' Winifred Wainwright said. 'Quite a whirlwind romance!'

'How long have you known Barney?' Candida asked Rilla.

'Only a month or so,' Rilla said.

'Quick work, indeed! I must say, as one of Barney's oldest and best friends, I am quite offended not to have been asked to the wedding.'

'It was very quiet.' Rilla was twisting her hands together nervously.

'Yes? Why was that?'

'Because I shall be sent away very shortly, and there was no time to arrange a large wedding,' Barney said, coming to Rilla's rescue. 'Besides, there's a war on, and it's not really the time for an enormous party.'

'I suppose you're right, although it's the first time I've ever heard you speak up for economy and restraint.' She turned to Mrs Wainwright. 'When I remember Barney's twenty-first birthday party, I do feel it's a pity that your talents couldn't have been used to make his wedding equally memorable.'

'Rilla's parents did it very nicely,' Dan said.

There was a slight pause and then Mrs Wainwright, in an effort to change the conversation, said, 'Do your nursing duties allow you time to play any tennis, Candida?'

'Oh, occasionally, but I miss my partner.'

'Candida and Barney were our local tennis champions,' Mrs Wainwright explained to Rilla. 'They played some splendid games together.'

'Indeed we did,' Candida drawled. She raised her glass to her lips and looked at Barney over the rim, her eyes glittering. 'Indeed we did. Of course, Barney is an exceptional player. *Quite* the fastest service in the game.'

Dan looked round quickly. His mother was still smiling; Rilla looked anxious but otherwise unconscious; Barney was staring at the toe of his riding boot.

'I must go,' Candida said. She stood up. 'Barney . . .'

'Are you riding Triton today?' Dan asked quickly. 'I haven't seen him for ages and you know I've always coveted him. I'll walk round to the stables with you and see you on your way.'

When he returned, Barney was on his own. He had helped himself to another drink and was downing it with the air of a man in dire need of fortification. Dan looked at him steadily, and Barney looked away.

'Been spreading yourself around a bit freely, haven't you, little brother?' Dan enquired. 'Or did I misunderstand that rather unpleasant innuendo?'

'You got it right.' Barney took another mouthful of whisky. 'Do you think Ma understood?'

'No, but then Candida has always been one of her favourites and she wouldn't be prepared to see any harm in her. She meant you to marry her, you know.'

'There was never any question of that.'

'I've sometimes wondered about Candida Blewett,' Dan said thoughtfully.

'If you've got as far as wondering and did nothing about it, you must be unique! Of course, she's always been a bit more circumspect with you. Being the elder son, you might have suited her as a permanency. I was never anything but what she said just now, a playfellow! It's true, we had some splendid times together. I'm far from regretting it, except that it was damned embarrassing meeting her out this morning and having to tell her I was married. She was much more put out about it than I thought she would be. Believe me, it wasn't my idea to bring her back here, but when she said she was coming anyway it seemed better to bring her myself and keep an eye on her.'

'Perhaps she took your little affair more seriously than you did?'

Barney looked sceptical. 'I think it's just a case of dog in the manger,' he said brutally. 'She doesn't want me herself, but she doesn't like to see me get away.'

He got no response to that remark and glancing at his brother he saw that Dan was merely looking thoughtful.

'Aren't I going to get a sermon about my wicked ways?' he asked with forced flippancy.

Dan looked mildly surprised. 'Have I ever preached to you?'

'No,' Barney admitted.

'I'm hardly in a position to do so. Looking back ten years, to when I was around your age, there are plenty of things for me to regret in my own life.'

'South American beauties?' Barney enquired with a more cheerful look on his face.

'Well, yes . . . but that wasn't what I was thinking about. It isn't easy to see you go off to fight a war and to know that if I hadn't turned myself into a crock by my own recklessness I could have gone as well.'

It was so rare for Dan to refer to his disability that the bitterness in his voice took Barney entirely by surprise.

'You're needed here,' he said awkwardly.

'Oh, yes, no doubt I shall be quite useful, but it isn't what I really want to do.' He glanced at Barney's troubled face and added on a lighter note, 'And let me tell you, I'd have been a damned sight better soldier than you, you pampered young lecher!'

Barney grimaced. 'I suppose you could say my sins have

caught up with me.' He swallowed some more whisky and then said in a gruff voice: 'I feel badly about what I've done to Rilla. You'll keep an eye on her, won't you?'

'Yes, of course.'

'She's a sweet kid. Not quite what I would have married in the ordinary way perhaps, but there's something about her ... I don't understand it myself, the way I feel about her. I suppose one day we'll have time to work it out.'

'I'll see she's all right while you're away.'

'And if anything should happen to me ...'

'It won't, but again I'd see she was all right.'

It was a commitment Dan took very seriously. Even more clearly than Rilla he saw the necessity for her to begin to live the sort of life appropriate to Barney's wife and he was pleased when his mother took up his suggestion and invited Rilla to join them at Appleyard.

She settled in, apparently without difficulty, but she was so quiet that it was impossible to discover whether she was happy or not. It came as a surprise to her to discover that Mrs Wainwright, far from being a lady of leisure, was extremely busy. She ran the Women's Institute in the village, she was an active member of the Women's Voluntary Service, helped to run a canteen for the influx of office workers in Cheltenham, did most of the gardening, kept bees, and did her best to see that Appleyard was maintained in something like its normal condition. She had a woman from the village to help with the cleaning three days a week, which Rilla would have considered a luxury if she had not been able to see for herself how demanding the old house could be, and she had old Agnes in the kitchen to do the cooking.

'She's almost past it,' Winifred Wainwright remarked. 'But it's inconceivable to pension her off, she'd die of boredom. Besides, I don't think I could do without her. Cooking has never been my favourite pastime. Thank goodness our evacuees cater for themselves.'

'Perhaps I could help?' Rilla suggested tentatively. 'I like cooking.'

She almost held her breath, willing Barney's mother to accept this offer of help. She wanted so much to be of use, but she was morbidly afraid of doing the wrong thing.

'I'd be glad if you'd keep an eye on her,' Winifred agreed carelessly. 'Agnes belongs to the "take a dozen eggs and half a pint of cream" school of cookery. She simply must learn to keep within the rations.'

Fortunately, Rilla was too diffident to put herself forward as a watchdog. She approached Agnes timidly and the old cook took it into her head that the bride was seeking lessons from her, which pleased her very much. Before long Rilla was spending most of her mornings in the kitchen, being treated rather like the kitchen maid Agnes would have had in better days.

It still did not fill up all the time Rilla had on her hands, but shortly afterwards she discovered her niche at Appleyard. Winifred, very smart in her green W.V.S. uniform, took a telephone message for Dan just as she was about to go out. She scribbled hurriedly on a piece of paper.

'Such a nuisance,' she said. 'I'm late already. Rilla, would you take this and put it on Dan's desk? He'll be back shortly.'

She thrust the piece of paper into Rilla's hand and hurried out. She was reduced now to riding a bicycle into town, pedalling furiously along the country lanes, and never allowing quite enough time to get to her appointments.

Rilla went round to the back of the house and crossed the stable yard to what she had learned to call 'the Estate Office.' She had never been inside Dan's office before and when she did so on this occasion she looked round with fascinated horror.

She placed the message Mrs Wainwright had given her in the middle of his desk, wondering as she did so whether Dan would actually see it among the chaos which surrounded the one small piece of paper.

He came in as she turned away from her shocked contemplation of the desk and she explained her errand.

'Thanks,' he said, but his mind was obviously on something else. He sat down at his desk. 'Somewhere in this lot there is a form from the War Agriculture Committee. I wonder how far down it is?'

'You're as untidy as Barney,' Rilla said severely. 'Haven't you got a filing system?'

'This is my filing system.' Dan said simply. 'I file by heap. My argument is that if I put everything down in one place then I always know where to look for it. Of course, it sometimes takes a little time to go right through the heap.'

'You ought to have a secretary,' Rilla said.

'I used to have a girl, but she's taken it into her head to join the W.A.A.F.'

'I trained as a secretary,' Rilla said. She would not venture to say more than that, but she looked at him hopefully.

'My dear Rilla, are you actually offering to help me?'

'If you think I could be of any use.'

'You'd be a life-saver,' Dan said frankly. 'I'm going out of my mind trying to keep track of all the new forms we are suddenly asked to fill in, and now the War Agriculture Committee are asking me to plough up a piece of ground that's been nothing but waste land for decades and to plant it with potatoes. Potatoes! We're dairy farmers round here. However . . . I suppose I shall have to give it a try. I'd be more than grateful for your help in the office.'

It developed into a routine which did more than anything else to help Rilla to settle in to Appleyard. She spent some time in the kitchen each morning, trying to prevent Agnes from grating a whole two-ounce ration of cheese into an unnecessary sauce, worked in the office in the afternoons and passed the evenings quietly knitting and listening to the wireless. Her letters to Barney began to be easier to write. She could describe

Dan's battles with the Agriculture Committee, knowing that he would understand the implications of the changes in farming pattern rather better than she did herself; she could tell him some of old Agnes's quainter sayings; and to her particular pleasure she was able to report that his dog, Fluke, had adopted her and followed her around everywhere, even flopping down with his head on her feet while she was typing letters for Dan in the Estate Office. The only thing she was not able to say was that Mrs Wainwright's attitude towards her had changed, even though it was by her invitation that Rilla was at Appleyard. Winifred accepted her presence, but took no pleasure in it. She made practical arrangements for the birth of the baby, took Rilla to see her own doctor and arranged for her to enter a nursing home when the time came. She made use of her, but otherwise ignored her as far as possible, just as she would have liked to ignore her evacuees in the other half of the house.

Rilla came into the room one day to find an argument going on between Dan and his mother.

'The house is ours!' Winifred was saying. 'Not mine, as you have recently reminded me, but you will, I hope, allow me the right to feel concerned about the way it's being treated. I see no reason why I shouldn't go and see for myself what those girls from the ministry are doing. I distinctly heard someone hammering yesterday!'

'You have to think of that part of the house as let,' Dan said. 'You can't walk in and out unless you ask permission first.'

'Permission! In my own house! They may be ruining the place!'

'The ministry has agreed to be responsible for any damage.' Dan still managed to hang on to his patience, but he was beginning to sound tired.

'I think I should go and inspect it, perhaps keep a record of what is being done. After all, I'm probably the only person who knows how Appleyard *ought* to be kept.'

'I'm sure you wouldn't like to put me into the position of having to apologize for anything you had done.' Dan spoke very quietly, but he succeeded in reducing Winifred to frustrated silence.

'What would be a good idea, would be if you were to ask our evacuees to come in and visit you occasionally, even just for a cup of tea.'

'I want nothing to do with them.'

'Then I will invite them and Rilla can entertain them. It would be good for her to have some younger company.'

He smiled at Rilla, but with a look of horror at the angry colour in Winifred's face she backed out of the room again.

'That was a very hurtful suggestion,' Winifred said. 'It's bad enough having that girl in the house, without trying to set her up as hostess at Appleyard, entertaining those other interlopers!'

'Not interlopers, our invited guests. You've had to be pleasant to people you haven't particularly liked in the past, and I've always admired your diplomacy. Can't you stretch a point now to help make these unfortunate girls feel a little more at home?'

'Unfortunate? Living here?'

'A long way from home,' Dan pointed out. 'Possibly not accustomed to living in the country, bored and lonely, and feeling, as they must, that they are not really wanted at Appleyard.'

Winifred bit her lip, torn between frustrated anger and a reluctant feeling that she was not living up to the part she had played in the past at Appleyard.

'I'll have them in on Sunday afternoons, three or four at a time,' she said at last. A thoughtful look passed over her face. 'With careful handling I might get myself invited into their part of the house so that I can have a look round.'

'You never give up, do you?' In spite of the misgivings he felt, Dan was smiling. 'All I ask is that if you see anything wrong you report it to me and let me handle it.'

The Sunday afternoon tea parties were stilted at first, but Winifred was too accomplished a hostess not to feel an obligation to make even unwanted guests feel at home. Rilla knew that the civil service girls laughed and called Winifred 'the Lady of the Manor' behind her back, but they were not ungrateful for the occasional break in the routine of their lives and, just as Dan had said, it was pleasant for her to have younger company from time to time. She was touched when she discovered that they were collaborating to knit a blanket for her coming baby.

Rilla's move to Appleyard coincided with a deterioration in the war situation. Finland, which had been invaded by Soviet Russia at the end of November and had initially put up a resistance that seemed to hold the Russian forces at bay, finally succumbed and sued for peace in March 1940. A month later, on 9 April, German forces began landing in Norway. Before the end of the day they had taken Oslo and all the major ports. In addition they had entered Denmark. It was the beginning of a catastrophic slide towards the fall of one European country after another to the advance of the German army.

Every night Rilla, Dan and Winifred gathered round the wireless to listen to the nine o'clock news. It gave them little cause for anything but anxiety. Indeed Barney, writing triumphantly that he was seeing action at last, seemed less concerned than they were, sitting in safety in the quiet English countryside.

'He sounds as if he's enjoying it,' Rilla said in puzzlement.

'Didn't you think he would?' Dan asked. 'Barney is a young man who likes action. Sitting around doing nothing doesn't agree with him.'

'He gets into mischief,' Winifred remarked, in an acid aside which Rilla acknowledged by a self-conscious blush.

By May she was heavily pregnant and she moved with a controlled dignity which Dan found touching.

'I've been hoping that Barney might get some leave,' she said wistfully one day. 'But I suppose it's not likely.'

'I'm afraid not,' Dan agreed. 'Things are going badly, Rilla.'

'Yes, I realize that,' she agreed. 'I . . . I'm not very good at geography. I don't think we did Europe at school. I think I'd find it easier to follow if we had a map.'

'Good idea,' he said. 'I'm sure there must be a map of Europe around, probably in the old schoolroom. I'll put it up on the wall of the office and we'll follow events as they happen.'

On 10 May 1940, German airborne troops struck against neutral Holland and Belgium. In five days Holland had capitulated. Dan stuck a Nazi swastika over that spot on the map.

'No use closing our eyes to the facts,' he said.

'I haven't had a letter from Barney this week,' Rilla said.

'I expect he's . . . busy,' Dan said. He was looking at the map with a frown on his face. 'I wish the news was a little more specific. I don't like the sound of this fighting in the Ardennes. I've been told it's an impossible terrain for tanks. If it wasn't for that I'd say it sounded ominously like a determined push into France.'

Day by day they watched the Allied armies, in the form of the little flags they had contrived, being pushed back and back towards the sea.

'I hoped things might improve once Churchill became Prime Minister,' Winifred remarked over breakfast one morning.

'It was already too late,' Dan said.

Rilla came in, a letter in her hand, her face radiant. 'I've heard from Barney,' she said. 'Only a little scribble, obviously written in an awful hurry, but he's all right.'

She was looking at Winifred and saw the spasm that crossed the older woman's face as relief fought with jealousy. 'He sends you his love,' she added hurriedly. She laughed, too happy to worry for long about Winifred's adverse reaction. 'And a pat on the head for Fluke.'

'What, nothing for me?' Dan enquired.

Rilla shook her head, suddenly overcome by a wave of emotion. 'I . . . I must get a hanky,' she said. 'Oh dear, how silly of me, to cry because I'm happy!'

She hurried out of the room. In the silence that followed Winifred said in a low voice, 'He might have written to me.'

'I think Barney's got his priorities right,' Dan said deliberately. 'Rilla was badly in need of some reassurance.'

'I'm his mother.'

'And she is his wife, and carrying his baby.' He met his mother's eyes fairly and squarely. 'The time is rapidly approaching when you are going to have to come to terms with that.'

'I've taken her into my home, made her welcome . . . '

Dan's eyebrows rose. 'Taken her into your home, yes; made her welcome, no.'

'I hate the sight of her,' Winifred said, all her bitterness coming to the surface. 'She seems to grow bigger every time I see her. Everyone must know by this time why Barney married her.'

'By "everyone" you mean people in the village, one or two farmers and a few of your friends. Ma, it's of no importance.'

'Not to you, perhaps. You don't care that Barney has ruined his life.'

'I don't agree that he has ruined his life. I've come to know Rilla pretty well over the last few months. She's been a tower of strength to me in the office. She's quick, neat, methodical and intelligent.'

'She's uneducated.'

'Nonsense! She just happens to have learnt different skills from the ones you value. When I think of some of the illiterate little birdwits who played at being debutantes in my young days, I think Rilla comes off quite well by comparison.'

'Oh, it's hopeless to talk to you,' Winifred said, getting up from the breakfast table. 'You're as infatuated with the girl as Barney is.'

'No, not that,' Dan said. 'But I do believe in giving credit where it's due and I think you are unjust to Rilla.'

'Don't let's talk about it any more,' Winifred said wearily. 'I don't want to quarrel with you.'

He looked at her with sudden attention. 'You look tired, Ma,' he said. 'You're doing too much.'

'I've been worried to death about Barney. You might make allowances for that. It's galling to get second-hand messages from him when I've been lying awake at night worrying about him.' She smiled slightly. 'Poor Dan, two emotional women to cope with—and over the breakfast table, too!'

By mutual consent they let the subject drop. To Dan, in spite of his concern for both of them, the poor relations between the two women seemed of little importance compared with the struggle taking place on the other side of the Channel. His misgivings about the fighting in the Ardennes had proved only too prophetic. Exploiting the mistaken belief that it could not be done, the German tanks broke through where they were least expected. Their advance continued with incredible speed until one evening a few days later, when Dan got up and switched off the wireless after the nine o'clock news, Winifred said incredulously, 'It isn't possible that France might fall, is it? Not *France!*'

Dan did not answer. In his opinion it was only too likely and he could only wonder that his mother found it necessary to ask the question.

'But that means . . . there will be no one left but us,' Rilla said, correctly interpreting his silence.

'What of it?' Winifred said. 'We're not beaten yet. And we won't be. If any Germans come here I shall shoot them myself.'

In spite of his forebodings Dan could not help smiling at her imperious tone. 'That's the spirit, Ma,' he said.

On 25 May the decision was taken that the British Expeditionary Force would retreat to the sea at Dunkirk. The following day the King of the Belgians began to sue for an armistice for his hard-pressed country, already almost entirely occupied by the victorious Germans.

'It's a race between us and the Germans,' Dan said, looking at the last tiny space on the map which was not overrun.

'If our army can get to Dunkirk and hold it, there's a chance of getting some of them away at least.'

'Barney . . . ' Rilla said.

He controlled a momentary irritation at her single-mindedness and smiled at her. 'I hope so.'

They were interrupted by the telephone. Dan answered it and seemed surprised when he discovered the identity of his caller.

'Greg! You old sea-horse! Where are you? I haven't heard from you for ages!'

The rest of his conversation was more cryptic, consisting mostly of long periods of silence while he listened to his friend on the other end of the line, interspersed by murmurs of assent. At last he said, 'Well, yes, of course, I'd be only too glad of the chance to go. It's damned frustrating, sitting here unable to lift a finger. When do you expect your sailing orders? Yes, I suppose the professionals are bound to delay calling in the amateurs as long as they can, but I quite agree with you that small boats will be necessary to act as ferries between the naval vessels and the shore. Yes, I remember it vividly—I should! That was the place where the drunken French sailor tried to lay you out with a wine bottle and I had to carry you on board and put out to sea single-handed! Right, I'll get my gear together and join you at Weymouth tomorrow.'

He put down the telephone, stood up and stretched himself. All of a sudden he looked younger, alert and vigorous, a man Rilla had not seen before.

'At last, something I can do!' he said. 'Oh, God, how I do hate not being able to join up, especially now that we are fighting for our lives. Rilla, if that interfering so-and-so from the War Ag Committee rings up, say I'll get in touch with him in a few days' time.'

'But where are you going?' she asked.

'Fishing.'

'Fishing?'

He paused in the doorway, his face alight with anticipation. 'Yes—for men.'

The rescue of the British Expeditionary Force from the beaches of Dunkirk by the Royal Navy, the Merchant Navy and a makeshift armada of little boats began with a dry announcement read out after the nine o'clock news on Tuesday, 14 May 1940:

> The Admiralty have made an order requiring all owners of self-propelled pleasure craft between thirty and one hundred feet in length to send any further particulars of them to the Admiralty within fourteen days from today, if they have not already been offered or requisitioned.

It was heard by Dan's friend, Gregory Parker, the fortunate possessor of a forty-foot motor yacht which had carried him round many European ports in the days before the war. He sent in the details requested and began to follow the movements of the British troops, as far as he could from the news which was given out, with even closer attention that he had before. His call to Dan had been urgent. The evacuation had already begun and the supply of small boats was proving inadequate to remove the numbers of men assembling on the vast sandy beaches around the port of Dunkirk.

It was a port the two men had visited before and neither of them underestimated the dangers of the task in front of them. It was a difficult harbour and a treacherous coast, littered with the wrecks of vessels which had run aground on the shifting sand banks. While the wide beaches would be useful for assembling the troops—and how many there would be was a question still unanswered when Dan and Greg set sail on 28 May—they also presented one of the major hazards of the operation, since they sloped so gently into the sea that only boats which drew the minimum depth of water could approach near enough to take up the men.

The main harbor of Dunkirk itself was already blocked and useless following an air attack on 20 May, which left only two possible embarkation points apart from the open beaches —a jetty to the west of the harbour and the long, narrow East Mole. To this East Mole, once it had been established that ships could berth alongside it, the naval destroyers inched their way, to load up with weary, battle-shocked troops. H.M.S. *Wakeful,* H.M.S. *Codrington,* H.M.S. *Harvester,* one after the other, they packed in the men and turned for home, while H.M.S. *McKay* stuck fast on a sand bank, and H.M.S. *Sabre* skimmed over the shoals with inches to spare and made for Dover.

On her second trip the *Wakeful,* already holed by an attack sustained on the return voyage from Dover to Dunkirk, was torpedoed. Torn apart by the explosion amidships, she sank in under a minute, and seven hundred troops, packed below decks, went down with her. Other ships in the vicinity began to search for survivors, and the German submarine U-62 closed in for a second kill. It was successful beyond the commander's expectation. Two torpedoes found a target in the destroyer *Grafton,* slicing away the stern and exploding in the wardroom. Taken by surprise, the other naval vessels cast round for the source of the attack. The minesweeper *Lydd* sighted what appeared to be a torpedo boat making an escape and opened fire, an example followed by the stricken *Grafton,* which was still afloat. It was an error in identification more malignant than the original attack. The supposed torpedo boat was the drifter *Comfort,* laden with survivors she had picked up from the *Wakeful.* Raked by machine gun bullets, rammed by the *Lydd,* the *Comfort* sank. Of her crew and the men she had rescued, only five survived.

The evacuation continued. Dan and Greg arrived at first light on May 29. It was unpleasant weather, with fog and drizzle, but it favoured their task, except that a heavy swell created difficulties in taking up the number of men it had been hoped the small boats could handle.

By midday the mist had cleared and eyes were turned apprehensively towards the clear sky, watching for the aircraft that would surely come.

Greg Parker, a former naval officer in his forties, with a jutting beard and a patch, which concealed the empty eye socket which had put him out of the navy—'as if they'd never heard of Nelson' he remarked bitterly—had had the forethought to don his old uniform jacket. In spite of the fact that it was worn over a dirty, white polo-necked sweater and ancient corduroy trousers, it gave him an authority to which he was not entitled, but which was of the greatest assistance in controlling men on the verge of panic. Nor had he forgotten his quarter-deck voice, and he used it to advantage when there was an attempt to rush his small boat.

'Hold back there! One at a time, and let's see a bit of discipline! Any man who makes a false move, I'll push his head under!'

The stampede subsided. There was even a reluctant laugh, and the soldiers, up to their armpits in sea water, some of them making their third or fourth attempt to climb aboard one of the rescuing boats, once more fell back into an orderly line.

'We'll be back in a minute, as soon as we've hoisted this lot aboard the destroyer,' Dan said consolingly.

He lost count of the trips they made, weighed down with weary, dirty men, cramped with hunger and thirst and red-eyed from lack of sleep. He was struck by the number of them who were still loaded with equipment and suggested to Greg as they returned yet again with an empty boat to the beach between Malo-les-Bains and Bray Dunes that it would be better to jettison all this unnecessary weight.

Greg shook his head. 'No,' he said decisively. 'Let them hold on to everything they can salvage. Good for morale. Separate a soldier from his boots and his rifle and he's finished. While he's still got them he's a fighting unit. Besides, those tiresome knapsacks have probably got personal possessions in them, things they'd not want to lose.'

He glanced up, towards the eastern sky. 'Here they come. I've been expecting this. Now we've really got trouble.'

The Stukas, fitted with sirens to add terror to their steeply-angled dives, screamed down on the mass of shipping and men and all hell broke loose. They concentrated on the harbour where the all-important East Mole was crammed with ships lying stem to stern. It was a target they could not miss. Against the thud of their exploding bombs, the fearful blaze of stricken ships, the retaliatory fire of the Vickers and Bofors guns, the little boats still crept forward towards the open beaches, towards the desperate men.

Greg commandeered a couple of tin helmets from somewhere. 'Not much protection against a hundred-pound bomb,' Dan remarked, but he perched the helmet on his head and was surprised by the psychological value of having something between him and the rain of bullets and shrapnel.

In a brief lull in the bombing, they picked up yet another load and began to make their precarious way back towards the ship they were helping to load. They passed the old Thames paddle-steamer *Crested Eagle.*

'Game old bird,' Greg said absent-mindedly. He raised his voice. 'Heads down! They're coming for us again.'

The huddled mass of men ducked as the screaming planes zoomed overhead, but they were not the target. It was the wallowing, overloaded *Crested Eagle* which was hit. The great wash from the explosion caught Greg's small craft and rocked it violently; they shipped water, but there was no damage. The *Crested Eagle,* men in flames leaping from her decks, crept on her way, almost unbelievably still capable of steering, until she reached the shallows, and the struggling, burning men could jump overboard and cool themselves in the bitter salt water out of which they had been hoisted such a short time before.

Without comment, Greg continued on his way.

'The men in the water . . . ' Dan said numbly.

'We're as full as we can hold already. We'll do what we can for them on the return trip.'

Again and again, they crept between ship and shore, until the light began to fail. On the last trip of the day, the men they were helping could hardly find the strength to climb the nets into the ship.

They watched the grey destroyer slide away into the gathering gloom.

'Right, that's our lot,' Greg said briskly.

'You're not giving up?' Dan asked in surprise.

'Not me! What I'm going to do is to stand out to sea where no one can give me any orders and have some food and a rest. Do you realize we haven't eaten since breakfast, my old son?'

'It's been a busy day,' Dan said through cracked lips.

He was conscious, now that the tension had eased, of great weariness and a pain in his chest which he knew came from his overtaxed lungs. Greg was right, they needed rest, and the thought of food brought a cramp of hunger to his stomach.

'I've stocked up for a week if necessary,' Greg said. 'Did a bit of pre-war hoarding which has come in very useful.'

'A week! Surely it can't go on that long? The Germans will overrun the beaches before that.'

'You never know.'

The contents of Greg's small galley revealed a forethought which did not surprise Dan, who had reason to know Greg's organizing flair from the past. Half an hour later, with a plate of hot tinned stew followed by tinned rice pudding inside him, with hands cupped round a steaming mug of cocoa laced with rum, he felt like a new man, except that he was having difficulty in keeping his eyes open.

'Those poor devils on the beaches,' he said. 'Some of them have already been without food and water for days.'

'The longer we keep up our strength, the more we shall be able to take off,' Greg pointed out. 'Water is one thing we have to go carefully on ourselves. Strictly for drinking, not for washing, I'm afraid. I always told you you should grow a beard like me.'

'I shall have one if we keep this up for a week,' Dan said with an ear-splitting yawn.

'Bunk time, old son.' The look Greg turned on Dan was kindly and a little anxious. It had been something of a gamble, asking Dan to join him on the *Glad Hand,* but he knew him well enough to believe that his dogged courage would carry him through. He was not going to risk the possibility of Dan cracking up now from lack of rest.

Dan woke just as the sky was beginning to show a faint greyness in the east. He stumbled on deck, yawning and stretching. The air was cold and dank. Dank . . . with sharpened attention Dan looked round him. Everything was covered in a thick layer of white mist, visibility was down to a few yards.

Greg chuckled. 'A gift from the gods, old son. A good old sea fog. Couldn't be better. Brew up the tea and we'll be on our way.'

Looking back afterwards, that was the last rest Dan could remember taking, but it had come at the right moment, after a shattering day. They picked their way forward through the shifting banks of mist, Greg cursing steadily in a way that Dan recognized as a good sign; when Greg was quiet, something was wrong. Their appearance as they loomed out of the fog was greeted by a faint cheer from the men on the shore.

They began the ferrying routine once more. The men with whom they were dealing now were fighting troops, fresh from the battlefields, and discipline seemed stricter than it had been the day before. The mist blew aside for a moment and Dan caught a glimpse of a tall young officer on the beach, marshaling the men and sending them forward in an orderly fashion. It might almost have been Barney, there was something familiar about his height and build, but the fog thickened again and he was lost to sight.

Dan put a question to the next man he helped on board, but the soldier shook his head. 'Sorry, sir, don't know a Lieutenant Wainwright. There was some young officer pushing us into line, but he wasn't one of my mob.' A faint grin showed for a moment on his cracked lips. 'Swears like a real trooper, whoever he is, and he knocked a man flat for trying to take some poor wounded bugger's water bottle—he'd lose his commission for that in peacetime. A right young fire-eater, but what his name was I couldn't tell you.'

Dan could spare no more time. It might have been Barney, it might not, but from that moment on he realized that he was scrutinizing each face as the men climbed aboard, in the faint hope that his brother might be amongst the rescued.

The East Mole was put out of action, which threw an even heavier burden on the small craft taking men from the beaches, but now they were reinforced by a whole flotilla of little boats, more than a thousand of them and more to come.

'How does it happen that we're here already?' Dan enquired, knowing the answer beforehand.

'We jumped the gun, old son.'

'I don't know how you managed to last as long as you did in the Royal Navy! Insubordination's your watchword!'

'Initiative,' Greg said in a hurt voice. 'We've been useful, haven't we?'

They had been useful. They went on being useful, until it began to seem as if they had never known anything but this ceaseless activity in the midst of a burning holocaust.

Attempts were made to rig up improvised jetties and the small craft lying alongside them were able to load troops without the men having to stand up to their necks in sea water. With the aid of these fragile constructions the troops could be loaded in a more orderly fashion. Dan had to strike desperate men on the knuckles forcing them to relinquish a hold on the side of the boat which threatened to swamp it.

The following day, hampered by a strong wind, they began taking French troops on board in addition to the British. It was a bad day for enemy action in the air. By this time they were beginning to be well-known, and the soldiers were eager to climb on board. Dan gathered that the little *Glad Hand* was believed to bear a charmed life and certainly, watching Greg steering nonchalantly through the burning wrecks which littered the coast, alternatively whistling under his breath and cursing steadily at the Huns overhead, it seemed as if there was an element of magic in their continued survival. The toll among the larger ships from bombs and torpedo attacks was fearful. Dazed, fear-stricken men were rescued from the beaches, loaded on to a ship and sent on their way for home and safety, only to be struck by torpedoes and thrown struggling into the sea. Some of them were picked up, some were not, and of those rescued a second time many were caught yet again between the bombers and the submarines.

Dan and Greg made their final effort on the night of 1 June. 'This is our lot,' Greg said as evening drew on. 'Not a hope of refuelling now and we're dead on our feet. We'll work through the night, but come the dawn it's England, home, and beauty for you and me, my old son.'

Only a few minutes later, their luck ran out. They were standing in close to the beach, about to start reloading, when the enemy aircraft swept overhead, strafing the crowded beach with machine guns. They passed over the water, bullets making a fantastic pattern of splashes as they hit the waves. The man at the head of the patient line gave a bubbling scream, threw up his hands and fell backwards, blood pouring from the hole which had been torn in his throat. The man behind him pushed his body out of the way and moved a step forward.

The planes turned in a wide arc and came back for a second attack. Dan, stooping over the bow of the boat, was knocked off his feet by what felt like a vicious blow on his shoulder. He tried to sit up, but his right arm was hanging uselessly by his side, with blood seeping through the rough wool of his jersey.

Greg left the wheel and came to him. His own face, down one side, was covered with blood.

'Just a splinter of wood,' he said in response to Dan's horrified gasp. 'Let's have a look at you, old son.' He took out a knife and ripped open the sleeve soaked in blood. 'Nasty. The bullet's gone right through, but I think the bone's broken.'

'I don't think it is.' Dan moved his arm cautiously. 'It was knocked numb, but I'm beginning to get movement back. It's damned painful, but nothing seems to be grating. Can you patch me up?'

Greg sat back on his heels. 'Are you game to carry on?'

Dan looked at him steadily. 'We said we'd work through the night and I think we must. I'll manage.'

Greg stood up. 'We've still got a first aid pack. I'll do what I can for you.'

He cupped his hands round his mouth and called to the waiting troops: 'Normal service will be resumed shortly.'

Decorated by a row of bullet holes, fortunately all above the water line, the *Glad Hand* went back into action. All through the night Dan kept up the gruelling programme, biting back the blistering invective that sprang to his lips as some stumbling soldier jostled his throbbing arm, but early in the morning of 2 June Greg loaded up with a lighter cargo of passengers than before and made for the English coast.

'With any luck we won't hit a mine,' he said with a nonchalance that would have seemed casual to anyone who had not witnessed his seamanship over the last few days. 'We'll make for Ramsgate, I think. Nice place, Ramsgate. I used to know a widow who lived there. Kept a boarding house; very hospitable.'

'I bet she was,' Dan said automatically. He passed his tongue over his dry lips. Their water was exhausted, their food was running low, and he needed medical attention. Greg was right, it was time to turn for home, and yet . . . there were still men waiting to be rescued. It was hard to leave them.

They put in to Ramsgate, one of a tiny fleet, and received a welcome which shook them profoundly. There seemed to be people everywhere, all eager to extend a helping hand. Someone had put up a makeshift banner: 'Welcome Home Our Heroes.'

'Cripes,' muttered one dazed soldier as he stepped ashore

from the battered *Glad Hand.* 'Don't they realize we've been beaten?'

'Beaten!' A woman who had heard him turned on him furiously, looking bitterly offended. She thrust a cup of steaming tea into his hand. 'Drink that and don't talk so daft! We haven't started fighting yet! Old Hitler doesn't know what he's let himself in for, now that our blood is up!'

Dan could not help smiling at the look on the man's face, but he was also aware of a change in atmosphere. The hot drinks and sandwiches worked a small miracle, but a lot more was due to the spirit that seemed to have got abroad. Tired backs straightened, heads were lifted, eyes that had been dull with defeat brightened. The kindness of the local people seemed unending. Half-naked, sea-soaked and barefoot men were given clothing and shoes, cigarettes were thrust on them, and offers of places to rest, but it was not the intention to allow crowds of survivors to build up at the Channel ports. As soon as they had had the minimum of rest and refreshment, they were collected together and taken off to the railway station.

'Notice something, old son?' Greg asked thoughtfully.

'They were marching,' Dan said.

'That's right. Not quite up to Guards' standard, but not bad considering what they've been through.'

Not bad, Dan thought, through a haze of fatigue and pain that dulled his brain. It had been worth it. He and Greg had done their bit and come through it safely—almost safely—and the men who had come home were still disciplined troops, not a demoralized mob. Only one question knocked unceasingly at his tired mind. Where was Barney?

Chapter 4

Once he was launched into action Barney proved himself to be a good soldier. Unlike the racehorse to which Colonel Franklyn had likened him, he was steadied by the sound of gunfire. He became sensible, careful of his men, but with an element of daring about him which kept them alert. His natural assurance stood him in good stead. He never doubted his ability to lead; and since this inbred assumption of authority was backed up by nerve and intelligence, he was given respect as well as obedience. He began to value the men under his command, to admire their stoicism and courage. He began to see the value of the lessons in instant obedience which had been hammered into him. He discovered that the laconic advice of his sergeant was worth having.

Sergeant Hillier, who had seen more service than all the rest of the platoon put together, was heard to remark that he was almost as good as a regular, which sounded like temperate praise, but actually placed Barney considerably higher in Sergeant Hillier's estimation than the majority of his fellow officers.

After a slow start, during a period when it was something of a privilege to be allowed to join French troops in a minor skirmish with the enemy, Barney's battalion saw some hard fighting in northern France. It was Barney's initiation into real warfare and he felt relieved that he came out of it well. He found it possible simultaneously to hate war and yet to find a curious enjoyment in it. On the credit side there was the sense of comradeship, the excitement of fighting for one's life, which had little to do with the mock battles he had taken part in during his O.T.C. days, an occasional pleasant sense of having outwitted the enemy. This last was rare. They were outnumbered and, worse than that, outmanoeuvred by the advancing German troops, and there was little exhilaration in constant retreat.

The invasion of Holland and Belgium focused attention on the north and disguised the really dangerous point of attack, through the hills of the Ardennes, outflanking the famous Maginot Line, on which the French had pinned their faith for the defence of their country, and on into the heart of France.

The British Expeditionary Force heard of the crossing of the Meuse at Sedan on 13 May with something like disbelief. The Allies had been outwitted and the Germans exploited their advantage to the full, racing towards the coast.

At about the time that Dan and Rilla set up the map on the Estate Office wall at Appleyard and began their anxious watch on the diminishing area in Allied hands, Barney's battalion withdrew, yet again, with orders to hold their position as long as possible.

'We might hang on for a week, but I doubt whether it will even be as long as that,' Martin Marshall said to Barney. His normally cheerful face looked gloomy. 'You know what's happening, don't you? We're being pushed into the sea.'

'I don't know what you're looking so down in the mouth

about,' Barney retorted. 'I'm the one who's just been given orders to move up the hill.'

Martin looked at the hillock scornfully. 'Call that a hill?'

'I call it a nasty exposed outpost.'

'Your chance of glory, old boy,' Martin pointed out. 'It'll encourage me no end to know that you're holding the Hun hordes at bay while I make . . . '

Barney joined in the chorus: ' . . . a strategic withdrawal to a prepared position.'

He collected his platoon together and they set off, moving cautiously over the rising ground. Their destination was a ruined farmhouse, consisting of little more than a bombed-out shell and outbuildings surrounding a courtyard.

'There's always a pong on these French farms,' Sergeant Hillier remarked as their noses were greeted by the odour of the midden in the centre of the courtyard.

They positioned look-outs with Bren guns, set up the light mortar, and settled down to wait. For the moment everything was quiet.

'Too quiet,' Barney said. 'Keep your eyes skinned. Something's bound to start soon.'

There was a cough from Sergeant Hillier, a sure sign that he had something to say.

'O.K., sergeant, what have I forgotten?' Barney asked with the frankness that had made him a popular officer.

'Might be a good idea if we searched the buildings, sir—such as they are.'

'The place looks empty enough,' Barney said. 'But I agree. Detail a party of men to go round—and, sergeant, if the poor devils who used to live here have left any of their belongings behind, they're to stay where they are, but, if there's anything in the eating or drinking line, we'll have it.'

The sergeant was back with his report while Barney was still raking the countryside with his binoculars, uneasy at this unaccustomed lull in activity.

'There's what looks like a couple of new graves round the

far side,' he said. 'Probably some of the family got killed in an air raid and the others buried them and moved out. No live-stock left, but there's a barrel of apples, a few turnips and half a dozen bottles of wine in the cellar.'

'What about water?'

'There's a pump that's still working—and the water seems O.K.'

'Good enough for a G.H.Q.' Barney commented. 'Tell the blokes they can have a few apples each, but if anyone touches the wine I'll chop his hand off. I don't want anyone falling asleep this afternoon. Where the devil are the Germans, ser-geant?'

'Collecting themselves together, I'd guess, sir. They made a massive push yesterday. Probably waiting for their supplies to catch up with them.'

It was dull work, hanging around waiting for something to happen. One of the men produced a pack of cards and four of them settled down to a game of pontoon. The flies were a nuisance. The midden steamed gently, but everyone grew used to that after a time. Periodically, Barney peered through his binoculars at the innocent-looking countryside, until at last something caught his eye and he looked again more closely, then without comment handed his glasses to Sergeant Hillier.

'Two o'clock of that clump of trees directly in front of us,' he said. 'What do you make of it?'

The sergeant focused the glasses. 'Flash of light on glass, sir,' he said. 'There's a road down there.'

'Yes, the trees hide it from view most of the way. Corporal Millet and you, Donaldson, do a quick reconnaissance. Keep low and use the cover of the trees and find out what's moving down there.'

The two men slipped away and began a quick, creeping run down the shallow slope towards the belt of trees.

'Everyone else keep out of sight. There's bound to be a reconnaissance plane over shortly.'

The corporal and his companion stumbled back breathlessly a few minutes later. 'Two armoured cars and a tank, sir,' Corporal Millet reported.

'Splendid. Send a signal to H.Q.' He glanced round. 'I'm going up to the top of the old chimney stack. From there I can see down into the only place where we're likely to catch them in the open.'

The sergeant coughed. 'A bit exposed up there, sir,' he suggested.

Barney looked up. 'Yes,' he agreed.

He climbed to the top of the massive chimney which had once formed the only source of heat for the living quarters. For a moment or two nothing seemed to stir in the valley below, then the first armoured car came into view on the clear stretch of road. Barney did not fool himself that the Germans were unaware of the presence of Allied forces in the area. He had a feeling that powerful German binoculars were focused on him personally. He called to Sergeant Hillier and the mortar opened fire.

The first car was hit, of that there was no doubt. It slewed across the road, hampering the advance of the vehicles behind it. Barney's little garrison trained their gun on the second car. The result was even more spectacular. It burst into flames. Barney spared one sickened thought for the men trapped inside it and then descended from his high perch. Two successes, but now retaliation was about to fall on them. The tank which had brought up the rear left the road and was bucketing towards them across the fields, crashing through the minor obstacles it encountered, its gun blazing. They opened fire, but Barney knew that their comparatively light weapons did not have the power to penetrate a heavily armoured tank. It would be a very lucky accident if they were able to do more than hinder its progress temporarily. They were all flat on the ground, taking what shelter they could, and the tank, with its devastating firing power, was getting nearer.

Amid the gunfire a new sound made itself heard. Barney

glanced up. 'Well, what do you know, the R.A.F.'s turned up on time for once!'

His facetious libel masked a feeling of profound relief. The aircraft zoomed overhead and they ducked low as a string of bombs was let loose. Craters appeared in the fields, a shower of earth and dust descended on them. The tank continued to advance.

'Cor, what a rotten aim,' Corporal Millet said, licking the dust from his dry lips, but he spoke prematurely. The tank lurched a yard or two, then there was a tremendous explosion and it disintegrated in a sickening shower of metal and torn flesh.

'Not bad,' Barney said. 'Two armoured cars and a tank out of action.' His hands were shaking slightly as he pushed his cap from his forehead. They had had a lucky escape.

It had been too easy. Nemesis arrived a minute or two later. The R.A.F. plane which had come to their aid was still in the air overhead. Out of the sun German fighters screamed towards it. It climbed and twisted, seeking a vantage point from which it could return the attack, but it was outnumbered by the German planes. One of the Stukas caught it full in its gun sights, there was a burst of machine gun fire and then the British aircraft dived for the ground, out of control and streaming a tail of smoke behind it. A white parachute broke from it and then another one, and drifted downwards, but Barney and his group of men had no time to decide whether the survivors were going to land behind enemy lines or among their own people. The German planes dived on their small outpost, engines screaming, bullets rattling and singing against the cobbled courtyard.

Barney picked himself up and spat out a mouthful of dust. 'Anyone hurt?' he called.

A chorus of reassuring answers came back, but one man did not speak. Corporal Millet lay on his back, his eyes wide open, an expression of total surprise on his face, quite dead.

They left him where he was. There was no time to do anything else. The murderous hail of machine gun bullets was on them again. This time one of the men manning a Bren gun yelped and clapped his hand to his leg. Barney crawled towards him. Blood was already seeping through his trouser leg and it was obvious that the bone was broken. Crouched in the corner of the wall, he and Sergeant Hillier fixed him up with a make-shift splint.

A bullet whistled through the gap of what had once been a window.

'That didn't come from the air,' Barney said. He took a cautious look through the open gap. A second bullet cracked into the plaster by the side of his head.

'Damn. It must be one of the Huns out of that first car we put out of action. Enterprising devil, he's got into the trees while we've been occupied, and I would guess he's shinned up one of them and is taking pot shots at us with a telescopic rifle. Very nasty. Do you think we can get him, Sergeant Hillier?'

'He's well within our range, sir. It's just a question of spotting him.'

Barney took off his cap and put it on the end of a length of splintered wood. 'Just like cowboys and Indians,' he remarked. 'Keep a sharp lookout, sergeant.'

He exposed the cap at the window. The next minute it was spun out of his hand as a bullet caught it squarely on the crown. Barney crawled along the ground and picked it up, looking thoughtfully at the jagged hole the bullet had inflicted on it.

'I've got him, sir,' Sergeant Hillier said. 'He's in the third beech tree from the left.'

'Right, then turn the mortar on the blighter. And everyone else keep their eyes skinned for any other activity.'

The mortar spoke once, twice and then a third time. The leaves on the trees in front of them were blown away, leaving bare, scarred branches. A body toppled slowly forward. Barney focused his glasses. He could see quite clearly the man's hands desperately trying to scrabble for a hold on the branches as he fell. He hit the ground, but he did not lie still. He lay on the grass writhing in agony.

'He's still alive,' Barney said.

'Up to his own side to do something about that,' Sergeant Hillier said.

It was a fine spring day, warm and sunny. Unbelievably, a bird was singing somewhere. They seemed to have been given a brief respite. Everything was quiet.

'I'm going down the hill for a look at the road up ahead,' Barney said.

He filled a water bottle with fresh water before he left. Sergeant Hillier watched him without comment. For all it seemed so quiet Barney took no chances. He squirmed over the ground, making use of such cover as there was. The wounded German marksman lay on the ground a little to his left. Barney approached him cautiously, but the man was beyond making any move against him. As Barney came up to him he opened his eyes and moved his head slightly. His lips moved, but no sound came out. Barney unscrewed the top of his water bottle and held it to his lips. He tried to swallow, but the water ran away down his chin. Barney slipped an arm under his shoulders and raised his head. This time he managed to take a little of the water. Intelligence returned to his eyes for a moment. He looked puzzled and slightly hostile. Barney could feel warm blood soaking through from the German's back on to his hand. He laid him down and wiped the blood away from his hand on the short, thick grass. There was little more he could do. The man obviously was not going to last much longer.

When he gained the cover of the trees, he stopped and put his binoculars up to his eyes. The road immediately in front of him was clear, but in the distance a line of lorries was on the move. Martin's words about holding back the Hun hordes came back to him and he grimaced. Not much chance of their little outpost holding up that lot for long. He went back up the hill. The German soldier was dead. Barney took time to collect his rifle with its telescopic sights and to remove the supply of ammunition, then he made a quick dash for the ruined farm-house.

'Lorry-loads of Germans coming up the road,' he said. 'See if you can raise H.Q. for me, sergeant, and I'll pass on the news.'

He also asked for further orders, not very hopefully. As he had feared, they were to stay where they were and to hold up the convoy for as long as possible. It came into sight a few minutes later, moving confidently down the road.

'They're going to have to stop to get those vehicles we shot up out of the way,' Sergeant Hillier said.

'Just what I was thinking,' Barney agreed. 'And if the chap in charge has any fighting sense at all he'll turn out some of the troops from the lorry at the rear, which will still be under cover of the trees, to attack us while we're shooting up the one in front, so keep your eyes skinned for anyone creeping through the woods.'

They waited until the leading lorry came to a halt and a party of Germans scrambled from the back to manhandle the remains of the armoured cars out of their path, then they opened fire. It gave Barney a certain grim satisfaction to see the way the Germans dived for cover, but he wasted no time on congratulating himself. With a terse order for the firing to continue, he turned his attention to the other side of the court-yard. Donaldson, in spite of his wounded leg, was doing good service as a look-out.

'They're coming, sir,' he said.

'Give me a couple of grenades,' Barney said. He stood up. With the powerful swing of his shoulders that had once scattered wickets on the village green, he lobbed the grenades into the trees. There were two shattering explosions, then a burst of rifle fire from the Germans. Behind him he could hear the mortar keeping up the attack on the lorries.

'Enemy aircraft approaching, sir.'

'Oh, hell!' Barney scrambled back to the Bren gun by the chimney. 'What's the situation on this side, sergeant?'

'We've put another lorry out of action, but they've got it

off the road, and toppled the remains of the two armoured cars into the ditch.'

The first bomb struck the ground between the farm and the belt of trees. 'Probably did more harm to their own side than to us,' Barney said breathlessly. 'What the bloody hell's happened to our own artillery? A sitting target, and they're not even trying.'

Another bomb exploded, this time on the other side of the building. When they picked themselves up the mortar had been knocked on its side and partly covered in crumbled brick. The man who had been firing it tried to speak, but bubbling bright red oozed out of his mouth. From his chest a fragment of shrapnel protruded. His head dropped forward and he died.

'Gun's out of action for the time being,' Sergeant Hillier said in a matter-of-fact voice.

As he spoke the British guns from their rear opened up at last. Shells whined over their heads. 'Bang on target,' Barney remarked. 'They must have been practising.'

'I think the Jerries are pulling out,' Sergeant Hillier said.

Below them the third and last lorry had been put into reverse. They could see grey-uniformed men who had survived the attack on the first two lorries scrambling into the back of the one that was getting away.

The shelling continued, but without scoring another hit, and it was out of range for the remaining guns in Barney's farmhouse fortress.

'Troops approaching from the rear, sir,' the look-out reported. 'Our own,' he added hastily.

A few minutes later, Martin Marshall stepped over what had been a ten-foot wall when Barney had moved into the farm earlier in the day.

'The rest of the company's been sent up to do a mopping-up operation,' he said.

'Well, thanks very much—now that we've done all the hard work!'

'What damage have you suffered?'

'Two dead, one wounded, mortar temporarily out of action, but we can fix that.'

Captain Alan Oldstaff came over the wall and repeated Martin's question. Barney got to his feet and answered mechanically. 'There are still some Germans among the trees,' he added.

'Right. We might get ourselves some prisoners. Rather a good show, on the whole.'

As he stumbled down the hill a couple of hours later, Barney discovered that he was dead tired. It had been a minor action, one of hundreds going on all the time, almost routine. More successful than some perhaps, but that had been as much a matter of luck as anything. Had it done any good? It might have held up the course of the war for a few hours, not much more than that, he thought cynically, but they had done what they had been asked to do and the damage they had inflicted was greater than they had sustained. Presumably, if they could always keep the scales tipped that way, they would eventually win.

There were letters waiting for him when he got down the hill. He felt a moment's surprised gratitude to the organization that eventually caught up with the mail, even though on this occasion it was a little out of date. There was a letter from Rilla, describing with some humor Dan's battles with the War Agricultural Committee. She was not a bad little letter-writer. He tried to remember what she looked like and conjured up a confused picture of dark silky hair, soft skin and large grey eyes. On the whole it was better not to think about how she had looked and felt. She made a passing reference to her state of health. He gathered that everything was going on as it should, but his ignorance of child-bearing was so profound that he could not picture Rilla as she must be by this time.

He put her letter away and went off to get some food. Once he had got that inside him perhaps he would be able to face the horrible, necessary task of writing to the families of the men who had died. At least he would be able to say they had died

98/

quickly and bravely. A figure materialized by his side. 'Yes, Sergeant Hillier, what is it?' he asked wearily.

'I thought you might like a bottle of wine, sir,' the sergeant said.

'I would! Thank you, sergeant.' Barney took it with inward amused admiration. Trust the old soldier not to forget his stomach. Sergeant Hillier would have considered it a mark of incompetence to leave behind anything so worth having as the half-dozen bottles of wine they had discovered in the cellar.

They were given a brief resumé of the situation the next morning.

'We've been caught on the hop,' Major Garner said. 'The Germans have done what everyone said was impossible and used tanks in the Ardennes, after fooling us that their main push was going to be in the north. They have driven right through between Arras and Abbeville. Communications with the British forces in the south have been severed. An attempt was made to strike south from Arras, but although some progress was made it has not been sustained. Some evacuation of troops from Boulogne and Calais has already taken place. For the next few days we shall be fighting a rearguard action, then we will withdraw to the perimeter of Dunkirk and prepare for total evacuation.'

There was a stifled murmur of surprise. Everyone had assumed that the British Expeditionary Force would withdraw to the coast and then, with their backs to the sea, make a stand and, if necessary, fight to the death.

'One other thing,' the Major went on. 'As you know, we have been on half-rations. There's nothing unique about this, the entire B.E.F. is on half-rations. Supplies are short and we are going to have to tighten our belts and make do with what we can get. Conditions everywhere are likely to be chaotic. The problem of refugees cluttering up the roads is something we've already encountered . . . ' Again there was a murmur of agreement. 'Yes, well, they're going to run out of places to move to shortly. Treat the local population as gently as you can. To them it looks as if we are running out on them. In fact, we've got to look upon this retreat as our best, possibly our only, chance to . . . ' he hesitated.

'*Reculer pour mieux sauter?*' Barney suggested.

'We don't all have your command of the French tongue, but I think you've got it right. If anyone makes insulting remarks—which they're bound to do—tell them we'll be back.'

It was difficult to believe in the possibility of a return trip as they fought their nightmare way towards the coast, just as it was difficult for the men fighting for their lives and the one remaining means of escape to understand that this overwhelming defeat could have happened so swiftly.

After the long-drawn-out period of little activity, skirmishing and minor engagements, the German attack, when it eventually came, had been devastatingly effective. From 10 May, when the German campaign opened with the invasion of neutral Holland and Belgium by airborne troops, it was only sixteen days before the Commander-in-chief of the British Army, General Lord Gort, was authorized by the Cabinet to put into effect a decision he had taken himself the day before, to retreat to Dunkirk and evacuate his forces by sea.

The attack on Holland and Belgium, successful though it was to prove, had in fact been a diversion away from the main push by the Panzer Corps. The daring nature of the strategy devised by General Heinz Guderian, using tanks and motorized infantry in the hilly and wooded terrain of the Ardennes, took the Allied command wholly by surprise. Resistance was negligible. On 13 May the Panzer Corps crossed the Meuse at Sédan and began striking into the heart of France. By the sixteenth the advance had progressed fifty miles and reached the River Oise, and by that time the Dutch had already capitulated. On 19 May Amiens fell to the Germans and the following day they reached the Channel and succeeded in cutting the communications of the Allied forces in Belgium with the army in the south.

The British Army still in Belgium, facing the advance of

infantry forces, was caught in the rear by the victorious Panzer Corps sweeping north up the Channel coast. On May 22 Boulogne was isolated by Guderian's advance. Calais followed the next day. Only one port remained open—Dunkirk—and the Germans were already at Gravelines, only ten miles away.

By Sunday, 26 May, tired, thirsty, hungry, unwashed and unshaven, the little force of which Barney Wainwright formed part had taken up its position at Wormhoudt a small town, on the line of defence known as the Canal Line. On the same day the evacuation from Dunkirk commenced, beginning with the men designated as 'useless mouths'—the men from the base organization, the training areas and the lines of communication. At Wormhoudt, as at other stopgap areas, the front-line troops fought on, battered from the air, assaulted by armoured contingents, which swirled round them and then, unbelievably, wavered to a halt. For some unfathomable reason the Germans were not pressing their advantage in order to overrun Dunkirk. Not that the fighting ceased. Outposts of the British and the remaining Allied armies still faced the unceasing onslaught and, somehow, held the opposing forces at bay.

At Wormhoudt they held out for two more days and then fell back on Wylder. The battle on this western front was fragmented, a matter of small, isolated pockets of resistance at divisional level, with little communication between the component parts. There were opportunities in plenty for officers of Barney's type, young, a little crazy with fatigue, reckless because this was the last throw and everything depended on it, to show the sort of dash and flair which carried their small units along for one more day, one more hour.

On the eastern front the Belgian Army capitulated. It became a race against time to evacuate the B.E.F. before the eastern and western forces of the Germans closed the gap and shut off their retreat. Mile by mile, sometimes it seemed more like inch by inch, Barney's division fought its way back towards the Dunkirk perimeter and took up their position on the Bergue-Furnes canal.

'Do you remember beds?' Barney asked Martin Marshall thoughtfully.

'Beds? Soft things, white, with pillows and sheets and blankets. We used to sleep in them.'

'Sleep! That's the word I've been trying to think of. I knew there was something I used to do that I've given up lately.'

They laughed, but they both knew that the situation was grim. They were too tired for sanity, and still the fight went on. When the word came that they were to leave for the beaches they were almost beyond moving.

'One more effort,' Barney said. His eyes were red-rimmed, he had four days' growth of beard on his chin, and his voice was little better than a croak. 'Come on, boys, the navy's waiting for us!'

They made the effort, but, although it was true that the navy was waiting for them, so was the Luftwaffe. They reached the wide, sandy beach at Bray Dunes and Barney's heart sank. Whatever he had expected, it was not this vast array of men, waiting with the dull patience of exhausted animals for the slow rescue. When the bombers and fighters arrived overhead and began strafing the beach it was all too familiar. They flung themselves down on the sand and then, when the attack had passed over, began the repugnant task of digging foxholes in the sand to provide a little cover against the next attack.

'I'll do a bit of prospecting,' Barney said. He looked along the crowded beach. He had got his men here, but what the hell was he supposed to do now? And where was everyone else from his division? He had lost track of them in the confusion. He was left with some thirty desperate men on his hands and no means that he could see of getting them food or water or organizing their escape.

It was a relief when he managed to track down a major from a totally different unit who could give him some guidance, but it was disconcerting to be put in charge of a stretch of beach and a miscellaneous collection of men who had lost touch with their own officers. He did his best to make contact with them, stumbling round the beach in the sand, establishing his tenuous authority. For the most part they were apathetic and yet there were signs of an astonishing resilience.

'I wouldn't say there was no *complaints,* if you was to ask, sir,' one grimy little cockney told him with the ghost of a grin. 'On the other 'and, the last seaside 'oliday I 'ad was at Bognor and I must say, taking it all in all, this is what you might call *livelier!*'

It was not much, but it was enough to raise a smile. Even more striking, another man, incapable of raising himself from the beach because of the extent of his fatigue, fumbled with the pack on his back as Barney approached, a look of relief on his face.

'I've got something here, sir,' he said. 'I've been saving it and now it's got to the point where I'm afraid to open it for fear of being rushed. If you'd take charge perhaps we could pass it round as far as it'll go.'

It was a tin of pineapple chunks. A large tin. It was better not to ask how it had been acquired. Barney could only wonder at the dogged endurance which had saved it until this last ditch. He opened it with reverent care. Succulent pineapple chunks, swimming in syrup.

'One chunk each, as far as it'll go, then a mouthful of juice,' Barney said.

'Don't forget yourself, sir,' the man said, watching with jealous eyes as the pieces of fruit disappeared. Barney hesitated, but there were limits beyond which self-denial could not go. He helped himself to the last chunk and chewed ecstatically as the heavenly sweet liquid ran down his parched throat.

He handed over the tin. 'Take a good swig,' he said. 'It was your tin.'

They finished it off regretfully. 'Now you're going to have to get on your feet and form a line into the sea,' Barney said.

He and Sergeant Hillier marshalled orderly lines which

shuffled slowly forward towards the little boats, which had started their ferry service again. From time to time they heard the noise of gunfire and bombing from the direction of the town.

'They're coming at us again!' Sergeant Hillier said. 'Bastards!'

'Get down!' Barney yelled above the screaming engines and the chattering machine gun bullets as the Stukas dived towards them once more. He and Sergeant Hillier flung themselves to the ground on the edge of the surf. When he was able to get up Barney was covered in wet sand. Sergeant Hillier did not move. A line of red trickled down his face and mingled with the sea water. Barney bent over him. He was wounded, but still alive. The patient line moved forward. Barney spoke to the nearest man.

'Give me a hand to get my sergeant up the beach where we can get some first aid for him.'

It was not until long afterwards that it occurred to him that by his prompt response to this order the man to whom he had spoken, a total stranger to him and to Sergeant Hillier, had given up his place in the line of those about to embark. He regretted then, too late, that he had not asked for his name and, in his anxiety for the man who had been his friend and mentor ever since he had joined the army, he had not so much as spoken a word of thanks. ·

There were medical orderlies among the dunes. He called one of them over and put the sergeant in his hands.

'Not much of a wound,' the orderly said cheerfully. 'I'll put a temporary dressing on it, and you can get it attended to when you arrive in England.'

His bland assumption that they were *en route* for home was reassuring, but although he might dismiss the wound as trivial compared with the crippling mutilations which had become commonplace to him it was bad enough. The sergeant regained consciousness, but he seemed dazed, and slow blood seeped through the dressing the orderly had placed on his head.

'I'll give you some water,' the orderly said. The eyes of the men round them watched avidly as he half-filled Sergeant Hillier's water bottle. Barney held the bottle to the sergeant's lips and he swallowed the precious liquid eagerly.

'Have some yourself, sir,' he said as he fell back.

The muscles of Barney's throat contracted longingly. He glanced round. He could not do it, not in front of all those pitiful eyes.

'Water is for the wounded,' he said. 'Thanks for the offer, but I'll hold out a bit longer.'

'I'm a liability now,' Sergeant Hillier said in a hoarse whisper. 'Might be better to have me carted off the beach and I'll take my chance of a move later.'

'Nonsense!' He moved his hand to clasp the wounded man lightly on the shoulder. 'You're going on the next ship out, if I have to carry you myself.'

He moved away, but he kept an eye on the sergeant, because he was worried by the way he lay so still and quiet. He was watching as one of the soldiers moved to the sergeant's side and crouched down. He saw his furtive look he gave before he began to fumble for the water bottle with its few precious drops of liquid. A shaft of vivid anger ran through Barney. He stepped forward and put his hand on the man's shoulder.

'Oh, no, you don't!' he said.

He caught the ugly look in the man's eye, saw the hasty movement just in time, and realized, too, the implications. He was the only officer in sight, the only person with even the semblance of authority. If he were overcome, anarchy might break loose, and the losers would be these poor, patient devils whose only hope was to retain a little discipline. Without pausing to think further, he swung up his fist and knocked the soldier backwards.

He picked up the fallen water bottle and tossed it to Sergeant Hillier.

As the soldier began to struggle to get to his feet in the loose, shifting sand, Barney said, 'Right. I'm moving you to the front of the queue to get you out of our sight. Get in the water.'

He saw the desire for revenge struggle with the man's realization that he had won himself an advantage. It was a relief when he turned away and shuffled into the place Barney had assigned to him.

Barney found Sergeant Hillier watching him when he looked round. 'You'd've been cashiered for that in peacetime,' the sergeant remarked. 'Silly devil. I'd have given him the water if he'd asked.'

Barney helped Sergeant Hillier to his feet and down to the water's edge. 'Give me a hand,' he said to the nearest soldier and the man moved to the sergeant's other side. They waded into the sea, first up to their waists and then, when it became obvious that the small boat for which they were making could come no nearer, up to their armpits.

'Keep your rifle out of the water!' the sergeant said to his other supporter, with something of the old rasp in his voice.

Over the top of his head the soldier caught Barney's eye and made a wry grimace. Together they hoisted the wounded man into the boat, then the other soldier climbed in. It seemed to be some sort of fishing vessel, manned by an elderly man and a very young boy.

'You're next, lieutenant,' the old man said.

Barney shook his head. 'No, I'm not coming yet. I've still got work to do on the beach. See you later!'

He turned and waded back and did not turn his head to watch the boat leave. The major who had put him in charge of that stretch of beach called out to him.

'You're still here? Good! Look, the East Mole in the town is back in action and loading is much faster there than it is from these flat beaches. Round up about two hundred men and march them off to Dunkirk port.'

Barney stared at him. 'These men have had just about all they can take,' he protested. 'I doubt if they can put one foot in front of another, let alone march for miles.'

'Get them along as best you can. I can assure you that it's their best chance of a quick getaway.'

He did as he was told. In a dull nightmare of fatigue he cursed and cajoled some two hundred weary men into a roughly military formation and led them off towards the vast pall of smoke which marked the site of the ruined port.

The East Mole presented an unbelievable sight. A conglomeration of ships, packed stem to stern, a long, long line of men shuffling forward towards them and, in the sea around, the wrecks of the vessels which had not survived the crippling air attacks, their hulls mere carcasses of twisted metal, some of them still burning. Barney looked up apprehensively. It might be faster to load up here, but it was obviously even more hazardous than on the open beaches. The only thing to cheer him was the feeling that this time he had done all that could be required of him, this time he could allow himself to go home.

Home. While they waited he passed the time by trying to remember it. Appleyard, peaceful and pleasant. Dan and his mother. Fluke, who would surely be ecstatic at his master's return. Rilla. Her name came last because she no longer held any reality for him. Rilla. Funny bunny. The girl he had married. And there was the baby to come soon.

He was going to find himself with a new lot of responsibilities on his shoulders once he got back to England. His tired brain refused to grapple with it. None of it seemed particularly important compared with the dire necessity for a night's sleep, even an hour's sleep, just a cessation of noises and danger and killing so that he could put his head down and forget.

He was so lost in his thoughts that the air raid took him by surprise. The aircraft fell on the massed men and ships, the anti-aircraft guns barked, the noise and destruction began again. Barney tried to lie down flat, but they were so packed that he could do no more than crouch low. He felt exposed and vulnerable on the narrow Mole. The evacuation was still continuing and the men behind him urged him and his companions forward.

He was on the ship, his feet were actually on the deck. He heard a naval officer say: 'About twenty more and that's as many as we can take,' and then they were hit.

He felt himself flung forward, as if by a giant hand, as the blast caught him; all the breath was driven out of his body. As he fell he was conscious of a searing pain in his right leg and then of everything sliding forward. His fingers scrabbled with desperate weakness at the tilting deck, but there was nothing to save him as he was flung into the water. He was still conscious as the oily sea closed round him and then something hit him on the head and he blacked out.

He did not regain consciousness when they dragged him out of the water, nor when they took him to the field hospital and set his broken leg. He was still wrapped in oblivion when the decision had to be made that of the remaining wounded only the walking cases could be evacuated: there was no room left for stretcher cases. He still believed when at last he came to himself that he would be put on a ship and taken home. He was too weak and disorientated to understand that the evacuation was over. He slept and woke and swallowed what was given to him with the blind obedience of a sick child, until at last one day he realized that the orderlies who fed him were German, that the doctors were German. He was in enemy hands. He lay on his back and stared up at the ceiling. His leg ached, but his head was clear. The first thought that came to him was: I'm a prisoner-of-war. The second thought was: I'm going to escape.

Chapter 5

It took weeks for the news of Barney's capture to filter through the correct channels and reach Appleyard. Dan returned from Dunkirk, grey-faced and very quiet, his wounded shoulder heavily padded and his arm immobilized. A little to his surprise—and hers, too—his mother burst into tears when she saw him.

'You ought to be used to seeing me come home in pieces,' he chided her. 'I've been doing it ever since I was a child, falling out of trees and into rivers, and goodness knows what.'

'This is different,' Winifred said, wiping her eyes. 'Dan, was it very bad?'

'Bad enough,' he admitted. 'But it was worth doing. Considering everything, we did quite well, you know.'

'Better than quite well. The latest figure I've heard for the troops rescued is three hundred and sixty-six thousand! All the same, it was a defeat—Churchill has made a speech reminding us of that.'

'Yes, indeed. The amount of equipment that had to be left behind was appalling. It'll take a lot of replacing.'

'And what comes next — invasion?'

'It's certainly a possibility. I should join the Local Defence Volunteers.'

'We've had no news of Barney,' Winifred said.

'There's hardly been time,' Dan said quickly. 'Even if he's in England he's probably still sleeping. I slept for fourteen hours myself after Greg and I got back to Weymouth.'

'I can't believe anything has happened to him.' The tears welled up and Winifred dabbed at her eyes again.

'Neither can I. I refuse to worry about him. Barney always falls on his feet. How is Rilla?'

'She's well enough,' Winifred said reluctantly. 'She's obviously fretting over Barney. I suppose she does care for him.'

'I'm sure she does,' Dan said.

He thought that perhaps their common anxiety for the same man might draw the two women closer together, but it did not seem to work that way. Rilla hardly ever spoke of him, but every day her grey eyes seemed to grow bigger in her pale face. Winifred found an outlet for her fears by constantly remarking that she was sure he would take them all by surprise by walking in one day. Rilla found her false cheerfulness acutely irritating, not realizing that her own silent misery was equally trying to Barney's mother. They avoided one another's company as far as possible and the coming baby was never referred to between them, even though the birth was now little more than a month away.

It was a fortunate thing that they were all three together when the telegram from the War Office arrived. It was addressed to Rilla, but Dan reached out and took it from her shaking fingers and ripped the envelope open.

'Barney is safe,' he said after a swift perusal of the message. 'Safe, but a prisoner-of-war.'

He looked up. His mother had buried her face in her hands, overcome by relief and distress, but Rilla gave him a tiny, tremulous smile and then slid from her chair to the floor unconscious.

She came to herself to find Dan and Mrs Wainwright bending over her. 'I'll call the doctor,' Dan said, getting to his feet, but Rilla stopped him.

'I'm all right,' she said. Her voice was weak, but her sickly pallor was already receding. 'It was just the shock and the relief after waiting so long for news.' She struggled to get her unwieldy body into a sitting position. 'Truly, I'm all right.'

'You'd better lie down,' Winifred said. She stood up. 'At least he's safe.'

'He'll hate being a prisoner,' Rilla said. 'Will we be able to write to him?'

'Of course.' Dan gave her a reassuring smile. 'We'll get the details very soon now. As Ma says, at least he's safe.'

To him it seemed that the two women seized too eagerly on this aspect of the news. Barney was safe, that was all that really mattered to them, although Rilla had had the perception to see that the state of imprisonment would be hateful to him. It was strange to think that he probably understood his brother's temperament better than either his wife or his mother. Barney would not sit down idly in captivity. He would expend all his energies towards escaping and Dan had the gravest misgivings about the danger he would run into.

That night Rilla had difficulty in sleeping. She had said that she was all right, but the shock of the War Office telegram coming after the long strain of waiting for news had jolted her more than she had wanted to admit. She tossed and turned and cried a little for Barney, so far away and facing unknown discomforts and brutality. She fell at last into an uneasy sleep, but towards dawn she woke to the first of a series of pains which, for all her ignorance, she recognized unmistakably as birth pangs. She lay for a time waiting to see what would happen, but at last, towards six o'clock, she got slowly out of bed, stood for a moment with her lips tightly pressed together and her hands against her distended stomach as another of the rhythmical movements moved up the scale of pain and down again, and then padded heavily along the corridor and tapped on Winifred's door.

Barney's son was born that afternoon, some five weeks premature, but a fine, healthy baby. Rilla was told that she had been lucky, that it had been an easy birth, a verdict with which she silently disagreed, but for all that it was a full fortnight before she and the child were allowed out of the nursing home to return to Appleyard—and with their return, the struggle for possession began.

After a brief conversation with the doctor, Winifred reluctantly abandoned a half-formed theory that the baby might not be Barney's after all. 'I suppose the child really was premature?' she demanded abruptly.

'Oh, certainly,' Dr. Barnes said in surprise. 'At least a month, probably rather more. However, he was well-developed, and he's made splendid progress since the birth. An unfortunate beginning, of course, but I don't think you need have any fears about him.'

She studied the baby surreptitiously when Rilla brought him back to Appleyard. He was very small, with that look of premature age so disconcerting in very young babies, but she rather thought she could detect a likeness to Barney, though his big, dark-grey eyes were like Rilla's. The first time she held him in her arms he looked up at her and blinked and she was astonished by the flood of warmth that ran through her. Barney had been an adorable baby. Bigger than this little shrimp, but then she had carried him the full term and she was a larger woman than fine-boned Rilla. With quickened interest she looked into the future and saw little Barney running about Appleyard, playing on the swing in the garden just as his father had done, climbing the trees, riding a bicycle, his first pony, going off to school, calling her Granny. She grew misty-eyed at the prospect and she surrendered the baby to his mother with the greatest reluctance.

'You'll call him Barnaby, of course,' she said, bending over the cot which had previously been used for both her own sons.

'No,' Rilla replied. She did not bother to explain that for her there could only be one Barnaby. 'He's going to be called Jonathan Leonard, after his two grandfathers.'

Winifred straightened up. It struck her as an affront that she should not have been consulted about the use of her dead husband's name.

'Were you going to call the baby after me if it had been a girl?' she enquired sarcastically.

'No,' Rilla said again. 'I don't really like the name Winifred very much. I was going to call her Deborah Edith after my aunt and my mother.'

Her tone was not conciliatory. She did not like the way Winifred had of walking into the room and picking up that baby, *her* baby; she did not like the advice she offered as if it constituted the law of the Medes and the Persians; and as the days wore on she became deeply uneasy about the role Winifred apparently foresaw for herself in the future.

It began innocuously enough with Dan remarking one morning as he left for the Estate Office that he was missing Rilla's expert assistance.

'Will you go back to helping Dan?' Mrs Wainwright asked casually after Dan had gone.

'I suppose so,' Rilla said. 'It's useful work, and it could hardly be more conveniently situated!'

'A little dull for you,' Winifred suggested. 'It's too soon after the baby's birth to think of anything else at the moment, but if you ever felt inclined to do some rather more interesting war work I am sure something could be arranged.'

'There's not much difference between working in an office in Cheltenham and working in an office here,' Rilla pointed out. 'Provided I'm not directed into something else—and I hardly think that will happen, because of Jon—I can probably be just as useful to Dan as to anyone else.'

'I was thinking of a more drastic change,' Winifred said. 'If you wanted to join one of the forces, or work in a factory, for instance—it would be a more lively life for you than mouldering away in the country.'

'But the baby . . .' Rilla said, genuinely amazed that Winifred should imagine she had any such ambitions.

'Little Jonathan could stay here, of course,' Winifred said smoothly. The eyes of the two women met. Winifred was smiling slightly, but there was an implacable air about her which frightened Rilla. She shook her head vehemently. 'I could never leave him,' she said.

The subject was not mentioned again, but the idea that Winifred wanted to separate her from her son had been planted in Rilla's mind. She became more possessive of him, refusing even the small amount of help she had accepted at first, and keeping all the care of him in her own hands. Everything about him was wonderful to her. She pored over all the tiny details of his body—the thin, surprised line of his eyebrows, the minute toe-nails, the whorls of his ears—and worshipped his perfection. She was awestricken by what she had done in bringing him into the world. If only Barney could have been there to see his son, right from the beginning, to observe as she did the changes which took place in him day by day, the visible unfolding of his mind and body.

Even Winifred's more well-intentioned gestures became suspect. She called to Rilla one day as she passed her bedroom door.

'I've been getting out the christening robe,' she said. She indicated the long white robe laid out on her bed. 'Such fine work! It was made for my husband's father—his portrait is the one that hangs on the stairs, you know—and it's been most carefully kept ever since. I used it for Dan and Barney. I thought we'd have the christening on the eighteenth of August. Not a party, of course, it would hardly be suitable in the circumstances . . .' She saw Rilla stiffen and went on hurriedly, '. . . with the war on and the baby's father not able to be present.'

Her explanation of her meaning was, as it happened, genuine, but it fell on deaf ears. Rilla was offended and with the little spirit of rebellion that had been growing in her ever since the birth of her baby she said, 'I've decided I'd like Jonathan to be christened in my own church at home.'

She had spoken on impulse, but it only needed Winifred's immediate opposition to make her obstinate. Even Dan failed to move her.

'My Mum and Dad want to see their grandson,' she said. 'I don't see any reason why I shouldn't take him to visit them for a week or two, and we can have the christening in Barbury.'

'I thought I was going to be godfather?' Dan said. 'I can't get away from here at the moment, not in the middle of harvest, Rilla.'

'I'll just have to have someone else then,' Rilla said.

She might have given in, since she foresaw that the journey to Barbury would be a difficult undertaking on crowded trains with a very young baby, if she had not immediately after this conversation gone upstairs and found Winifred with Jonathan on her lap.

'He was such a wet boy, I thought I'd change him,' she said. 'Poor little mite, I'm sure he was uncomfortable.'

Rilla was immediately on the defensive. 'I'd prefer to do it myself,' she said stiffly. 'I don't think it's good for a baby to have a lot of strange people handling him.'

'I'm hardly a stranger,' Winifred said. With ill grace she handed the baby over to Rilla and went away, disgruntled and affronted.

Rilla sat down with the baby on her lap and looked down at him with eyes that blurred with tears. The baby wrinkled up his nose and yawned.

'You're Mummy's own darling little man and nobody shall take you away from me, nobody!' Rilla said in a fierce whisper.

'Horrid Granny isn't going to have you.'

It sounded ridiculous, even to her own ears, and certainly Jonathan Leonard was entirely indifferent as to who changed his nappies, as long as he was comfortable and well fed, but the gulf between Rilla and Winifred seemed to be widening rather than diminishing. Rilla longed for the easy, uncomplicated affection of her own family. She wanted her mother. They could talk on equal terms now. She wanted to tell her about her confinement, to have her views on the way the baby was developing, to know that her father had recovered from his hurt embarrassment over her pregnancy and that her mother was reconciled to her decision to move to Appleyard.

As to whether she would return permanently to Appleyard, she was not sure. The reasons for doing so remained unchanged, but she had never foreseen that she might be called upon to make a home there for years without any possibility of Barney returning for an occasional leave, nor had she foreseen Winifred's possessive attitude over her grandson.

She felt that it would help her to decide what to do if she could get away for a time and so she stuck to her determination to take Jonathan to visit her parents in the face of both Winifred and Dan's opposition.

'There have already been air raids,' Dan pointed out. 'It's foolhardy to run into danger unnecessarily.'

'There's been nothing near Barbury—not really near,' Rilla said defensively. 'And we've had warnings round here, too.'

'It would be much simpler for your parents to come here.' He thought that she looked doubtful and added gently, 'This is your home, Rilla. You can ask anyone you like to stay, and we'd always be pleased to see your family.'

'That's good of you,' she said gratefully. 'But, Dan, I want to get away—just for a little while. I want to think about what I'm going to do next. I want . . . I want my *own* people, and in many ways it will be easier to go now while Jon is tiny than to wait until he's too big for me to carry.'

She got her way, but there were times on her long, slow journey when she regretted it. The compensation came when Edith and Len met her at the terminus in London and Edith held out her arms for her grandson, her face beaming with delight.

'Sound asleep, the little treasure!' she exclaimed. 'Has he been good? Have you had a good journey? You must be tired to death, love, coming all that way. How are you feeling?'

'I'm fine,' Rilla said, 'I'll be glad to get home. Careful of that case, Da, I've got a box of half a dozen eggs in it wrapped up in Jon's clean nappies.'

'Eggs!' Edith exclaimed. 'You lucky girl, that's what comes of living in the country! They're worth their weight in gold round our way.'

It was, as Rilla had said, a relief to get him to Barbury at last, but something seemed to have happened to the house where she had lived all her life before going to Appleyard. The rooms had shrunk. It had grown shabbier and more cluttered. It was spotlessly clean, of course, but Rilla was no longer accustomed to sitting with her elbows on the table for a long chat after a meal and before the dirty dishes were removed. The bathroom at 62 Sudbury Road was a cold, narrow room, and the hot water supply was limited. At Appleyard she had had all the hot water she wanted, she could bathe Jon without worrying about him catching cold, and without knocking her elbow against the wash basin. And there was ample drying space for the nappies which hung in damp, depressing rows in the kitchen at Sudbury Road. She had forgotten how small the garden was, especially now that a section of it was taken up by the Anderson air-raid shelter.

'Nasty thing,' Edith said distastefully. 'I shan't go into it unless I have to.'

The war seemed nearer in Barbury. At Appleyard, in spite of Dan having taken part in the evacuation of Dunkirk and Barney's imprisonment, in spite of the black-out, the evacuees, and the shortages, she had been cushioned against what she now saw of the consistant daily grind to keep ordinary life going. She was shocked to discover how much of her mother's time was taken up with queueing for necessities and the occasional small luxuries, such as the solitary orange which Edith bore home in triumph and insisted Rilla should eat.

Rilla divided it up carefully and refused to touch it until Edith, Len, and Joyce had all taken a section each.

'And that's enough,' Edith said firmly. 'Eat it up, Rilla, and don't argue. It'll do you good. I'd like to see a bit more colour in your cheeks than you've got at the moment, my girl.'

The look she gave her daughter was full of anxiety. When they were alone she said bluntly, 'It's early days yet, of course, and it's only to be expected that you should feel a bit pulled down after a premature birth, but you don't look right to me. There's nothing wrong, is there? You've seen the doctor? Everything's as it should be?'

'Oh, yes, I'm perfectly all right,' Rilla assured her, but her voice lacked conviction.

'Then I suppose you're fretting about that husband of yours?'

Rilla turned her head away. 'I've not heard from him yet. Just the official message to say he's a prisoner, that's all. Oh, Mum, he was *wounded* and I don't even know what's the matter with him.'

The tears she had been holding back overflowed. Edith put her arm round her daughter's shoulders and patted her consolingly. 'There, there, I thought that was it,' she said. 'Have a good cry, love. You'll feel better then.'

'He doesn't even know he's got a son,' Rilla wept.

'It'll be a lovely surprise for him when he hears the news,' Edith said. 'Now, come on, love, pull yourself together. It's hard, I know, and you little more than a baby yourself, but there's thousands in the same boat and some worse off than you. It won't do any good to fret yourself into being ill. You've got someone else besides yourself to think of now. There's that lovely baby depending on you.'

'Mrs Wainwright wants to take him away from me,' Rilla said.

Haltingly she repeated her conversation with Barney's mother about going away to do war work and leaving Jon in her care.

'She may have meant it well,' Mrs Gray said slowly. 'Those sort of people think nothing of handing their kids over to a nurse to look after. Then again, you are a bit jealous of him, aren't you? You gave me a bit of a look the other day when I picked Jon up because he was crying. You didn't like it, did you?'

'Not much,' Rilla admitted. 'But, of course, it's different when it's you, Mum.'

'Is it? I'm not so sure. You'd probably find I'd be just as much of an interfering nuisance if you was to live here. It's only natural. Us older ones think we know it all because we've been through it already, and the young mothers don't like being told. I've never met Barney's Mum and I must admit she sounds a right snooty bit of goods, but I do feel for her, you know. It's hard, very hard, to have your son taken away from you and put in a prison camp. I expect she feels it, poor thing. Only natural she should want a bit of a cuddle of his baby for comfort.'

'I suppose so,' Rilla admitted reluctantly. 'But she doesn't like me. She still resents Barney having married me. I get the impression she wants to push me out and take Jon over.'

'Bear with her,' her mother advised. 'You've got to go on living there, after all.'

'I suppose I must,' Rilla said.

'You'd be daft to do anything else. From what you've said since you've been here you seem to be very comfortably situated, and no matter what they may say food *is* easier in the country—look at those eggs you brought us, the first shell eggs I've seen for three months. There's fruit and vegetables, too, and don't tell me they don't get a bit extra when there's things like pigs being killed, because I won't believe you.'

She saw that Rilla still looked doubtful and went on, 'I

won't say we wouldn't have you back here and welcome if it was necessary, but there's no doubt you're better off where you are.'

It was true. Rilla bowed to the inevitable and began to think about making her return to Appleyard during the week after Jon's christening. She had wanted Dan to be the principal godfather, but since Dan had said very firmly that it was quite impossible for him to leave Appleyard in the middle of the first grain harvest some of his land had seen in the last eighty years, Rilla's father was to stand in for him as proxy, with one of Rilla's cousins as the other godfather and Joyce as godmother.

Joyce was unexpectedly enthusiastic about her nephew. She was as fascinated by his smallness and completeness as Rilla herself.

'I think you're ever so lucky, Rilla,' she said enviously. 'I never thought much of babies before, but he's *gorgeous!*'

'It isn't all honey,' Rilla said drily. 'Having a baby in wartime, I mean, with a husband somewhere overseas.'

She had always had an uncomplicated affection for her younger sister, but now she felt separated from her by an immeasurable gulf of experience. Joyce had not known the guilty delight of Rilla's union with Barney, nor the first horror of finding herself pregnant, nor the long months in an alien environment, upset by all the little ailments of child-bearing, nor the pain of birth, nor the terrible helpless love she felt for the small being she had brought into the world, a love which dragged at her entrails and made her feel she would defend him to the last drop of her blood against anything that threatened him.

Dinah was equally admiring, but to Rilla she seemed changed. They had only been separated for six months, but Rilla could hardly believe that she had once regarded this flashy, vulgar little girl as her best friend. She remembered now how often Dinah's ways had grated on her. Dinah seemed to have become even more aggressive, or had Rilla grown accustomed to gentler ways?

'So the baby came even earlier than he was expected?' Mrs Gloster asked.

'Much earlier,' Mrs Gray said firmly. 'Still, he's a healthy little mite. We're getting him christened on Sunday, and Rilla's taking him back to his Dad's home the week after.'

'Is it very grand, Rill?' Dinah asked.

'It is rather,' Rilla admitted. 'But homelike, in spite of that. It's a beautiful house and there's a big garden for Jon to play in when he gets older.'

'A bit dull for you, though,' Dinah suggested. 'Cor, I couldn't stand having a husband shut up in a prison camp. I'd go nuts. Especially living with his family to keep an eye on me and see I didn't have any fun.'

'I don't want any fun,' Rilla said shortly. 'Not without Barney.'

'It's not a natural life, say what you like,' Mrs Gloster said.

For all its drawbacks, Rilla was surprised to find that she was looking forward to her return to Appleyard. She had grown fond of the place for its own sake, but this short time away from it had shown her that it was where she now felt most at home. It was no longer alien, but the natural center of her existence. It was there she felt closest to Barney, not here in her own small, cluttered home amongst her well-meaning but uncomprehending family.

Quite apart from anything else, she felt safe at Appleyard. She had been alarmed since she arrived at Barbury by the frequency with which the air-raid sirens sounded. Although nothing very much seemed to happen in their immediate vicinity, the possibility of enemy action from the aeroplanes which were regularly attacking the R.A.F. stations in the south-east could not be ignored. Dan had been right, she ought not to have come, even though the brief visit had been of considerable value to her in putting things into perspective. She had begun to see from her own mother's attitude that it was the natural prerogative of grandmothers to believe they knew what was best for babies, and, even though she was convinced of an additional element of jealous possessiveness in Winifred Wainwright's interference, she could not help recognizing that Edith was just as ready to intervene and offer advice whether wanted or not. She would have to try to be more tolerant, especially if she was to continue to live and work at Appleyard. It was comforting to think that she not only had a place in which to live, but also a job to keep her occupied. A useful job, too. Dan had already told her how much she was missed. He would be glad to see her back.

In this more philosophical frame of mind she felt able to relax and the last few days of her visit home were more enjoyable than the first. Only one small thing marred the important event of Jonathan Leonard's christening: Rilla's Aunt Debbie was unable to attend. She had suffered from intermittent pains somewhere vaguely referred to as 'her insides' for some time and shortly before Rilla's return to Barbury she had been taken to hospital for a gall-bladder operation.

'You ought to go and see her before you leave, Rilla,' Edith said. 'You can't take the baby though. I don't think they'd allow him into the ward. It's a pity because she'd love to see him.'

'If the snapshots of the christening turn out all right, I could take them to the hospital,' Rilla suggested.

'Good idea. We could both go on Thursday when there's evening visiting. Your Dad will be off to his L.D.V. as soon as he's had his tea, but Joyce will be here to give an eye to Jon.'

Rilla looked doubtful, but she remembered her resolution to be less possessive about her tiny son, and so she agreed to the arrangement. She gave Joyce nervous instructions about what to do with the baby during the short time she would be left alone with him, a little worried by her sister's matter-of-fact acceptance of the enormous responsibility that was being handed over to her.

'Don't be such a fuss-pot,' Joyce said. 'I know one end of a baby from the other! He seems to spend most of his time sleeping. I don't suppose he'll even know you are out of the house.'

Almost as a last thought, Rilla said as they went out of the door, 'If there should be an air raid . . .'

'I'll take Jon out to the shelter.'

'It's damp out there,' Edith said. 'Better just sit under the stairs until the "All Clear" goes. Not that anything is likely to happen, but it's just as well to be careful.'

The Battle of Britain had begun. Hitler's order, issued on 1 August, had been for the Luftwaffe to 'destroy the enemy Air Force as soon as possible.' Goering had launched the great offensive which was intended to carry out this instruction on 13 August and had labelled the day 'Eagle Day.' The German bombers flew into the attack on the R.A.F. stations in south-east England, but at that time the raids were not near enough to Barbury to cause the Grays anything more than slight inconvenience from air raid warnings which seemed to have little to do with them. Overhead, the fighters of the R.A.F. fought their battles in a blue sky criss-crossed by white vapour trails and their successes caused consternation in the Luftwaffe. Whatever tactics they adopted, it seemed that their losses were always heavier than those of the British and Allied squadrons. The easy victory of which they had been confident began to look more difficult to achieve than had been anticipated. Goering growled and fumed, but the dreaded Spitfires continued to appear out of nowhere to shoot down his bombers and fighters.

On the fine Thursday evening in the middle of August when Rilla and her mother went to visit Edith's sister in hospital the German bombers were making for Croydon; Croydon, the site of the first civilian airport in England, almost obsolete now, surrounded by houses and light industry; Croydon, just a few miles away from Barbury.

Aunt Debbie lacked her customary pink cheeks, but she was still her placid self. She exclaimed suitably over the pictures of Jon looking alternatively cross and bored in the arms of various people outside the church after the christening.

'Pity I can't see him,' she said regretfully. 'But that sister's a real dragon, she won't let any children into her ward. Never mind, Rilla, you'll have to bring him to me for a visit some time.

I've got the room to put you up and it'll make a nice change for you.'

From the restless movement her mother made on her uncomfortable hospital chair, Rilla guessed that this suggestion did not find much favour in her eyes. If Rilla was coming to Barbury she would stay with Edith and Len, or Edith would want to know the reason why.

When they left the hospital the sun was still shining. 'A nice evening,' Rilla remarked. 'Aunt Debbie seems to be getting on all right, doesn't she?'

'A bit dragged down, I thought,' Edith said.

They walked towards the bus stop. 'I hope we don't have to wait long.'

She had hardly spoken when the sirens began to sound.

'Oh, no!' Rilla exclaimed. 'Oh, Mum, how awful! I must get home to Jon.'

'If it's a proper raid the buses will stop running,' Mrs Gray said. She looked anxiously up into the sky. 'We can start walking, if you like, but I expect we'll be stopped and shoved down a shelter.'

It was just as she had feared. They had only gone a few hundred yards down the road when an imperative whistle stopped them in their tracks.

'Didn't you hear the warning?' the warden demanded. 'Take cover, please.'

'I *must* get home,' Rilla said again.

'If you want to get home in one piece, then get down the shelter,' he said. 'Come along now, there's a public shelter round the next corner. And hurry!'

They obeyed him, even though Rilla looked mutinous. 'It'll probably be nothing but another dog fight overhead,' she said.

'I expect so, in which case it'll only be a short alert,' Mrs Gray said, trying to reassure herself as well as Rilla.

It was a short raid, but it was a severe one. In half an hour on that bright August evening sixty-two people were killed. The sound of the bombs was audible only as an occasional dull thud in the safety of the brick-built shelter where Rilla and her mother were waiting.

'It doesn't sound as if it's anywhere near here,' Mrs Gray said.

'Not all that far away,' Rilla said. She twisted her hands together. 'Not in Barbury, though—is it?'

'No, no, I'm sure it's not,' Edith said quickly.

It was true that the target was not the little town of Barbury, but to one German bomber from his damaged plane, one target was much like another. There were gas-works in Barbury, he could see them quite plainly below him in the brilliant evening sunshine. He had had to turn away from his primary objective and it was imperative that he lighten his load to improve his chances of a safe return to home base. He ordered the bombs away and was only slightly irritated to see that he had not achieved a direct hit on the works beneath him.

In the shelter Rilla and Mrs Gray looked at one another fearfully. The explosions had been much nearer than the earlier ones.

'Sound's a very deceptive thing,' Edith said. 'Probably that was just as many miles away as the others.'

The time they spent waiting for the 'All Clear' to sound seemed interminable, but at last it came and they emerged, blinded in the clear light, from the dimness of the shelter. The hospital, and the shelter where they had taken refuge, stood on a hill to the south of Barbury. Looking down towards the town they could see a column of smoke in the north.

'Not far from the gasworks,' Edith said. 'I hope your Dad's all right. He's on duty there tonight.'

They began to walk faster and faster, until they were almost running. There were few people about, not a bus to be seen. The nearer they got to Sudbury Road the more ominous it began to look. In the High Street a fire engine passed them, and an ambulance. Neither of them spoke. Edith was breathing heavily with the effort of keeping up with Rilla. Rilla was hardly conscious of moving her feet. All her mind was bent towards the house where she had left Jon.

They turned into Sudbury Road and found their way barred. Rilla did not pause, but when she tried to go round the side of the barrier she was stopped.

'Now, then,' the policeman said. 'You can't go down there, miss.'

She turned wide, unseeing eyes on him. 'I've got to get home to my baby,' she said.

His attention sharpened. 'You live down there?'

She nodded, her hand on the rope of the barrier, sure that he would let her pass.

'What number?'

'Number sixty-two,' Edith answered him. Her eyes were fixed on his face, but Rilla was staring down the road. There was glass everywhere, bricks and rubble and tumbled walls. There was a great gaping hole.

The policeman looked away. 'Sorry,' he repeated mechanically. 'You can't go down the road now. As you can see, it's not safe. I'll . . . I'll let you know as soon as it's been cleared.'

'Which house has been hit?' Edith asked. She held her breath for his reply, but the policeman was not committing himself.

'I don't rightly know,' he lied. 'I don't know either if there's been any casualties, so it's no use asking me.' He paused helplessly. 'Perhaps you could just tell me who was in your house,' he suggested.

'My daughter, Joyce Gray.'

'Age?'

'Fourteen. And my little grandson. He's only a few weeks old.'

'Six weeks,' Rilla said. 'He needs me.' She turned her enormous eyes on the sweating policeman. 'I've got to go to him.'

Before he could stop her, she had ducked under the barrier and started down the road at a run. The policeman gave a shout and one of the A.R.P. workers, his face grey with dust and a shovel in his hand, looked round.

'Stop her!' the policeman called. He caught up with them as the A.R.P. man grasped Rilla's arm and held her back.

'Mother of a baby in Number sixty-two,' he said breathlessly. The eyes of the two men met.

'Better for you to leave it to us,' the A.R.P. man said awkwardly to Rilla, but it seemed as if she did not hear him.

She shook herself free, but this time the policeman, accustomed to dealing with struggling prisoners, took hold of her and held her pinioned. There was only one thought in his mind—that at all costs she must be stopped from seeing what had happened at Number 62. She fought him frantically until at last, with merciful cruelty, he brought up his fist and knocked her senseless.

They fetched Len from the gasworks and tried to put Edith and Rilla into his care, but Rilla clutched his arm and begged: 'Dad, *you* go. They won't let me in. Jon may be buried. He's so little—they might miss him. He'll be crying for me. He'll be hungry and frightened. Why won't they let me go and find him?'

Len touched her bruised chin. 'You've hurt yourself,' he said.

'Fainted and hit her face on a brick,' the policeman said glibly.

Rilla was looking at him with eyes so dilated by shock that they seemed black. She shook his arm, her fingers working frantically into the flesh beneath his sleeve, as she insisted that he must go and look for Jon, and he saw that the words that poured out of her were being used to hide her understanding of something she could not face. He freed himself and went down the road in company with the policeman.

'Tell me what's happened,' he said.

'Direct hit,' the policeman said reluctantly. 'I'm sorry to have to tell you, but anyone inside didn't have a chance.'

'What about the shelter?'

'Flattened. But there was no one in it.'

'I've got to go and see.'

The policeman abandoned his official stance. He removed his helmet and wiped his sweating forehead. 'Christ, mate, I wouldn't if I was you.'

'I've got to be able to tell my daughter that I've seen for myself.'

'I can't let you.'

'It's my grandson, my daughter. I have the right.'

He walked steadily down the road towards the home where he and Edith had lived together in growing affection through the years, the little house with its hard-won comforts, the place where his two girls had been born and grown up. There was nothing there now but a ruined shell. The new wallpaper he had put up in the front room just before the war broke out showed up incongruously bright on a wall left partially standing. They showed him a minute blue bootee soaked in blood and he nodded; it had belonged to Jon. They showed him a piece of a flowered cotton frock and a length of hair, Joyce's hair, and he nodded again, and then, very carefully, like a drunken man negotiating a tightrope, he walked back up the road again.

He met the question in Rilla's desperate eyes with a steady look. 'You've got to be a very brave girl,' he said. 'Jon and Joyce have been killed.' He felt Edith's hand on his arm and pressed it against his ribs. He took a deep breath.

'I've seen them both,' he said. 'It was the blast that killed them. They wouldn't have known a thing about it. They look quite peaceful, like they'd gone to sleep together. Joyce was holding the little nipper, he wouldn't have been frightened.'

'Can't I see him?' Rilla whispered. 'I want to see him, Dad.'

'Better not. Remember him like he was. Like we're going to remember Joyce, Mum and me.'

Dan came to the funeral and was shocked by the sight of Rilla's white, still face.

It was a perfect summer's day. The sun shone, the sky was blue. The grass in the churchyard had been cut that morning and the fresh smell of it hung in the air. Only the dark yew trees struck a sombre note amongst the white gravestones.

There was only one coffin. It seemed a touching thought to Dan, that the two young creatures who had died together should be buried with one another.

The Vicar led the small procession towards the newly-dug grave.

'Underneath are the everlasting arms,' he intoned.

Dan envied him the certainty in his voice. Edith had a handkerchief pressed to her eyes and Len had to hold her arm to guide her. Rilla walked alone.

When they reached the grave she stood apart from everyone else. Her lack of support filled Dan with pity, but when he went to stand beside her she moved away and he realized that she did not want his sympathy.

Only one thing disturbed her rigid composure during the service. A robin flew down to the newly-turned earth, flirted its tail and pecked hopefully for food. It seemed quite unafraid, looking about with a bright, round eye, but when the coffin was lowered the movement disturbed it. It flew up on to the branch of a hawthorn tree and began to sing. Dan saw Rilla's eyes following its flight and as the shrill, sweet song rose in the air she moved her head from side to side and half-lifted her hand as if she wanted to make it stop, then she pressed her lips tightly together and stared at the ground and the moment passed.

Dan tried once more to help her with a hand under her elbow as she got into the car after they had left the churchyard, but Rilla shook him off, almost impatiently, as if all contact was unwelcome to her.

It was when he brought up the question of her return to

Appleyard that he began to have some understanding of her state of mind.

'I don't think I'll come back,' Rilla said in a dull, flat voice. 'There's not much point, is there? You only wanted me there because you thought it was the proper place for Barney's son to be brought up, and your mother thought it was a way of getting hold of the baby. Now there isn't a baby. Barney needn't have married me.'

'None of that is true,' Dan said. 'We do want you back.' He got no response and so he added deliberately, 'I've got a letter for you from Barney.'

She made a movement of her hand, as if to keep something away from her, and he saw that she was afraid of anything that might break through the barrier she had built around herself. It made him hesitate to hand over the letter. 'You'll have to remember that he wrote before . . . before this terrible disaster,' he warned her.

She held out her hand and he gave her the thin letter card which was all Barney had been able to send. There was no room for him to say much, but he had written it out of despair, and the longing for his freedom came through. He told Rilla that he missed her, that he had been counting the days until the baby was due and was anxious for her safety, and begged her to take care of herself and the child. It broke Rilla.

'He didn't even know Jon had been born,' she said. 'Oh, Dan, Dan, by this time he must have had my letter telling him what a wonderful son he'd got and now I've got to write and tell him that he's dead, and it was my fault, my fault!'

'You were in no way to blame,' Dan said, bewildered by her passionate outburst.

'I shouldn't have brought him here! You warned me and I wouldn't listen. I killed him, my little son, my little baby!'

It was a relief when Edith came and took over. Her arms closed around Rilla. 'It's all right,' she said to Dan. 'You leave her to me.'

'Try to make her see that it wasn't her fault,' Dan said.

Edith nodded her head. 'That's a silly thing to say,' she said to Rilla with determination, but with a quivering voice. 'You might just as well blame me for letting you come here. Oh, love, I know how you feel! I've been cursing myself for telling Joyce not to go down the shelter. Because it was damp! It keeps me awake at night, thinking perhaps . . . perhaps it might have saved them. Your Dad says it wouldn't . . . I don't know, perhaps he's just trying to comfort me.' The two women sat huddled together on the sofa in the sitting room of Debbie's house, where they were staying until a fresh home could be found for them. Rilla stirred in her mother's arms. 'I've been selfish,' she said. 'Not thinking much about Joyce. I'm sorry, Mum, it's just as bad for you as it is for me.'

'Worse in a way,' Edith said. 'Jon was a little love, but we'd had Joyce for fourteen years. All those years of bringing her up. She was a naughty baby and your Dad was so good with her, walking up and down with her at night to give me a rest. My little girl . . . I was a bit sharp with her sometimes, but she would answer me back. Just the age for it, of course, but you were always more docile than she was and it irritated me when she was so uppity. Now I remember the times I snapped at her and I could bite my tongue out. But what's the use of thinking like that? We've got to go on living, you and me, love. I've got to look after Len. He's taken it badly, for all he doesn't say much. And you've got to keep young Barney from getting too despondent. Bad enough for him, poor young chap, being shut up in that nasty Germany and hearing such dreadful news, without having to worry about you going to pieces as well.'

She gave Rilla another hug and then stood up. 'Go and wash your face,' she said. 'There's all the tea things to wash up still. That's one thing, there's always something to be done. It keeps your mind off thinking.'

She was touched by Dan's concern for them. 'What will you do?' he asked. 'Where will you live?'

'We'll go on living in Barbury,' Edith said. 'Len's got his work here, you see. He doesn't like being in a reserved occupation, but they won't let him go. There's one or two houses to be had, if you know the right people. We've got word of one already, up the top end of Sudbury Road.' A faint, bitter smile touched the corners of her mouth. 'The better end. I always wanted to live up the other end of the road. What we'll do for furniture I don't know. We lost everything. All my nice home.' Again she paused and then squared her shoulders resolutely. 'We'll manage, I dare say.'

'We've got an attic full of unwanted furniture at Appleyard,' Dan said. 'I'd like to make a suggestion, Mrs Gray. Will you and Len come back with me to Appleyard? I think you both ought to get away, if only for a week or two, and if you come, Rilla will come. She needs you at the moment, but I still hope that she will make her home with us eventually. You could look through the unwanted stuff we've got stowed away and see if there's anything that would be useful to you. Then, when you are ready to come back, we can see whether Rilla wishes to come with you or to stay with us.'

'It's good of you,' Edith said. 'I'll have to talk to Len. You're right, he ought to get away. He's not been sleeping very well, starting up in the night and calling out, enough to make you jump out of your skin. A bit of a holiday in the country'd do him the world of good.'

In one respect the short visit to Appleyard was a success: Len turned out to be more of a countryman than anyone had suspected. He proved infinitely easier to entertain than Edith. Dan took him out with a gun and he shot a couple of rabbits and a wood pigeon and felt that the target practice he had put in with the Local Defence Volunteers had been well worthwhile. He found the gardening tools and put in some hard work on a patch of ground intended for winter vegetables. 'Not potatoes,' Dan said. 'I never want to see another potato as long as I live!' He dropped in to the village pub and, since his story was known, was treated with awkward compassion. No one spoke of the air raid or his loss, but the silent current of sympathy was expressed by a 'What's yours?' that would normally not have been uttered for a cautious month or more.

It was Edith who was bored. She had an idea that by doing housework she would be demeaning herself and letting Rilla down and so, although her instinct was to seize a duster and brighten up the rooms, she forced herself to sit with idle hands, looking out of the window at a scene which was undeniably beautiful, but which, for Edith, might just as well have been the Sahara Desert.

'If this is life in the country, you can have it,' she said at the end of the first week. 'Honestly, Rilla, I don't know how you stood it all those months. Nothing to do, no one to see. Oh, it's restful, I'll give you that, and it's doing your Dad good, but if I was to have the choice of a holiday, in ordinary times, I mean, I must say I'd prefer somewhere like Margate where you've got the sea and a bit of life.'

'I like it,' Rilla said.

There was a short pause. 'You'll be staying on then?' Edith asked.

'No. I'd rather come back to Barbury with you. I can help you get settled in the new house. Then . . . I don't know. Find a job, I suppose.'

She was adamant about this decision. Dan pointed out that he still had a worthwhile job for her to do at Appleyard, but she shook her head.

'Mum needs me just now,' she said. 'It'll be terrible for her, going back to Barbury to a different house, and Joyce not being there.'

Put like that it was not a thing Dan could argue against. They had met in the Estate Office. Dan had just come in from the fields. He looked and felt tired and sweaty. His injured shoulder had healed, but it was still tender and he had been putting too much strain on it, and his bad leg ached abominably. In other circumstances he might have made more of an effort to discuss the matter dispassionately with Rilla. As it was, he felt unequal to the argument and the rest of their conversation silenced him completely.

She was holding a large brown paper parcel. 'I was looking for some string,' she said. 'Do you have something I can use to put round this parcel?'

'String has practically disappeared, but I think I can find you a little bit,' he said. 'Is it to go through the post?'

'No. In fact, you can probably have the string back once it's been delivered. It's a parcel for your mother to take to the W.V.S. Dan, will you give it to her?'

If he had been less tired and preoccupied it would not have been necessary for him to ask, 'What's in the parcel?'

'Baby clothes,' Rilla said in the careful, even voice she always used when they came near to mentioning Jon. 'It seems a pity to waste them.'

He understood then the reason why she had asked him to deliver the parcel to his mother. Winifred's bitterness over the death of her grandson had been almost entirely directed towards Rilla. They preserved a precarious peace by not mentioning the subject. Would it be better to bring it out into the open by insisting on Rilla handing over the parcel herself? Had Rilla been going to stay it might have been worth the possibility of a painful scene for the sake of the reconciliation that might ensue from it. As it was, Dan said wearily, 'I'll take the parcel myself next time I'm in Cheltenham.'

He looked at Rilla's unresponsive face and added, 'Ma feels it too, you know, Rilla.'

She looked up quickly. 'Yes, I know that. We just don't seem to be able to talk about it. She blames me and I agree with her. If I could defend myself it might be easier. I can't go on living here, Dan.'

'No, perhaps not, in the circumstances. I shall miss you.'

She smiled faintly, obviously not really believing him, and yet it was true. He had come to enjoy Rilla's quiet company in the period before Jon's birth. When they had been following the German advance on the map together they had had long talks about Europe. She had been eager to listen to his reminiscences of places he had visited himself. He had found her naïve, but acutely responsive. It had been interesting to see how quickly her mind expanded to new ideas and impressions. It occurred to him now that there was no one in his immediate vicinity to whom he could talk in the same way. Relations with his mother were strained, perhaps not permanently, but certainly for the time being. Most of his contemporaries were in the forces. With a wry smile, Dan admitted to himself that the war's gift to him had been a crippling loneliness.

Rilla returned home to Barbury, composed and quiet, and helped her parents to settle in to their new home, but there could be no question of taking up the old threads again.

'What are you going to do, Rill?' Dinah asked. 'I think you're nuts myself, coming back here to all the air raids and everything when you had such a cushy number in the country, but as long as you're here, why don't you come into the factory with me?'

Dinah had abandoned Maison Julie and was working in a factory a mile or two outside Barbury. She was frank about what they produced. 'Shell cases mostly. We're not supposed to talk about it, but how can you keep something secret with three hundred people in the know? You'd be surprised what a lot of work there is to them when all they're going to do is explode and be destroyed. It's hard work at first and the noise gets you down, but you get used to it. It's ever so patriotic and the money's smashing.'

Rilla turned her enormous, grave eyes on her friend and considered this proposition thoughtfully. 'I couldn't do that,' she said. 'Making things to kill people, I can't do that.'

Dinah went away after that, in something of a huff. 'Making things to kill people,' it was not a nice way to talk about all her hard work at the factory. It was soppy. Thinking like that was no way to win the war. Rilla had changed since the days when she had always followed Dinah's lead. Of course, she had had a terrible shock, losing her little baby like that, but it seemed to Dinah that she had got a bit above herself, living with her grand in-laws. Too good now to muck up her hands and do a bit of dirty work.

The conversation increased the distance between Rilla and her former friend, but it had the effect of crystallizing Rilla's own thoughts about what she would do with her life.

'The way things are going, I'm bound to be called up or directed into war work,' she said to her mother and father. 'I don't want to make munitions and if I join up it could mean that I'm helping to free some man to go and get wounded or killed or taken prisoner. I know, Dad, don't bother to tell me, that we can't win the war without soldiers and guns and fighting, but that's not for me. I'm going to be a nurse.'

Chapter 6

Barney's wounds were slow to heal and, once he was fully aware of his situation, he did not try to hurry the process, realizing that he was far better off in hospital than he would have been anywhere else. The situation was confused; the Germans were not prepared for the vast numbers of prisoners they had on their hands. It was better to keep quiet, to benefit from the care of the French medical staff in the hospital at Lille, to which he had been transferred, and to wait until he could see more clearly how he was going to escape.

He was in hospital when his baby was born, but at that time he had had no letters from home and he remained unaware of the news for some weeks. He wrote to Rilla as soon as he was strong enough and there seemed some hope of a letter getting through. He supposed that the birth must be drawing near and he felt a spasm of compassion for her. She was at Appleyard, he was pleased about that. If only he too could have been there!

He thought of his home constantly and tried to imagine how Rilla fitted in. From the letters he had received before his capture it sounded as if she had made quite a niche for herself. Strange, that had been the last thing he'd expected.

The news of the baby's birth was late in reaching him because Rilla had had to wait until she had an address to which to send his letters. The news of the child's death reached him almost simultaneously. By that time he was on his feet, moving cautiously around the ward with the aid of a stick. When he had read the letters, one from Dan with all the details, one from Rilla, very short and stilted, every small phrase betraying her anguished grief, he hobbled out of the ward and down to the W.C., the only place where he could be alone. He bolted the door and leaned his forehead against the white-tiled wall; with one fist he beat against the cold, hard surface trying to find an outlet for his helpless anger. All those long months when Rilla had carried the child. If this was to be the end of it, they need never have married. The thought filled him with shame.

In the few months between their wedding and the time when the real fighting had started with the irruption of the German offensive, he had not been faithful to her. Fighting had been more than sporadic, and it had been possible to get leave. A return to England was not really feasible, and most of his cheerful, footloose contemporaries had made a bee-line for Paris. Barney had decided to pay a visit to Yvette Gallimard, not, unfortunately, at the villa in the south of France where they had both been guests just before the war, but at her home in Dijon.

He sensed, when he telephoned her from the station to announce his arrival, that she was a little surprised by the visit, and not entirely pleased, but he thought she would soon get over that once they were together. He invited her to dine with him and she agreed to meet him at a restaurant nearby.

He wondered whether there was another lover in the offing, which would be a nuisance and spoil the plans he had made for his leave. At least there was no husband to worry about. Yvette was a childless widow in her late thirties, a little older than Barney realized; charming, good-looking, well-dressed, and amusing; very much in demand as a guest; and only just beginning to scrutinize herself in the looking glass for signs of encroaching middle age. She was not rich, but she had enough money to make her independent. She occasionally helped a friend who ran an art gallery and she was knowledge-able about modern painting. She was *mondaine,* frivolous, cyni-cal, very much a Frenchwoman and, at that time, deeply trou-bled by her country's situation. She had regarded her brief affair with Barney as nothing more than a holiday diversion. It had amused her and gratified her vanity to attract this good-looking young Englishman in the face of competition from the young girls in the party. They had all wanted him. It had given her a glow of satisfaction to know that he had eyes for no one but her.

She looked at him on the other side of the table that night in Dijon and remembered that it had hurt, just a little, to part with him. He was a tiresome, careless boy, but he had intelli-gence and sensitivity as well as a hard, sun-tanned body and a vigour which she had found just a little fatiguing. It had been a satisfying episode, but she was not entirely sure that she wanted to take it up again, not now, when the circumstances were so different.

It was disconcerting to have to admit to finding him even more attractive than he had been the previous summer. He had hardened, become more mature; there was an edge of ruthless-ness about him which sent a *frisson* along her nerve ends. He had the look of a fighting man, even though he could not have seen much real action. She had the feeling that, whereas it had been she who had dictated the progress of their Riviera affair, now Barney would take charge, and the idea was not unappeal-ing. She decided to let matters take their course, to sit back and see how he would handle the situation.

'I will tell you something, *mon cher ami,*' she said over the dinner she allowed him to buy for her. 'You are a very big rascal. You amuse yourself with me on the Côte d'Azur, and me too, I enjoyed it very much, and then you think to yourself this woman she is very good, very nice in bed, but she is too old for me so I will go back to England and forget all about her. And now, you have time on your hands, and without a word, without a telephone call, you appear and you think you will pick up where you left off. You do not think to yourself that perhaps I have better things to do than to amuse a little boy, no matter how handsome he looks in his smart British uniform? Tell me now what you have been doing all this long time when you have not taken the trouble to keep in touch with me?'

'I've been fairly busy,' Barney said. 'For one thing, I got married.'

'*Tiens!*' Yvette looked blankly astonished. She examined him carefully. 'You have not at all the air of a married man,' she said. 'I do not understand it. Still less do I understand why you come to see me. Perhaps I have wronged you, *mon cher* Barney, perhaps after all it is a visit of pure friendship.'

'Not altogether,' Barney said. He hesitated and then he gave her a baldly factual account of his marriage.

'I see,' Yvette said thoughtfully. 'And now you are a little cross with yourself that you married this sad little girl, and you think there is no reason why you should not take your pleasure where you will, and so you come to see me. I am not a cheap *cocotte*, Lieutenant Wainwright.'

'You are probably the most attractive woman I shall ever know,' Barney said. He took her hand and kissed it lightly. 'If you are sending me away, I suppose I shall have to accept it with as much grace as I can muster. As for poor Rilla, it was partly your fault, you know. If I hadn't been missing you so badly, I might never have become involved with her.'

'You are altogether wicked, and I dislike you very much indeed,' Yvette said. His lips moved against her hand. She removed it from his grasp, but Barney sensed that she was having to make an effort not to smile and he had the comfortable conviction that it would not be necessary to start looking for a hotel room for the weekend.

The memory of this brief interlude did not trouble him when he returned to his unit. It was only after he had had the news of the baby's death that he felt guilty, though he told himself there was no reason why he should. When he had married Rilla it had been with a private reservation that it need not alter his way of life when they were apart. He had not expected to feel so strongly about the loss of the child for whose sake he had married her. It hardened the resolve he had already taken, that at all costs he must escape from his captivity and return to the fight.

It had been gradually borne in on him as he became convalescent that he was almost the only Britisher amongst a contingent of French.

'An accident of war,' one of his companions told him. 'You were dragged out of the sea by one of our boys and we kept you with us. We were the rearguard. We were promised that when at last the end came we would be taken off on a ship to England, but there were too many of us. All the little rats came out of their holes when they got wind that the last ships were leaving, and we, who had fought for their precious little lives, we, the fighting men, were left behind. Now, what is there for us? As long a stay as possible in hospital—and, thank God, the medical staff are very co-operative about that, you will find—then most likely deportation to Germany.'

'I suppose I shall be sent to join a British prisoner-of-war camp,' Barney said doubtfully. 'I must make some enquiries.'

'Discreet, I beg, *mon vieux*,' Jacques begged him. 'We do not want to draw attention to ourselves, you understand.'

The result of Barney's careful questions made him thoughtful. There seemed every possibility that he would, eventually, find himself in a camp for British prisoners in as distant a spot as the Germans could devise, far away on the Polish border perhaps, where even the most intractable prisoner would have difficulty in escaping. The French, on the other hand, were likely to remain closer at hand. Other restraints besides barbed wire could be placed on them. If they escaped they might find their way home, but what would that profit them? Their country was occupied, they could be picked up again quite easily. Even worse, if they failed to reappear, reprisals could be imposed on their families.

Barney started to concentrate on building up his strength and getting back his walking ability. His leg had been broken in two places, and his concussion had been severe, but his bones knitted together, his torn flesh renewed itself, his headaches and black-outs subsided. Finally he was left with only a long scar on his leg and a little patch of hair on his right temple that had turned white and gave an odd touch of distinction to his young face.

They received a visit from a German medical team and, in spite of the French doctors' attempts to persuade them that all the patients were still unfit, Barney and six of the twelve cases in his ward were told they would be moved out the following day. He was pleased to see that the Germans were put out by the discovery of a British Army officer amongst the Frenchmen.

'I do not understand how it has happened that you have remained here so long,' the German officer in charge remarked. 'However, it is of no importance. You will be taken to Germany and there your case will be properly documented.'

There was something about his bland faith in the efficiency of the German system that irked Barney. He was not going to be reduced to the level of a card in an index by fussy little clerks like this one.

He dressed and shuffled downstairs the next day with his wardmates, but he climbed onto the lorry which was waiting for them only after a swift look round had confirmed that there was no point in making a dash for the hospital gates, since they were guarded by two armed German soldiers.

There were more soldiers at the station, and again he could see no hope of escape. It was the first time his French companions had been outside the hospital and seen for themselves the grey uniforms of their enemies in their own streets. It reduced most of them to silent misery and he found them unhappy companions.

They stumbled stiffly out of the lorry which had taken them to the station, dressed in a weird conglomeration of clothes which had been handed out at random when they left the hospital. Barney had collected a pair of black trousers, rather too large for him, a good quality brown-tweed jacket and a blue and white striped shirt. Most of his companions looked equally shabby; few of them were wearing any semblance of uniform.

They found that they were only part of a larger contingent which had been rounded up from points all round the city. They were formed up into lines and ordered to wait. They waited, in dull resentment, until darkness began to fall and at last the round-up was complete. Slowly they began to shuffle forward. Barney saw that they were passing by a couple of small tables where two earnest clerks in uniform, similar to the medical man he had despised, were checking their names against a list. It would be his turn soon. He looked round. There were armed soldiers standing by the tables. There were more, looking bored, walking up and down the lines of prisoners. Again there seemed no possibility of making a successful bolt for it.

He weighed up his chances of making a quick dash onto the railway track and had just decided that it would be too risky when the air raid warning sounded. He saw some of the soldiers looking up apprehensively, but no one gave them any orders about taking shelter. The slow line moved forward again.

The guns started. They could see bursting shells and flak in the air and hear the sound of aircraft overhead. There were only six people between him and the busy little clerk waiting to check his identity when the bombs fell. Prisoners and guards flung themselves to the ground. Afterwards, Barney remembered feeling a strong sense of indignation that he should be under attack from his own side. The danger, the noise, the

/143

screams of the injured were all too familiar. He had been through all this before. Something swished down through the darkness and he huddled closer to the ground. There was an ear-splitting explosion; the earth rocked beneath him.

He could not believe, when the reverberations of the explosion had died away, that he was still alive. He wiped the dirt away from his eyes and moved cautiously. He was not only alive, but unhurt. He lifted his head. All round him was a scene of carnage. One of the bombs had landed in the middle of the yard, destroying Germans and French alike. He could hear the groans of the wounded and dying. One of the bodies near him moved and Barney crawled forward to see if there was anything he could do to help, but it was obvious that the man was not going to survive. He tried to speak, but nothing he said was intelligible. A bubbling stream of blood came out of his mouth and he died. Barney looked round. No one was paying any attention to him. This might be his moment to get away, now while the panic and confusion lasted.

He found that he was shaking with the shock of his near escape and took a moment to pull himself together. He must think calmly. He would not get very far as Lieutenant Barnaby Wainwright. Better by far if he could to assume a French identity. The dead man who had tried to speak to him was tall, dark and had probably been in his mid-twenties. Barney felt in his pocket. His papers were still intact. In his benumbed state, Barney could not decide whether it would be better to plant his own identification on the Frenchman or to retain it. In the end, he decided not to part with it.

He crawled away to a place where some burning wood supplied a flicker of light. He appeared to have stolen the papers of Jean-Luc Ferrier, aged twenty-six, a native of Lyons. An ambulance came clanging up the street. There were shouts and a confusion of movement as the survivors began to stumble over the dead and wounded in the darkness. He began to make his way towards the railway track.

He almost made it. If the raid had lasted another ten

minutes, he would have been away from the railway station, but his luck ran out as he stumbled over the last few yards of debris. A voice challenged him sharply, and when he did not stop he heard the ominous sound of a rifle bolt being rammed home. Again he was challenged, and this time he stopped. Recapture was better than a bullet between the shoulder blades.

Not until he was taken for further interrogation did it occur to him that he could still use his assumed identity. His French was fluent. At a pinch he could pass as a Frenchman, at least to the Germans. It would probably save him from being sent off to a distant camp.

His questioning was perfunctory. The German officer knew perfectly well that he had been trying to make a run for it, but there were more urgent matters on his mind. Barney gave his name firmly as 'Jean-Luc Ferrier' and it was accepted without question. He was hurried off with the surviving members of his party.

This time they were loaded onto a train, but the progress they made was slow. A man who had climbed up on a companion's shoulders to look out of the window high up in their truck reported that, as far as he could make out, considerable damage had been inflicted on the sidings. He seemed pleased about it. Barney decided to say as little as possible until he had had time to size up his new companions. He had little hope of sustaining his deception amongst a crowd of Frenchmen. Would they give him away? He thought not.

They were treated like cattle but, like cattle, they were fed and watered. He managed to secure a place on the floor of the railway truck, sitting with his back against the creaking wall. He still had his British identification on him and reason now told him that a double identity could be a dangerous thing. He did not want to run the risk of being shot as a spy. He felt the rough wooden boards beneath him. There was undoubtedly a gap between them. He could see right through to the track rushing by below. Trying not to draw attention to what he was doing, he fed his British papers through the gap. Two minutes later the identity of Second Lieutenant Barnaby Wainwright had disappeared, and only Jean-Luc Ferrier remained.

He stared again at the floor of the truck 'We might be able to lever these boards up,' he said to his nearest companion.

The man looked at him with lacklustre eyes. 'What for?'

'To escape.'

His neighbour merely shrugged. Clearly the idea had no interest for him, but another man said, 'I'm game.'

They cleared a space and began working on the wooden floor. One board came away in a splintering rush, but that did not provide a big enough space for a man to pass through. They were hard at work on a second one when the train began to slow down.

'This could be our chance,' Barney said.

The Frenchman succeeded in enlarging the hole and dropped down onto the track just as the train stopped. He crouched there, leaving no room for Barney. They could hear voices and the sound of running footsteps and then the rattle of a machine gun.

'Someone else trying to get away—and not succeeding,' said one of the prisoners in the truck.

Barney bent down and spoke to his fellow escaper. 'Crawl along the track so that I can get out, then lie down flat until the train has passed over us,' he said.

The man looked up, his face glistening with sweat. Instead of taking Barney's advice, he crawled out between the wheels and began to run. The machine gun spoke again. They heard a choking cry and then silence. The next moment the key turned in the padlock on the outside and the door of their truck slid open.

A German officer stood there, a revolver in his hand, backed by two armed guards. He spoke tersely in German.

'If anyone else attempts to escape, you will all be shot,' one of the guards behind him interpreted.

The door slammed shut and they sank back into the mindless torpor from which this brief excitement had roused them, made more uncomfortable now by the rush of cold air through the hole in the floor and sickened by the death of their companion.

They crossed the Rhine and Barney began to despair. He was out of a country in which the citizens were at least nominally friendly and into Nazi Germany where every man's hand would be against him.

The camp in which they eventually found themselves was not large. About one hundred men in all were settled in huts in a barbed wire compound. They were too tired and confused to take much notice of one another that night, but the following morning Barney saw some curious glances directed towards him. They were given a breakfast of black bread and ersatz coffee, they assembled for a head count and then they were addressed by the commandant.

They had become prisoners, he told them, because of their unwarranted resistance to the rightful territorial claims of the Third Reich. Their country was beaten, they had been deserted by their allies, they would not be returning to their homes until Germany's victory was won. In the meantime they would work, for the most part on farms. The harder they worked, the sooner the war would be over, and the sooner they would be able to go home.

When it was over they were dismissed. For the rest of the day, it seemed, they were, as the commandant put it with an unfortunate turn of phrase, 'at liberty.'

Barney found himself in the middle of a little group of men, being shunted unobtrusively towards a far corner of the compound. He guessed what was coming and went along with them without resistance. They surrounded him, apparently nothing more than a casual knot of men, but he saw the hard purpose in their eyes and hoped that his story would be believed.

One of them appeared to have been chosen to interrogate him. 'You told the Boche your name was Jean-Luc Ferrier. Is that true?' he demanded.

'No,' Barney said with careful clarity. 'I am Lieutenant Barnaby Wainwright, a British officer.'

There was a slight but perceptible easing of tension.

'What's your game?' his questioner asked.

They listened intently as he explained his reasons for the exchange of identity. He looked round the circle of faces. 'Will you support me?' he asked.

'We'll have to talk it over. If there's any danger in it for us, we may decide to ditch you.'

'We can't turn him in to the Boche,' another voice protested.

He left them to talk it over, not sure what the outcome would be. They were not exactly hostile to him, but neither were they particularly friendly. He heard someone ask, 'Why should we do anything for a British officer after the way they let us down?' and bit back a scathing retort.

They kept him waiting half a day before they told him their decision: they would not reveal his deception. It was a relief, and yet what had he gained? He was still a prisoner. He still had to find the means of escape and it was now November.

The days resolved themselves into a routine. They lived in the camp and were sent out in batches each day to work in the fields, but as the winter drew on there was less for them to do. His anxiety to get away faded a little. It began to look as if he would have to sit out the winter, but in the spring, without fail, he would make his move.

The cold was bitter. There was one stove with a tin chimney in each hut, but the fuel they were given was never enough. The huts were new, built of bare wooden boards, and the wind howled through the cracks. They stuffed the spaces with rags, but that did not stop the snow creeping in. It melted and froze again, so that there were days when icicles hung inside the huts.

Outside there was nothing but an empty yard surrounded by barbed wire. Sometimes they walked round and round the perimeter, but usually they were out working during daylight, and in the evenings they lay on their bunks, writing letters when they had paper and ink, reading when they had a book, talking about their homes and families and their lives before they had joined the army, about women, about food, but gradually they grew more taciturn. As the winter wore on there were more and more men who spent hours doing nothing but lying on their backs in silence and staring at the ceiling.

They were starved of news and what they heard through letters was not encouraging. Hungary and Romania joined the Axis. The Commandant made sure they heard about that. There were stories of the British having opened an offensive in North Africa and rumours that it was going well, but to counter that there were reports of fearsome raids on England, London in particular, and Barney, with the memory of the carnage in the railway yard fresh in his mind, wondered how long the people at home could hold out in the face of such horror.

It would have cheered him if he could have seen the way the civilian population was weathering the storm. There was a spirit abroad in Britain compounded of grim determination not to be beaten by 'that Hitler' and a peculiar and cheerful impudence in the face of anything he could inflict on them. Shopkeepers with walls and windows destroyed put up notices saying 'Business as usual'; bombed a second time, they amended them to 'Still open for business'; until someone with little left but a tarpaulin over a skeleton frame of a building thought of improving the wording to 'Even more open than usual.'

The raid in which Jon and Joyce had been killed had been the first daylight raid in the London area. It signalled the start of the Blitz. From then on the sirens sounded night after night, and the population took to the shelters. In the mornings they emerged, pinched and wan, surveyed the scenes of wreckage all round them, shook themselves and made a joke, and plodded off home to see what was left of the houses they had left the night before. It seemed that nothing could daunt their obstinate determination to carry on as usual. Office workers from the suburbs, mostly elderly men and young girls, battled their way to work in spite of bombed railway lines and torn-up roads.

They tramped over the damaged bridges, picked their way through the debris and, if their places of work had survived, shook the dust and splintered glass out of their files and settled down to the day's work. Shops stayed open, although it became usual for them to close at four o'clock so as to allow staff and customers to reach home before the nightly raid began. Public services operated, with gas, electricity and water restored by what at times seemed like miraculous means after a main had been blasted, although there were periods when housewives in a damaged street had to queue for water at a stand-pipe, cook as best they could over an open fire or, if they were old-fashioned and lucky, a kitchen range, and pass as much of the evening as they were able to spend out of the shelter by the light of a candle. An indoor shelter, the Morrison, named after the new Home Secretary, Mr Herbert Morrison, proved popular. The metal sides and top, with a wire mesh on one side, resembled a cage, but it was a relief to be able to spend the nights in the privacy of one's own home with some degree of safety and, if the space it provided was too confined for comfort, at least it was warm.

All over the country, ordinary men and women who had volunteered as A.R.P. wardens, as demolition workers, as W.V.S., as first-aid workers, rose above their everyday selves and gave that little extra they had not known they had in them. The Fire Brigade turned out night after night; ambulance drivers, many of them women, drove through a hail of shrapnel and developed instant reflexes when suddenly encountering a fresh hole in the road.

People became tired, desperately tired, but there was no thought of defeat in their minds. The first excitement at actually being under fire had given way to a grimmer appreciation of what the German menace really meant, but no one talked of giving in. It would take a little time, things would probably get worse before they got better, but hardly a soul in the whole British Isles doubted the ultimate outcome of this bitter struggle.

The Local Defence Volunteers, which both Dan and Len Gray had joined, had been renamed the Home Guard, and their uniforms and equipment had improved since the days when they had turned out wearing their working clothes and carrying anything from an ancient fowling piece to a pitchfork. Dan, given the rank of captain, was proud of his little band of local stalwarts, appreciating the effort it took for men who had been on their feet for a long working day to appear regularly for drill and instruction, especially when in their quiet country district there was little for them to do but watch for the invasion which did not come.

The fields round the village of Chatwood were ploughed, the rows of autumn stubble disappeared; the yellow leaves grew brown and brittle, collecting in drifts under the hedges; the villagers began to talk among themselves about what kind of a Christmas it was going to be. Sergeant Hobbs, on Home Guard duty in the church tower, saw flashes of gunfire on the distant horizon and heard a vibration in the air from falling bombs and thought sympathetically about the poor devils in the Midlands towns who were getting it again. He leaned against the parapet and wondered whether he dared light a cigarette. He was struggling with this temptation when he heard the sound of an aeroplane overhead. It was approaching the village, but slowly, its engines coughing and spluttering. It sounded as if it were in trouble. He was not certain, because of the way it kept cutting out, but he thought he recognized the distinctive sound of a Heinkel. He peered up into the darkness and suddenly he saw a patch of light, coming nearer. It was the plane and it was on fire. The light grew larger and brighter. The aircraft was diving for the ground. There was an explosion, a brilliant yellow flare, and it broke up in mid-air. Instinctively he ducked, but it was further away than it looked. The pieces, scattered over a wide distance, fell harmlessly over the quiet fields.

At dawn that day they were all out gathering up as much of the burnt-out plane as could be located. The twisted fuselage was discovered and established beyond doubt to be the wreck of a Heinkel. It contained three burnt and mutilated bodies.

Sergeant Hobbs came hurrying across the field. 'Message just came through, sir,' he said to Dan. He surveyed the wreckage of the plane with satisfaction. 'A Heinkel,' he said. 'I told you that was what it was.'

'Apparently the navigator parachuted to safety and has been picked up on the other side of Cheltenham,' Dan said, reading through the message. 'He says there was a crew of five. Which raises an interesting question: there's one missing, and from the disposition of the bodies it looks as if it must be the pilot. Where is he?'

'You reckon he baled out, sir?' Sergeant Hobbs asked eagerly.

'I think he must have done. Whether or not he came down in this area is another question, but I think it calls for a search.'

'Mr Wainwright, Mr Wainwright!' A boy came running across the field, waving his arms and shouting, 'We've found a parachute!' He took them back to the place where he and his brother had found the parachute, bundled up and thrust under a hedge on Dan's own land.

'We were just having a look round before we went to school, and we saw this flash of white,' he explained. 'And we thought . . .' He stopped, perceiving that he had arrived at an awkward moment in his explanation.

'That it might be a rabbit caught in one of your Dad's snares which he's told you to check because he'd been on duty all night and not had a chance to get round,' Dan supplied helpfully.

Willy Barminster shuffled his feet, conscious of grins from the listening men, and hurried on: 'We had a look, like, and there it was all bundled away.'

'Willy said we oughter say nothing about it, because it would come in right useful,' the other little boy remarked.

'No, I didn't,' Willy hotly disputed. 'Who does it belong to, Mr Wainwright? Is it finders, keepers?'

'Strictly speaking, I believe not,' Dan said. 'However, I've got more important things to think about with a German airman on the loose. If it were to disappear, I don't know that I'd be particularly worried. But, Willy, there's good stuff in those parachutes; it's to be given to your Mum, not wasted on making tents for playing cowboys and Indians or anything like that.'

'Can we help look for the German?' the smaller boy enquired.

'Indeed you can't! You've done your bit and we're very grateful to you, but this man is probably armed and I can't risk one of you being taken hostage. Go on down to the village and pass the word round for everyone to be on the alert, and then go to school!'

He watched them scamper away, reasonably certain that they would be safe on the clear path between the farmland and the village. He lifted his eyes to the line of the hills beyond Appleyard. It seemed likely that the parachutist would have made for the open country. But how far had he managed to get?

They spread out and began a systematic search. It was Reg Barminster, with his keen poacher's eye, who saw the tracks. A broken twig, a few bent blades of grass, an overhanging branch pushed to one side. 'Straight up the hill and going clumsy-like,' he said.

'Injured, perhaps?'

'Could be. There's a spot of blood and, look, another one. If he's got any sense he'll give up easy enough. What chance has he got?'

Not much chance, in Dan's opinion, but that was not to say the man would not choose to put up a fight. He moved forward cautiously.

From the shelter of a small copse of trees Kurt Moltke watched the hunt begin. He withdrew further into the shadow of the trees and then took refuge underneath a hawthorn bush overgrown with brambles and ivy. He winced as the thorns tore at his unprotected face when he crawled into his hiding place. He was moving cautiously and he knew that his only chance of remaining undetected was to keep perfectly still. No hope of running away, his ankle had been broken when he had made his parachute landing in darkness on the rough ground. He had done well to get as far as this. If he could stick it out until darkness fell again he would try one of the outlying farms he had seen for food. What then? Germany was a long way across the sea. He doubted in his saner moments whether he would ever see it again, but he was suffering from shock and a blow on the head and there were long periods when he was light-headed with pain and believed that he could take on the entire British Army and order them to put him in a boat for home. The cowardly British, who had run away at Dunkirk, would be no match for one of the Luftwaffe's highly-trained pilots. The fact that that summer the R.A.F. had proved more than a match for the Luftwaffe was something he did not acknowledge, even though at the back of his mind he knew that Goering's strategy had not been a success.

He reached the furthest point to which he could retreat and felt for the revolver strapped to his side. The pain from his injured ankle ran up his leg in excruciating waves. He shifted around on the dry, rustling leaves, trying to find a comfortable position in which to sit out the long day.

His cover was good and he might have remained hidden if it had not been for Fluke. Barney's dog, having lost both his master and his newly-acquired mistress, had turned to Dan for companionship. It was not a strictly military arrangement, but he had been adopted by the Chatwood Home Guards as their mascot and he was usually somewhere around when they had their exercises.

On this occasion he was supposed to be tied up at Apple-yard, but he had got loose and set out across the fields, bent on a little sport and exercise. He bounded over the fields, long black ears flapping, and was only slightly put out by Dan's unusually stern command to him to come to heel. He looked up, alert and eager to please, his tail wagging busily as he tried to take in the rules of this new game. Dan moved forward into the shadow of the small group of trees, every sense alert. Fluke padded after him, snuffling hopefully at various beguiling smells. He paused, stiffening as he caught the scent of blood and fear from beneath the thick bushes. He growled, low in his throat.

Dan, warned of danger, approached the overgrown bushes cautiously, his gun at the ready.

"Come on out," he ordered.

There was no response. With an excited yelp, Fluke burrowed through the undergrowth and came face to face with the German flyer, frozen into immobility, his injured leg thrust out in front of him. He lifted the hand which held the gun in an unmistakably menacing gesture and, with an hysterical flurry of barks, Fluke flung himself into the attack. With a judgement that could not have been bettered he seized the outstretched leg in its leather flying boot between his teeth and began to worry it.

Kurt's finger was already on the trigger. As the intolerable pain engulfed him he jerked his hand up in a reflex action that was to prove disastrous for him and shot the little dog through the head. It gave Dan just the space of time he needed to break through the prickly branches and seize the initiative.

For one split second the two men regarded one another. Kurt, a young, blond giant in the best Aryan tradition, a dyed-in-the-wool Nazi, arrogant, sure of himself, totally convinced of the rightness of the war in which he was involved, but at that moment crazy with pain and sure that this was his last moment on earth; and Dan, every natural instinct outraged by the savage reprisal on the helpless little animal. In that moment of confrontation he remembered many things: Rilla and her dead baby, Barney in his prison camp, the hospital ships he had seen deliberately bombed at Dunkirk, the helpless men mowed down by machine gun bullets, the sufferings of the homeless refugees. He lifted his rifle higher.

Just for a second Kurt let his arrogant guard slip. Believing that this grim-faced man was about to shoot him, he let his nervousness betray him and ran his tongue over his dry lips. In that one tiny moment of weakness Dan saw him suddenly in a different light. He was an enemy, but he was no older than Barney. He was hurt and he was afraid. With his eyes still fixed on the tired young face with its red-rimmed eyes and blond stubble on the chin, Dan felt for his whistle and blew a long blast to fetch help.

They were not particularly gentle with him when they saw what he had done to Fluke, but after they had dragged him out of his prickly hiding place they carried him down the hill to the police station and called in the local doctor, who spoke a little German.

Out of his bewilderment as he surveyed this bunch of amateur soldiers who crowded round for a sight of their capture, Kurt looked up at Dan and achieved a flicker of his old arrogance. He made a remark with a sneering lift of his upper lip, which Dan did not understand.

"He says something about your weakness being the reason why we will lose the war," the doctor reported with a puzzled frown.

Dan smiled faintly. "No," he said. "Tell him, if your German will run to it, that, on the contrary, it is the reason why we've got to win."

Chapter 7

On her first day as a probationer Rilla was convinced that she had made a mistake in thinking she could ever become a nurse. She had laced her flat-heeled black shoes too tightly and her feet hurt; her legs ached with the unaccustomed standing; the elastic belt which circled her waist was too tight; the starched collar of her uniform rasped her neck; and the little bit of stiffened muslin perched on top of her head was surely going to fall off at any moment in spite of all the hair pins. She looked and felt harassed and nervous. With a sinking heart, she contemplated the possibility that she might not be able to keep going. It would be dreadful if she had to give up, all the more so because it had not been easy to persuade the matron of St Oswulf's Hospital to take her.

'We need nurses,' Miss Earlingham had said frankly at their initial interview. 'Your educational level and your personal attributes seem to be what we are looking for. Two things

157

make me hesitate. One is the fact that you are married, but in wartime—and particularly since your husband has the misfortune to be a prisoner-of-war—I think that need not be an obstacle. The other thing, and this is the real stumbling block, is the very terrible loss you have experienced. I must put this to you bluntly. Your training will, of necessity, take you into obstetrics. Do you think you can face it?'

Rilla had paused to consider. It was true that when she had volunteered for nursing training she had been thinking more in terms of attending wounded soldiers.

'We are beginning to get a lot of civilian casualties from air raids, too,' Miss Earlingham said, watching her closely. 'Would that distress you unduly?'

'I think I can come to terms with it,' Rilla said slowly. 'After all, it's *because* I lost Jon—my baby—and my sister that I decided to go into nursing. You are right, of course. It won't be easy to see other women with their babies, and perhaps it will be hard, the first time, to handle a little child. I think I can do it now that I've begun to face up to what I've lost. At first, I was too numb to feel anything, then I had a time when I couldn't stop crying, but there's a sort of calm in me now. I feel as if the worst that could possibly happen to me has already happened, and I've lived through it. More than that, I've found out that whatever happens you can't stop yourself from going on living. Your heart goes on beating even though you think it's broken, your lungs go on pumping air, you have to have food.'

'Some people can't accept that, and then they have nervous breakdowns,' the matron had said, interested by this quiet analysis of extreme grief.

'There were moments when I could have turned my back on reality,' Rilla admitted. 'But there were other people to think about besides myself. I couldn't add to what Mum and Dad were going through, and then there was Barney—my husband —he might still want me when he comes back.'

Miss Earlingham caught the implications of that betraying

'might' and gave her a sharp look. So all was not well with the marriage. It might not stand the strain of long separation. In that case, Mrs Wainwright might be glad of a profession to fall back on. She seemed a sensible child, unexpectedly thoughtful, thrust into maturity sooner than most girls. The signs were that she would make a good nurse. She indicated on the file in front of her that Rilla was to be accepted.

It took a week for Rilla to find her feet and a month before she admitted cautiously to herself that, in spite of the slogging hard work, she was enjoying her training. It was not all bed pans and vomit bowls. The lectures were usually interesting, though she shared the common outrage at being required to attend them in what was supposed to be her free time, and she enjoyed her contact with the patients.

She found it strange to live in the nurses' home, surrounded by women, a stranger experience to her than to some of the other girls, who had come straight from home or even from boarding school, and it was more difficult than she had imagined to bridge the gulf caused by her wider experience. She was as young as any of them, but how much older she felt. They were a cheerful, friendly bunch of girls, but she could not join in their giggling over an encounter with one of the better-looking doctors, nor sympathize with their agonizing over their boy-friends.

She discovered one other girl whose circumstances were similar to her own. Rilla was still trying to settle down in these unfamiliar surroundings when one of the other newcomers asked, with a touch of diffidence, 'I noticed that you were "Mrs" Wainwright. Are you perhaps, like me, a widow?'

Rilla looked up quickly from the textbook on anatomy she had been thumbing through with a sinking heart as she realized how much there was to learn. The girl who had spoken to her was rather older than the rest of the group, probably approaching her mid-twenties. Rilla tried to remember her name. Ann something.

'I'm Ann Lauriston,' the other girl said helpfully. 'My husband was in the Royal Navy. His ship went down in the Atlantic.'

'I'm terribly sorry,' Rilla said. 'No, my husband is alive, but he's a prisoner-of-war.'

'Oh, that's hard,' Ann said sympathetically.

They smiled at one another, and Rilla began to feel that here perhaps was someone with whom she had something in common. Ann was a tall girl, taller than Rilla, and very slender. There was a touch of style about her, even in that stiff uniform, Rilla thought. Her skirt was exactly the right length for her long legs, and she seemed to have managed her cap rather better than most of the newcomers. It sat lightly on top of her head like a fly-away butterfly, not at all like the creased and precarious bit of rag to which Rilla felt she had reduced hers. She had red hair, cut short and curling naturally up the back of her head, very blue eyes, and a fine pink and white complexion with a scattering of freckles over her nose.

Her accent puzzled Rilla.

'Are you Canadian?' she asked.

Ann shook her head. 'A lot of people make that mistake —mainly, I guess, because they don't expect to find an American in London right now. I'm from the United States, but I married an Englishman and England became my home. When Tom was killed it seemed to me that the least I could do was to stay on and do what I could to help.'

'Didn't your parents want you to go back to America?'

'They sure did! I think I've won them over now, but Mom in particular is still jittery about me being here in London.'

'How did you come to marry an Englishman?'

'He was a naval attaché in Washington. Dad is a senator.' She paused and smiled as if at a pleasant memory. 'Don't ever let anyone tell you the British are slow! I was rushed off my feet! But I've never regretted it.'

'Not even now?'

'Because he's dead? No. I'm grateful for what I had.' She

glanced round the chattering crowd of girls in the dining room where she and Rilla had chanced to sit down at the same table. 'I'm older than most of our group by several years. I've only just begun to realize what a difference it makes.'

'I feel it, too,' Rilla said. She looked wistfully at her contemporaries. 'They seem so untouched.'

Ann looked at her curiously. There was something about the way she spoke and something about her manner that suggested more than a husband out of touch in a prisoner-of-war camp. It was several weeks before she learned the full story, and when she did she understood both Rilla's look of suffering and her compassion for anyone in trouble.

Christmas came, the first Christmas Rilla had ever spent away from home. Even in wartime the hospital staff went to a great deal of effort to ensure that everyone who was well enough enjoyed it to the full. Rilla's neat fingers came in useful on her ward in preparing decorations, and when she was persuaded to add her small, sweet singing voice to the choir of nurses who toured the wards singing carols on Christmas morning, she felt as much part of a family as she had ever done in the past.

Even so, there were some aspects of the festive season which passed her by. She did not go to the hospital ball and a hopeful approach from a student with mistletoe in his hand met with a decidedly cool rebuff.

She and Ann shared this reluctance to join in the social life of the hospital and since they did not allow themselves any of the distractions in which the other girls took part they were soon star pupils. They recited lists of bones to one another and described symptoms from which the other had to diagnose a disease. Occasionally they allowed themselves a visit to a cinema, but neither of them would accept an invitation from any of the medical students who approached them.

'One day perhaps,' Ann said to Rilla. 'One day, I may be able to start thinking of another man, but not yet—and not one of these boys. They seem to think that because I've had a husband I'm in special need of their attentions.'

'As if they were doing you a favour,' Rilla agreed. 'I've had the same approach made to me. It makes you laugh, doesn't it?'

'It makes me cross,' Ann said. 'All right, so I miss having Tom, but it's *Tom* I miss. Wanting him isn't something that's going to be satisfied by a quick fumble from an overheated kid in a white coat.'

Since she employed the same forthright turn of speech to her would-be suitors she was soon free of them, and it seemed that she did not regret it.

Rilla was able to confide to Ann some of her doubts and fears about her future with Barney. Ann had been married when she was nineteen, not much older than Rilla, but she had had her Tom for four years before he disappeared in the cold grey Atlantic.

'Just time to settle down into being a real married couple, in spite of him being away at sea,' she said wistfully. 'I can see how difficult it must be for you to know how things are going to turn out, Rilla. You and Barney hardly knew one another before you were separated.'

'That's true,' Rilla agreed. 'I hang on to the fact that he still keeps writing to me—at least, he has until now, but there seems to be some sort of hold-up at the moment, probably because he's been moved—and we manage to find things to say in our letters. But I know I've changed, and I think I shall change still more if he is away for a really long time.'

'Do you still love him?'

'I don't really know. Sometimes I think about the few times we were together and what I remember seems wonderful, and at other times it seems like something I must have dreamt. Nothing much that happened to me between the time I met Barney and the time Jon was born seems quite real any more and I can scarcely remember what I was like before Barney came along.'

'So, when he comes home, he may find himself with an entirely different Rilla?'

'Come to that, I may find myself with a completely different Barney.' She sighed and then smiled. 'I knew nothing about real life before, I can see that now, but no one could say that about me since I started nursing! There's nothing like it for showing your rock-bottom reality!'

'I understand now why they call this period basic training,' Ann agreed.

'I do think someone ought to give the patients an idea of which nurses are which,' Rilla said. 'It terrifies me, the way they address us all as "nurse" and expect us all to be experts.'

'What do you suggest—that we wear "L" plates?' Ann inquired.

'I suppose it wouldn't do much for morale,' Rilla admitted. 'As it is, I had one old dear the other day accusing me of practising on her—which was true! I'm going on Men's Surgical next week, where you are now. What's it like?'

'I've enjoyed it. Most of the patients are real sweeties and sister is a cheerful old girl. There'll be a different staff nurse by the time you get there, the one I've had is going on nights.'

It seemed to Rilla the following Monday morning, when she was due to start work on Andrew Ward, that nothing could go right. She had had a bad night, disturbed by an air raid, and instead of remaining awake when the 'All Clear' sounded she fell into a heavy sleep and did not hear her alarm clock. When Ann became worried at not seeing her around and knocked on her door she struggled out of a confused dream and then started up in horror as she realized the time.

She scrambled into her clothes, decided to forget about breakfast, and rushed off to her new ward with a hasty word of thanks to Ann in passing. She arrived at Andrew Ward only ten minutes late, but she was out of breath and she lacked her usual neatness. She hoped that Sister Cuthbert would live up to her reputation of being what Ann had called her—a cheerful old girl—but it was not Sister Cuthbert who confronted her when she looked into the office.

The staff nurse behind the desk, temporarily in charge during the sister's absence, was a tall, cool blonde. She looked up as Rilla came in and her eyes narrowed.

'Ah, yes, Nurse Wainwright,' she said. 'You are supposed to arrive on time, you know.'

'I'm sorry,' Rilla stammered. For one moment she was not sure, and then she said hesitantly, 'I know you, don't I? Didn't we meet . . . ?'

'At Appleyard,' Candida Blewett agreed. 'When you were Barney Wainwright's child bride.'

Her insolent gaze wandered over Rilla, lingering thoughtfully on the hastily-donned uniform. Rilla flushed painfully, only too aware of the short-comings in her appearance.

'I overslept,' she said and then wished she had kept silent.

A derisive smile crossed Candida's face, but she did not comment on this. Instead, she said, 'I was under the impression you were pregnant. Where did you jettison the baby?'

'He was killed in an air raid.' The flat, uncompromising answer disconcerted Candida.

'I hadn't heard,' she said. She hurried on to a different subject. 'Do you have any news of Barney? I know he was taken prisoner at Dunkirk, of course.'

'I hear from him regularly,' Rilla lied. It was not true; she had not heard from Barney for weeks and the thought was a constant nagging worry at the back of her mind. 'He was all right last time he wrote.'

'Oh, hardly all right, surely? Poor dear Barney, locked up without a woman! It hardly bears thinking about!'

A suspicion, unwelcome and unacknowledged before, which had been sown in Rilla's mind at their first meeting, about Barney's past relations with Candida, returned to her again. Candida spoke as if she knew all about him. He had been Rilla's first love and she had always closed her mind to the fact that she could not have been the first woman he had known. She had never thought about them, those other girls. Now she felt certain that Candida had been one of them and the thought was so distasteful that she felt physically sick.

She was dismissed with a sweet, false smile as soon as

Sister Cuthbert bustled into the room and demanded to know why her nurses were gossiping in the office instead of being out on the ward.

'Nurse Wainwright was a little behindhand this morning,' Candida said. 'She overslept, poor dear. One remembers so clearly how fatiguing one found one's own first few months.'

But I've been here for the last quarter of an hour, Rilla thought rebelliously as Sister Cuthbert looked pointedly at the clock.

She did the best she could to catch up on the wasted minutes, but she was feeling hungry after missing her breakfast. The patients were not as well supplied with fruit and biscuits as they would have been in peacetime, but one of them was displaying a magnificent box of chocolates.

'All the way from America,' he said proudly. 'My niece sent it, which I think was real good of her, considering she's not set eyes on me for the last ten years. Have one, Nurse.'

'We're not supposed to,' Rilla said, but she eyed the box longingly.

'Go on! To tell you the truth, I don't care much for chocolates, but it was a kind thought.'

Seeing that it would give him real pleasure if she accepted, Rilla selected one of the sweets and put it in her mouth. Unfortunately it had a hard centre. She was still chewing when Candida caught her.

'Eating, nurse? On the ward? On duty? Surely you've been taught better than that?'

'He would have been disappointed if I'd said no,' Rilla excused herself.

'My dear, the story of my life in one sentence! "He would have been disappointed if I'd said no!"'

Rilla swallowed convulsively, choked and began coughing helplessly, her eyes streaming.

'You'd better go and get yourself a drink of water,' Candida said. She sighed. 'I'll carry on here.'

When Rilla returned Sister Cuthbert was on the ward. She

looked up with as much of a frown as her jolly face would assume and said, 'I know you are still very new, nurse, but you mustn't go wandering around leaving staff nurse to do your chores, you know. Nurse Blewett has better things to do than the small tasks we are able to leave to you.'

It was the first of many such pinpricks. Rilla could do nothing right and her anxiety made her nervous. She had only to sense Candida watching her to spill the tea, drop the thermometer on the floor and once, disastrously, throw away a specimen of urine that was wanted for testing. What made it so difficult to combat was that Candida did nothing. Her presence alone ensured that Rilla went to pieces. Such criticisms as she made of Rilla's work were justified. She was careless, she was over-anxious.

Her poor performance puzzled Sister Cuthbert. 'She came to me with a good report from her last ward,' she said to Candida. 'I can't think what's the matter with her. Keep a close eye on her, won't you?'

'Oh, yes, I will,' Candida promised.

Something about her readiness to keep watch on Rilla disturbed Sister Cuthbert. There was something wrong. There was an atmosphere she did not like on her ward. In her turn she kept watch, and her eyes were fixed not on Rilla, but on Candida Blewett.

Candida did not bother to analyze her rancour towards the little girl Barney had married. She despised her for her defencelessness, and it annoyed her that Rilla had trapped Barney into marriage, even though Candida had never seriously considered him for herself. Not as a husband. She was herself on edge, her nerves stretched taut by the long bombardment they were enduring, exposed to the suffering of the injured, missing the comfortable life to which she was accustomed. Everything was bloody; she felt miserable; it was all too easy to take it out on little Rilla Wainwright.

She had a day off and Rilla's work picked up. Sister Cuthbert looked even more thoughtful.

'Did I gather from something I overheard the other day that you knew Nurse Blewett before you met her here?' she asked casually.

'Not really,' Rilla said. 'I met her once. She knew . . . she knows my husband . . . my husband's family very well.'

Sister Cuthbert said nothing, but she was fully alive to the implications of that stammering little speech. There was something. Jealousy? It was difficult to imagine Candida Blewett being jealous of Rilla and yet, if the younger girl had captured a man she fancied for herself, it might be all the more galling for Candida to know that, on the face of it, she had most of the advantages. She was not exactly a beauty, but even in wartime she retained something of the glossy sheen of a monied background, and she was attractive to men. There had been one or two whispers during her training about the swathe she was cutting through the medical students, and not only the students if all Sister Cuthbert had heard was true. Sister Cuthbert blinked her big brown eyes, which gave nothing away—Candida insisted, in her drawling voice, that she chewed the cud as an aid to thought—and began to make plans.

'You're due for a rest period, aren't you?' she asked Rilla. 'What are you going to do? Go home to your family?'

'No, I'm going into the country to visit my husband's home,' Rilla said.

'An excellent idea. A bit of peace and quiet will do you good. I see you will be coming back to me for another couple of weeks on your return.' She picked up a piece of paper from her desk and looked at it with studied care. 'Nurse Blewett will be doing a spell in the theatre by that time. She'll be pleased about that. She's a good theatre nurse. In fact, I think I shall recommend that she concentrates on theatre work.'

She glanced up and caught the look of intense relief on Rilla's face. Not such a bad little thing and, in her way, far more beautiful than Candida Blewett would ever be. Too eager to please perhaps, that's why she had taken it so hard when her work had been poor. It was to be hoped that she would settle again now.

With the prospect of being free of Candida on her return, Rilla went off to Appleyard in a comparatively happy frame of mind. What Sister Cuthbert had said was quite true, she was very much in need of a period of peace and quiet. The incessant bombing, the horror of the casualties, added to the strain of her inexperience and the unpleasantness from Candida, had reduced her to a state of quivering nervousness.

She had thought at first that she ought to go to her own home, but her mother had urged her to accept Dan's standing invitation to go to Appleyard for the sake of the better rest it would give her.

'Besides,' Edith said. 'You ought to keep in touch with Barney's family.'

'Mrs Wainwright still hates me.'

'Poor woman. I feel for her. Now that I've met her I can see she's not a person you could ever feel at home with exactly, but she's her own worst enemy in my opinion. Keep friendly with her, love—or as friendly as she'll let you. It won't do for you to be at outs with his mother when Barney comes home.'

Rilla sighed and agreed. At least it would be nice to see Dan again. And Appleyard. In fact, if it had not been for Winifred's continuing hostility she could really have looked forward to this brief holiday. Quite apart from which, she would be able to find out whether they had had any letters from Barney. She had been without news now since November— nearly three months—and she was deeply unhappy about it.

The train was late, slow and crowded. Rilla had been on duty all day and she had hoped to be able to sit down and rest on the train to Cheltenham. To her dismay, by the time she had fought her way on to the train there, was not a seat to be had. The small suitcase she had packed for the weekend was not strong enough to sit on. She managed to secure a place in the corridor and leant against the handrail by the window. As the train moved out of Paddington she surreptitiously slid one foot out of her shoe and rubbed it against the other. The train gave a jerk and when she put her foot down her shoe had slid away from her. Scarlet in the face, she had to search for it among the baggage dumped in the corridor for lack of space on the racks.

'Here you are, Cinderella,' a soldier said at last. He grinned as he handed back the well-worn shoe. 'Call me Prince Charming and I'll put it on for you.'

She grimaced as she slipped it back on her foot.

'I know,' he said sympathetically. 'Your feet are killing you!'

'They are,' Rilla admitted.

'Been standing all day?'

'Yes, I'm a nurse.'

She felt a sudden thrill of pride at being able to say that. She might still be a raw recruit, but it was true—she was a nurse.

''Nuff said,' the soldier said. 'Bill! Little lady here's a nurse! Who we going to throw out to get a seat for her?'

Bill considered. 'There's Jimmy got a seat in there,' he suggested. 'Lazy b . . . bloke. Doesn't deserve to sit down.'

'Right! Let's get him out of it.'

He began to slide open the compartment door but Rilla clutched his arm in alarm. 'Oh, no!' she said. 'You mustn't . . . I'm perfectly all right, honestly I am. I don't want to take anyone's seat.'

The soldier ignored this protest. He tapped the shoulder of a soldier who was dozing peacefully in the corner.

'Come on then, Jimmy boy,' he said. 'Let's be 'aving yer. We've got a little nurse here, been on duty all day . . .' he glanced at Rilla. 'That's right, ain't it, you've been on duty all day?'

Rilla nodded, speechless with embarrassment at the upheaval she was causing.

'Are you going to sit there like the lord of the manor and let this poor girl stand up, or are you going to be a gentleman and give her your seat?'

Jimmy blinked in a bemused way. Then he grinned. 'I'll take her on my lap, if you like?' he offered.

'You'll take her on your lap! As if she'd look at the likes of you! Let the poor girl sit down.'

Jimmy got to his feet with a resigned shrug. Rilla tried to refuse the proffered seat, but he would not hear of it. He disappeared into the corridor, where the dim blue lights cast an unhealthy glow over the faces of his companions, and Rilla sat down with heartfelt relief in the comfort of a corner seat.

Dan was waiting for her at the station. 'I managed to bring the car to meet you,' he said.

'What luxury! How did you justify that?'

'I've got a sack of potatoes in the boot. I'm delivering them —somewhere—if anyone asks. However, I don't think we'll be stopped and, in any case, I'm by way of being a local hero since I captured our parachutist, so I think I can get away with a minor infringement of the regulations.'

'As an alternative to getting a medal,' Rilla agreed. 'Your parachutist must have caused quite a stir in Chatwood.'

'Our moment of glory,' Dan agreed. 'Poor chap, I don't think he quite understands what it's all about, but the village has adopted him! They sent him a Christmas parcel! I'd give a lot to know what a convinced young Nazi thinks of that sort of muddle-headed kindness from his enemies, especially after what he did.' Before he started the car Dan paused and laid his hand over the top of one of Rilla's. 'Rilla, I think I'd better break this to you straight-away and quickly. Fluke is dead.'

'Oh, no! Not dear old Fluke! What happened to him?'

'He attacked the German and he shot him.'

'How horrible!' There was a brief pause and then she added in a low voice, 'They destroy everything.'

'I know how you feel. Poor Fluke, he was much more of a hero than I was. If it hadn't been for him, I would have had that bullet myself, I think.'

'Have you told Barney?' It was a roundabout way of asking whether Barney had written to Dan and his mother and not to her and she waited for Dan's reply with a quickened heart.

'I'd like to keep it from him,' Dan said slowly. 'As a matter of fact, we haven't heard from him recently. How about you?'

'I haven't had any letters either,' Rilla said. She was not quite sure which was uppermost in her mind, relief that Barney had not merely stopped writing to her or new anxiety because his silence extended to the rest of his family. 'Not since November when he wrote to say he was leaving hospital.'

'Of course, he's in a proper prisoner-of-war camp in Germany now,' Dan said as he started the car. 'It may be more difficult for letters to get through.'

'It's been nearly three months. You don't think anything could be wrong?'

'We would have been notified,' Dan said with automatic reassurance. He hoped Rilla would not realize how worried he was. He had always anticipated that Barney would attempt to escape. Had he done so and, if so, where was he? Crossing Germany in the bitter winter weather would be foolhardy and hazardous, but Dan would take no odds against his brother attempting it.

'Can you make any enquiries?' Rilla was asking.

'It might be better not to—not yet,' Dan said.

Rilla could see no reason for this, but she trusted Dan's judgement and so, in spite of her anxiety, she agreed to wait.

'Do you think our letters still get through to him?' she asked.

'It's possible. In which case, it's important to keep writing. You won't give up, will you, Rilla?'

'Of course not. Did you imagine I would?'

They were moving out of the town. It was totally dark, but Dan knew the way too well to feel any uncertainty about his route. All the same, for a time he appeared to find it necessary to concentrate on his driving and did not reply to Rilla's question immediately.

'When we last met you said something about it having been unnecessary for Barney to have married you,' he said carefully.

'I was afraid you might decide to . . . opt out. I was relieved when you wrote and said you would come for the weekend. At least you've decided to keep in touch with us!'

'I shan't, as you say, opt out, while Barney is a prisoner-of-war,' Rilla said slowly. 'When he comes back, then I don't know what will happen. I don't know what Barney will want to do. There's something I want to ask you, Dan, but not just now. I'm tired and a bit on edge and I think it will be better to leave it until I've had a chance to rest.'

'Have the raids been very bad?'

'Yes, they have. We seem to get no respite. I can't tell you how much I'm looking forward to a night without a warning.'

'I hope we live up to expectations! Ma has gone away for the weekend, by the way.'

It was said with all the casualness in the world, but Rilla was not deceived. 'Is she still as bitter as ever about me taking Jon into danger?' she asked.

'Quite honestly, I think not, but she's too stubborn to admit that her attitude is unreasonable. She's driving herself too hard. I'm not sorry she's gone away for a rest. Agnes is looking forward to seeing you.'

It started as a pleasant, restful weekend. Dan deliberately ignored some of the multitude of tasks that waited for him and gave Rilla as much of his company as she seemed to want. She was tired out when she arrived on the Friday night and was glad to go to bed early and to sleep late the next morning. She woke up with a start and remembered her first visit to Appleyard, when she had slept late into the morning, though not for the same reason.

Lying there, still half-asleep, in the bed she had shared with Barney, she was suddenly visited by a wave of desire for him so strong that it jolted her stark awake out of her drowsy day-dreams. In all the long months of her pregnancy and the dull acceptance of her grief, she had never before had this vivid physical remembrance of him. She could almost feel the warmth of his long body against hers; she remembered his laughter and his gentle, teasing hands, and the hardness and urgency of his desire for her. She twisted her limbs restlessly under the bed-clothes and then threw the covers back and got out of bed. She stood up so quickly that she felt a little dizzy. She stood for a moment, her hands pressed against her temples, until she had recovered her balance.

When she went downstairs, she seemed rested and relaxed by her long sleep, but inside she felt tense and restless. When her hand brushed against Dan's by accident, she jumped as if stung.

He took her over to the Estate Office to show her how well he was continuing the systems she had introduced and she laughed at him when he was unable to find the file for which he was looking. He looked round at her and his rueful grin was extremely attractive. He was as tall as Barney, but much thinner, and there were lines on his face.

'You look tired,' she said abruptly.

'It's been a hard winter,' he answered absent-mindedly. 'Where the dickens have I put that file?'

'Does your shoulder still hurt you?'

'No, I never think about it.' He looked round again, his eyebrows raised in surprise. 'Why this sudden interest in my health?'

'Oh, I don't know. Professional interest perhaps. I thought you looked a bit ... drawn. You've always been so good to me. The least I can do is take an interest in you in return.'

'Thank you.' He touched her cheek with a careless hand as he went past. 'Here it is! I must have put it down while I answered the telephone and forgotten about it.'

'You'll be back to filing by heap unless you take care,' Rilla warned him.

They spent the rest of the morning in the office with Dan half-working and half-chatting, bringing Rilla up to date with developments at Appleyard since she had given up her work for him.

'I used to think potatoes were my least favourite crop,' he

said. 'But that was before I discovered Brussels sprouts. Never volunteer to pick sprouts, Rilla. The little beasts hold the frost you have to stoop to strip them off the stalks and you end up with frostbite and lumbago. By the way, I mustn't forget that I've got a special message for you from Greg Parker. He wants to invite you to take a holiday at his house in Weymouth.'

'But I don't know him,' Rilla said.

'He's a very old friend, not only a friend of mine, but of Barney's, too. He'd like to meet you and, if possible, to do something for you.'

'He feels sorry for me.'

'Is that any reason to turn down a well-meant invitation?'

'No,' Rilla admitted. 'As a matter of fact, I've been wondering what to do with the week I'm due in June.'

'You can always come here, you know that.'

'I wouldn't like to put your mother to the trouble of going away for a whole week! Besides, I'd like to go somewhere completely different. But to go and stay with a man I've never met . . . I don't know. He's not married, is he?'

'No, Greg lives on his own. Perhaps I should explain that he invited me to go, too.'

Rilla's face lit up. 'Oh, that would make all the difference! Do say you'll go, Dan.'

'I doubt if I can manage a week, but perhaps I could get away for a long weekend. Let me have the date of your holiday, and I'll get in touch with Greg and see what can be arranged. I feel, like you, that it would do me good to have a change of scene.'

Dan found that the absence of his mother during Rilla's visit lowered the tension considerably as far as he was concerned. He felt able to relax and enjoy her company. She was a companionable youngster. It was surprising to realize how much they had come to share during the time she had spent at Appleyard. It helped to clear his mind to be able to explain some of his problems to her. Barney was scarcely mentioned.

On an impulse he raided the wine cellar for one of his few remaining bottles of French wine to liven up their rabbit stew on Saturday night. Rilla appreciated the gesture, although it was somewhat wasted on her uneducated palate. She wore her pink *crêpe* wedding dress and Dan, to her surprise, remembered it and raised his glass in a toast and told her that she looked lovely.

It was true, he thought, twisting the stem of his glass idly between his fingers as he watched her over the dinner table. She had always had the promise of beauty, and now that promise had been fulfilled. Most of the time he had known her she had been thickened by pregnancy, her breasts heavy with milk after Jon's birth, but now she was as slim as a reed. She had acquired a touch of poise which had been lacking when he had first known her. Her hair was as silky as ever and her skin as fine and pale, with the creamy lustre of his mother's cherished pearls. She had always had lovely eyes, but now when Rilla gave you her full attention, especially when she was serious, there was something about them which stopped the heart. Barney had picked a winner; he must be eating his heart out in prison.

It was not a comfortable thought. Dan had a sudden feeling of guilt that he should be sitting there, tired, it was true, and harassed by a multitude of cares, but safe and well, eating good food, drinking good wine, and admiring his brother's wife. There was no harm in it, of course. He had always had a fondness for Rilla. He felt protective towards her. Barney would expect him to take an interest in her; indeed, he had asked him to do so. It was his bad luck that this weekend he had begun to notice that she was attractive as a woman, not just appealing as a sister-in-law.

He had been silent for so long that Rilla said tentatively: 'Dan . . .?'

He looked up quickly. 'Sorry, I was day-dreaming. One of the faults one develops from living too much alone.'

The wine had loosened Rilla's tongue. 'Why do you live alone?' she asked. 'I've sometimes wondered . . . Why haven't you got married, Dan?'

'Difficult to say. I played the field when I was younger, getting married was not on the cards.'

'Like Barney,' Rilla said evenly. 'Only you were luckier than he was.'

'I shan't take any notice of that,' Dan said. 'Except to say that, in my opinion, Barney's luck was decidedly in when he met you.' He hurried on. 'Then I had a long period when I was a semi-invalid. Now, I don't meet many girls and the ones I do don't appeal to me—or are already spoken for.'

She met his smiling eyes and realized with a jolt that he included her. Dan found her attractive? She had always discounted his compliments as nothing more than kindness. Was it really possible that he was serious about thinking her beautiful? It was a troubling thought, but by no means unpleasant. Because she was thrown off balance, she hurried on to the subject she had been hoping to find the courage to bring up over the weekend.

'There's one girl you know who works with me in the hospital,' she said abruptly. 'Candida Blewett.'

'Ah, yes. Candida.'

As an answer it could hardly have been more non-committal, but Rilla was cheered by the realization that Dan did not particularly like Candida either.

'Not one of your old flames?' she enquired.

'By no means.'

'One of Barney's perhaps?'

Dan hesitated. 'They saw a lot of one another at one time,' he said. 'They were tennis partners.'

'There was more to it than that, I think. Candida doesn't like me and I think—I'm almost sure—that it's because of Barney. Dan, I must know: were Candida and Barney in love with one another before he met me?'

'No.'

Rilla was pleating the edge of the white damask table-cloth between her fingers, her dark head bent. 'I think perhaps you are wrong about that,' she said. 'Candida has been throwing out hints—it's a dreadful thing to say, but I believe she meant me to understand that she had actually . . . you know . . . been to bed with Barney.'

'What do you expect me to say to that, apart from "no comment"?'

She looked up quickly. 'You think it's true. But then she must have been in love with him?'

'Not necessarily.'

'I don't understand. She *couldn't* . . . surely?'

'I assure you it can be done,' Dan said drily. He finished off his wine in one long swallow. 'This is not something you and I can talk about, Rilla. If you must know about Barney's past love life you will have to ask him, although if you take my advice you'll leave the subject strictly alone.'

There was a slight constraint between them for the rest of the evening. Rilla felt she had been reproved, and it upset her. They listened to the wireless, played a game of halma, but they did not quite settle back into the friendly ease she had always known with Dan. Without being aware of what she was doing, she exerted herself to charm him back into the pleasant relationship they had always enjoyed. She told him little anecdotes about the hospital which made him laugh and after she had turned on the wireless for the nine o'clock news she subsided with graceful ease on the hearthrug, a trick she had picked up from Ann, who was much addicted to sitting on the floor, and leaned back against his chair. Her silky hair was almost touching his hand. Dan moved slightly, reflecting with rueful inner amusement that while the view down the open neck of Rilla's dress, of which she was obviously quite unconscious, was quite delightful, it was not a suitable spectacle for a lonely old bachelor.

Still conscious of a constraint in the atmosphere, Rilla tried to put it right when they said good night. She paused at the bottom of the dark staircase, waiting for Dan.

'I must bolt the front door and make sure old Agnes hasn't left the gas on in the kitchen,' Dan said. 'She's beginning to be careless about little things like that. Good night, Rilla.'

She was standing on the bottom stair, which brought her up to his level. Impulsively, she leaned forward and kissed him on the cheek. For one moment, as she drew back, he looked straight into her eyes, his face expressionless, and then he reached out and pulled her to him and kissed her on the lips.

She was too taken by surprise to be conscious of any other emotion. There was no room for anything but astonishment that this demanding mouth belonged to Dan, kind Dan, who had treated her with unfailing courtesy. She moved against him, fitting herself to his hard, lean body, and then he released her, just at the moment when the realization hit her of how much she was liking it. He stepped back and she clutched at the banister to regain her balance.

He was years older than she was and infinitely more experienced. There was only one thought in his head: that the threatened disaster must at all costs be avoided.

'Well, that was very pleasant,' he said with a jauntiness which would not have deceived Rilla if she had been more in command of herself. 'Thank you, dear Rilla. I shall consider it the equivalent of the kiss under the mistletoe I didn't get at Christmas. Good night, sleep well, and I'll see you in the morning.'

He fumbled a little blindly with the bolts on the front door, hearing her behind him going slowly up the stairs, and then, instead of following her, went back into the drawing-room and sat hour after lonely hour staring into the dying fire.

Rilla left quite early on Sunday. In order to make sure of getting back to the nurses' home before the nightly raid began, she explained. There was nothing in Dan's demeanour to show that he regarded the kiss he had given her as anything more than what he had called it, a seasonal caress to be forgotten as quickly as it had been given, but Rilla had had the frightening experience of finding herself on the edge of an abyss she had not even suspected. She had, on one and the same day, made two discoveries: that she was physically hungry for her husband, and that it would be possible for that hunger to be satisfied by another man. It must not happen, she told herself. Not with anyone, and above all, not with Dan.

She was attracted to him—why had it never occurred to her before that he was an overwhelmingly attractive man?—but she did not feel the fervent romantic love she had felt for Barney, the sort of love which up till then she had believed necessary before any love-making could take place. She had been naïve. Dan had implied as much when she had asked him about Candida. Barney and Candida had satisfied an urge without any of the love there had been between Rilla and Barney. An unwelcome doubt about the quality of Barney's love for her came into her mind and was quickly dismissed. He had loved her, just as much as she had loved him. It was necessary to believe that and to forget how it had felt to have Dan's arms, not Barney's, close round her. Above all, to close her mind to the warmth of her response.

She did not go to Appleyard again. She and Dan corresponded in a desultory fashion, mainly to ask one another whether there was any word from Barney, and the answer was always no. His long silence preyed on Rilla's nerves. Something must have happened to him, but what? The suspense was as bad, and even more prolonged, than it had been after Dunkirk and even when Dan, not knowing whether he was acting for the best or not, put some inquiries in hand, still nothing could be discovered about what had happened to him.

The spring came and was beautiful, even in bomb-stricken London. In the bomb craters the wild flowers bloomed and then, in May 1941, there came at last a relief from the incessant raids. It was difficult to believe at first, as one quiet night succeeded another.

'I slept from ten o'clock to seven o'clock, right through the night without a single break,' Ann said disbelievingly.

'I still wake up about every two or three hours and listen to the quietness,' Rilla admitted.

They were beginning to feel like old hands at the nursing game by this time, with the first six months of their training behind them. First-year examinations in November were beginning to cast a shadow. They still studied together and spent a lot of their free time in one another's company. Ann had once or twice accepted invitations from such young men as came their way, but Rilla, with a new wariness since her weekend at Appleyard, still remained aloof. It was a strain and it took its toll of her. She was a little too taut, a little too fine-drawn and she looked for the letters which did not come from Barney with a pitiful anxiety. She visited her home fairly regularly, but it was not the same somehow. For one thing, Edith had taken the revolutionary step of going out to work.

'No sense in sitting around moping,' she said briskly, and joined Dinah in the munitions factory.

'We're better off now, your Dad and me, than we've ever been since we got married,' she confided to Rilla. 'The house is the best we've ever had—and very lucky we were to get it, before everyone else got bombed out and joined the queue—and the furniture Dan gave us may be old, but it's better quality than anything we've ever been able to afford. We could be very comfortable.'

'But you're not?' Rilla asked.

'Can't be, can we, with the raids every night and Joyce and little Jon buried up the road, and now this worry about your Barney. I can't rest until that Hitler's beaten. That's why I'm in the factory, that and not wanting to sit around at home with nothing much to do all day.'

'She works all the hours God sends,' Len grumbled to Rilla. 'She earns a fortune—more than I do, some weeks—and what for, I ask you? There's nothing to spend it on. Oh, well, it's always been her way. There's no still in her when she's in trouble.'

'What about you, Dad?' Rilla asked. 'Are you all right?'

He squeezed her hand with one of his awkward gestures of affection. 'I'm all right, girl. Have you heard from young Barney yet?'

'Not a word since November. I'm sick with worry when I have time to think about it, which fortunately isn't often. I'm like Mum, I suppose; when there's something wrong I try to work it off.'

She felt anxious about her parents, but there was little she could do to help them in their grief and there was not much point in going home on her days off if Mum was not there. Almost imperceptibly she had begun to drift away from them.

'I don't know why it is,' she confided to Ann. 'I don't feel at home in Barbury any more. Perhaps it's because Mum and Dad are living in a different house. And it seems so strange to go home and find Mum out working. She was always at home when we got in from school—*always*. Now, if I go down during the day, I have to let myself into an empty house and wait for her to get home. It's not the same. She likes to talk about the factory and she thinks some of the things the girls say are screamingly funny and somehow it doesn't mean a thing to me.'

'It's only natural, I guess, once you start having a life of your own.'

'We haven't got a life of our own, have we?' Rilla asked. 'Only the hospital. Ann, do you still miss Tom?'

'Yes, of course,' Ann answered in surprise. She looked at Rilla's averted head and said slowly, 'Oh, I see what you mean. Yes, it doesn't get much better.'

'I thought perhaps it was just me,' Rilla said. 'I begin to understand why some women go off the rails.'

'At least your Barney is alive,' Ann said wistfully. 'One day he'll come back to you.'

'I'm beginning to wonder if he is alive,' Rilla said in a low voice. 'I don't know what I am—a wife or a widow. It was bad enough when I knew where he was and what had happened to him. Now, I'm even more in limbo than I was before.'

Because of her decision to avoid Dan's company the invitation which came to Rilla from Greg Parker filled her with dismay. She had hoped that the idea had been forgotten, but Dan, with an enthusiasm he had afterwards regretted, had written off immediately on the Saturday morning of their weekend together to tell Greg when she was due to take her holiday and committing himself to spending at least part of it with her and Greg. His efforts to get out of this promise met with no success.

'Can't get away? Nonsense, old chap, of course you can,' Greg said. 'No one's as indispensable as all that. How long is it since you had a holiday? Not since I took you off to Dunkirk, I bet.'

'Some holiday!' Dan commented.

'Well, I don't promise this will be as lively, but the thing is, your sister-in-law has asked if she can bring a friend with her, another nurse. Now, one girl I can cope with, but if there are two of them I need a bit of help, so you come along and help me look after them.'

Dan wavered and allowed himself to be persuaded. He could do with a day or two away from Appleyard and Greg was always good company. The presence of one of Rilla's friends from the hospital would make it look quite natural for him to leave Rilla to be entertained by Greg. Besides which, he still worried about Rilla. He wanted to see her, to judge her state of mind and to see how she was bearing up under the strain of Barney's continued absence.

He arrived a little ahead of the girls on a Friday evening when the early summer sun flooded Greg's white-painted house with sunshine. He was not particularly surprised when Greg, with a hospitable flourish, produced a bottle of whisky.

'You old scrounger. If there was only one bottle of whisky in the United Kingdom it would end up in your hands. Yes, I will have a drink, and you can make it a stiff one. If I'm here to relax I may as well start off as I mean to go on.'

There was a ring at the front doorbell and Greg went to answer it. Dan got to his feet as he showed the girls in. The sun was in his eyes, but he saw a tall girl with an aureole of flame-coloured hair. She moved to one side and Rilla was behind her.

Dan was dismayed by his reaction to the sight of her. He had believed that because he was on his guard and was expecting to see her it would have no effect on him, but when she stood in front of him in the doorway, looking pale and tired, with her hair swinging forward against her cheek, and her great, troubled eyes fixed on his face, his sharp physical response shocked him. He stepped forward mechanically, saying the right things and smiling, but when Ann was introduced to him he turned to her with relief, more than ever determined to devote himself to her in the days he was going to be forced to spend under the same roof as Rilla.

He took another look at her, this girl who so unexpectedly turned out to be an American, at her long slim legs and bright red hair, the dusting of freckles over her nose and her wide, smiling mouth. For any man in his right mind, he reflected, it ought to be no hardship to concentrate on Ann Lauriston.

They passed all too quickly, the lazy, golden days. They managed to find a place to swim, in spite of the defences all round the coast. Ann, in particular, loved the water and swam like a fish. Greg, looking, as Dan told him unkindly, for all the world like a walrus, wallowed in the shallows with Rilla, who was not a strong swimmer; but Dan, with his eyes on the darting, twisting figure of the slim girl who was Rilla's friend, drove himself through the water to dive underneath and all round her until she turned over on her back to float on the surface and begged him to give up.

'You're a real mermaid,' he said, floating by her side.

'I love it and it's ages since I was in the sea.'

'We'd better turn back,' Dan said reluctantly. 'If we go out much further we'll find ourselves in a minefield or, the way you move through the water, you may be mistaken for a torpedo.'

'Oh, Dan, don't!' Ann begged. 'I was trying to forget about the war.'

'Sorry. Come on, I'll race you to the shore.'

He beat her easily and was waiting as she came up out of the sea, pulling off the white rubber cap she had worn to protect her hair. Her old green swimsuit clung to her figure and the sunlight caught her bright hair and showed up the golden freckles across her nose. She saw him watching her and refused to allow herself to be confused by his approval. She looked him straight in the eye, her chin tilted with a hint of a challenge, and then blushed vividly as Dan accepted the challenge and looked her over with open admiration, a broad smile on his face.

She dropped her cap and picked up her towel, which she draped round her shoulders. She felt slightly cross and slightly amused and just a little bit breathless. It was a long time since she had allowed herself to be disturbed by any man. Why had Rilla never told her how attractive her brother-in-law was? She had said he was kind, and nice, and that he had been good to her. She had never mentioned his height or the slight hesitation in his walk, or the thick, dark hair which grew so neatly on his head, and the long-fingered, sensitive hands, and the dark, thoughtful eyes which looked right into you and asked a question and then smiled because the involuntary answer seemed to please him. But then, of course, Rilla's mind was entirely taken up by his brother. Or was it? Watching Rilla and Dan carefully avoiding one another's company over the next three days, Ann came to a conclusion which troubled her and, for some reason, was hurtful.

They parted the best of friends, she and Dan. He even suggested that the next time Rilla visited Appleyard, Ann should come with her.

Before she could stop herself, Ann had asked, 'Because you need a chaperone?'

For once he did not smile when he looked at her. 'Am I so transparent?' he asked gravely.

'There's an atmosphere. You shy away from one another.'

He paused to consider before he said carefully, 'Rilla exerts a very strong field of attraction. I got too near and gave myself a shock, and her too. Understandably, she is now a little wary of me. I shan't make the same mistake again.'

'There's something about Rilla,' Ann agreed. 'Most of the men who are well enough perk up when they see a pretty nurse, but there's real competition to catch Rilla's eye.'

'Fortunately, she is scarcely aware of it herself. If she ever started to use that power deliberately she would be a very dangerous woman.' He was smiling again. 'But then she wouldn't be the Rilla we both know and are both fond of.'

Ann agreed quietly. She did not want to talk about it any more, but Dan added abruptly, 'If you come to Appleyard, come for your own sake, because it would please you and because I want to see you there.'

Again she agreed, but she doubted whether she would accept the invitation if it ever came.

Chapter 8

The other men in the *Arbeitskommando* where Barney was dragging out the miserable winter days sometimes received letters and even parcels from their families. Barney had nothing, until he thought of writing to Yvette under his assumed name. He addressed her as *'ma chère tante,'* but his letter contained a specific reference to his leave in March and the good time they had had together; he trusted that her quick wits would see through the deception.

In due course she replied and sent him a parcel. It was not much, but it contained some cigarettes which he was able to barter for extra food, a sweater of pre-war quality, a bar of chocolate and a couple of crime novels.

There was also a letter, but the tone in which it was written was chilling. 'I would prefer you not to write again,' Yvette said. 'In the circumstances, there is little I can do for you.' He tried to tell himself that Yvette must have some very good

Barney drank little and kept his wits about him. After an hour old Jakob was entertaining them with drinking songs, by two o'clock he was fast asleep and at least two of the prisoners had followed his example. Barney got to his feet and sauntered away.

He reconnoitred carefully as he came in sight of the house. There was no one there. The farm dog was loose in the yard, but he too seemed to have been affected by the heat of the day and lay panting in a patch of shade. He raised his head as Barney approached, and growled warningly, but Barney went up to him boldly and spoke and he thumped his tail and subsided. Barney had already noted where Frau Berblinger hid the key. He reached up and there it was, on the ledge over the door.

There was an angry bark and the dog came hurtling across the yard. He landed at Barney's heels, snarling and snapping, as Barney tried to fit the key in the lock. Barney kicked backwards without looking round and felt his foot meet flesh. There was an anguished yelp, a moment's silence and then the dog attacked again. He leaped up and a searing pain ran through Barney's arm. He staggered, pulled off balance, but he had got the door open. The dog's teeth were tearing at his flesh. With his free hand he caught hold of the collar it wore and tore himself free.

The hold he had on the collar half throttled the animal. Barney flung it away from him and it landed on its side in the dust. He stepped inside and slammed the door shut. He leaned his back against it, breathing quickly. Blood was running down his arm and the jagged tooth-marks were turning blue. Outside, the dog had started to bark again. He heard the thud of its body against the wood as it made a vain attempt to get at him through the door.

He went into the kitchen and held his arm under the tap. Then he found a clean linen cloth and tore it into a rough bandage. Fixing it round his arm with one hand was difficult, but he pulled the knot tight with his teeth and decided it would do well enough. His only fear was that the frenzied barking, carrying across the fields, would bring old Jakob home to see what was wrong.

Food was his main necessity. He found the larder and helped himself to a loaf of bread, a bottle of the wine which had proved such a good friend to him, a small round cheese, and a jar of bottled plums. He stuffed them into a straw bag and added a knife, fork and spoon, then he went upstairs.

He felt a twinge of compunction as he went through old Jakob's scanty store of clothes. He told himself that the man was his enemy, but it was difficult to think of him in that light. He was a cheerful old chap and he had been good to Barney, as far as he was able. It was his misfortune that his Sunday boots were exactly what Barney needed.

He had less compunction about taking an ancient waterproof cape, some socks and a spare shirt from the other bedroom since these presumably belonged to the soldier-husband, but money was another thing he found it difficult to take. He shut his mind to the uncomfortable feeling that he was nothing better than a common thief and helped himself to Frau Berblinger's spare cash.

When he left the house he was wearing old Jakob's boots with his extra pair of socks, he had the straw shopping bag slung over one shoulder and he was carrying a battered suitcase which contained, besides his spare clothes, old Jakob's shaving tackle, matches and a small metal dish and an ancient school atlas with reasonably detailed maps of the area he hoped to cover.

He had been walking for about half an hour when he heard the sound of an engine behind him. He glanced over his shoulder. Coming along the road was a bus. He had not realized that this minor road was served by the local buses. Was it worth trying to shorten his journey by taking the bus, or would it be a mistake? He made a swift decision and held up his hand. The dilapidated old vehicle slowed down. Its destination was stated on the front: Bergzabern. Barney climbed on board and felt for his money. 'Bergzabern,' he demanded boldly. His money was accepted without question, he was given a ticket. There were half a dozen people, all old men or women, on the bus and he took a seat well away from any of them. He thought that one or two of them looked at him curiously and guessed that strangers were few in that part of the country, but no one questioned him and they wheezed and bounced along without mishap.

He had been a little afraid of not realizing when they had arrived at their destination and thus drawing attention to himself, but when they arrived there was no mistaking it. Everyone got up to get out and Barney joined them. The square was crowded with people. He glanced out of the window as he awaited his turn to alight and got a shock. Among the people waiting to board the bus for its return journey were Frau Berblinger and the young boy, Paul. The alighting passengers were shuffling forward. Barney kept his head down, as if he were watching for the step; he lifted his suitcase high on his shoulder, out of the way of the other passengers, hiding his face from those waiting to get on.

He took a quick look and saw that the boy was pulling at Frau Berblinger's arm, making his unintelligible noises. She shook him off, intent on securing a place on the bus. Barney turned quickly towards the back of the bus and lost himself in the crowd.

There were soldiers about, and even though he should have expected that in a town close to the frontier the sight of the grey uniforms made his stomach muscles tense.

The market was still in progress. He forced himself to walk round it and purchased half a kilo of grapes to add to his store of food. He dared not ask for anything else, being ignorant of the rationing system.

He found his way out of the town. There were hills to the west and he wanted to be among them by nightfall. In some ways it was a relief to be free of the town; in others it was not. All the time he had been among the crowd he had feared a hand on his shoulder, but once the people were left behind he felt lonely and conspicuous. He found a track which led him steadily upwards through the trees. Old Jakob's boots were quite comfortable for walking, but as the path grew steeper he found the suitcase an encumbrance and he thought it would look suspicious to anyone he met.

He paused near the summit of the hill he had been climbing. The sun was sinking ahead of him, so he was walking west. He must not go too far in that direction, because the frontier lay to the south. He had had no food since the middle of the day and he decided to eat while he thought about the next stage of his journey. He had some bread and cheese, a swig or two of wine and some of the grapes. It all tasted so different from anything he had had in recent months. Perhaps it really was better, perhaps it was the exhilaration of his freedom which gave it an extra savour.

He was not alone on the wooded slopes. He had heard voices calling more than once and now he could hear people coming up the hill towards him. His instinct was to hide. It would look suspicious if they had already caught sight of him, but if they stopped to speak his poor German would give him away immediately. He bundled away the remains of his food and dived for the bushes.

They came into sight a minute later, two soldiers and a couple of girls. They were scuffling among themselves, the men trying to get an arm round the girls. Barney ducked his head down and hoped they would go on past, well clear of him, but he heard a burst of laughter and when he peered out between the leaves he saw that one of the soldiers was holding his girl back to let the other couple get ahead of them. As soon as they disappeared round a bend he pulled her close and began to kiss her.

Barney put his head down again and waited. He heard more sounds of muffled giggles and protests. The next time he looked the soldier had both his hands inside the girl's blouse and was squeezing her big breasts. She broke away from him and he chased her into the shelter of the bushes on the opposite side of the path away from Barney. There was an excited squeal and the sound of breaking twigs as they crashed through the bushes and he got her down on the ground.

Moving cautiously, Barney collected his things together. Sticking out from the bushes opposite he could see a pair of boots, soles uppermost, and the baggy ends of a pair of loosened trousers. As far as he could judge, the soldier was hard at it and unlikely to notice anything short of a clap of thunder. He crept through the cover on his side of the track as far as the bend and then took to the path again.

Somewhere around ten o'clock, after stumbling a couple of times over hidden tree roots in the gathering dark, he decided to call a halt. He had some more grapes, a piece of bread and a mouthful of wine, wrapped himself up in the waterproof cape and stretched out. At first the little noises of the forest disturbed him, but he soon grew used to the occasional rustlings around him and went off to sleep with a feeling of achievement that had eluded him for a long time.

It was a warm night, but he woke up about four o'clock feeling stiff and cold. The air was chilly and there was a little mist clinging to the ground between the trees. He stood up and stamped and stretched, wishing he had something hot to drink. It was quite light and promised to be another fine day.

He began to go down hill, quite steeply, but as he was now walking due south he was not particularly worried about that. In the valley the path crossed a stream. He was worried by the way his arm had stiffened up in the night and he decided to stop and take a look at it. He had to soak the rough bandage before he could get it to come away from his skin. Underneath, the wound looked red and puffy, but he decided the stiffness was mostly due to bruising.

He stripped off his shirt and plunged his head and shoulders in the chilly water, gasping from the shock of it. He used the shirt to dry himself and took a clean one out of his suitcase, but before he put it on he scooped up some water in his metal dish, collected some loose twigs, lit a fire and heated up some water for shaving.

He grinned to himself as he reflected that on a hiking holiday he would certainly not have bothered to shave, but it was important to present a good appearance to the world and so he shaved as meticulously as he could by touch, cursing himself for not having thought to steal a mirror while he was raiding the farmhouse. He washed out the dish, heated some fresh water and had a curious breakfast of stale bread soaked in a mixture of hot water and wine, with a piece of strong cheese.

He felt heartened by this meal and by his wash. He packed up carefully and set off once more. The way now lay along the valley by the stream, with steep hills on either side of him. It was not bad going, though muddy in places, and he made good time. He reached a wider track and knew that he must keep alert, but it was still early, even for a country district, and he appeared to be the only person abroad.

The track was now a small but definite road and he caught a glimpse of a rooftop or two ahead of him. He pressed on and then came to a sudden halt. There was something else besides houses ahead of him: fortifications. With a sickening shock he realized he had reached the Maginot Line.

The Maginot Line—on which the French had bent all their hopes of defence, and which the Germans had outflanked so easily, taking them all by surprise by their thrust through the Ardennes. Of course he would have to cross it. There was the Siegfried Line as well, which the Germans had built to face the French fortifications. No wonder there had been soldiers at Bergzabern. It must at one time have been right on the edge of the defences, perhaps a garrison town.

He sat down in dejection to think what to do. The Maginot Line had been built to keep out the Germans, but it had been a failure. It served little purpose now. The enemy was inside the country it had been intended to defend. The Germans would have little reason to keep it manned. They might be using the forts as barracks for their troops, but it seemed unlikely to Barney that they would keep many men tied up on a frontier that needed no defence. He decided to try a little reconnaissance.

He hid his shopping bag and suitcase and moved forward carefully, using the cover of the trees as much as possible and keeping off the track he had been using. Everything seemed quiet. There was a wide, cleared area with concrete tank traps and trenches and barbed wire which formed defences on both the German and French sides of the border, but no major buildings and, as far as he could see, no soldiers. He went back and fetched his luggage. He was determined to get across now, if he could; otherwise he thought he might have to wait until night-fall and he did not particularly look forward to a day spent lurking in the woods, nor to getting through the barbed wire and tank traps in the dark.

He set out, dodging in and out of trenches, using his suitcase to batter a way through the bent and rusting wire, scratched and bleeding, and always with the feeling that there must be eyes watching him through the dark slits of the silent concrete towers. At every moment he expected to be challenged, a shout to him to halt, the rattle of a machine gun, the whine of a rifle bullet. He stopped once to get his breath back, standing doubled over with the air tearing through his lungs. Something moved and he whirled round to face it. It was a tattered poster, caught on the wire and moving in the wind. He went on.

He could not believe it, he really could not believe that his luck had held, when he found himself on the far side of the line. He was in France. He was still not safe, but he had got clean away from his camp and he had crossed his first frontier. He was so elated that he had to pull himself up sharply. It would not do to grow careless now.

He walked steadily all day, keeping fairly high and veering west. The suitcase became more and more of a liability. He shoved it wearily from one hand to another and regretted that he had not rigged up some sort of pack for his back instead. By the early afternoon he saw that he was coming to a more populated area. He wondered whether it was time to descend to the valley and then found that the decision was being taken out of his hands by the lie of the land, unless he followed the lines of the Vosges to the west, which he did not want to do.

He made his way down towards a group of houses. It was not much of a place, but it was served by the railway line and there was a station. He decided to take a chance. There were people about in the streets, but to his relief they took no interest in him. As he looked round it was obvious that this was country which had felt the hand of war. Tanks had passed through these streets, bullets had pockmarked the walls, there were gaps amongst the buildings and holes filled with rubble which told a mute story of battles fought and lost. He approached the railway station warily, keeping an eye open for soldiers or police.

Two men were coming towards him, chatting to one another. As they drew level with him, one of them called out a greeting to a third man on the other side of the street, who crossed over and stood talking to them. Barney forced himself to walk past them, hiding the shock they had given him. They were speaking German.

It took him a minute or two to work it out. He had crossed the frontier, but he had been only too correct when he thought to himself that the frontier no longer existed. He was in Alsace. The Germans had always maintained that Alsace and Lorraine rightly belonged to them. It was possible that the men he had seen were native-born Alsatians who happened to speak German amongst themselves, but to Barney it seemed far more likely that while he had been out of touch in the *Arbeitskommando* the area had been colonized by the victorious Germans. In which case, the sooner he got out of it the better and he would give up his hope of catching a train.

He paused by the entrance to the railway station, looked idly at a tattered timetable, which was probably out of date, and then walked briskly away. He felt hideously conspicuous, but no one challenged him, and he was just beginning to feel reassured when he saw his first German soldier. He rode past Barney on a bicycle, an overweight man with a roll of fat at the back of his neck, his immense grey-trousered behind overhanging the bicycle saddle on either side. Barney watched him disappearing down the street and wished fervently that he was back among the trees and hills which had served him in such good stead for the last couple of days. He wished it still more as he continued down the road and saw that the German soldier had dismounted and he would have to walk past him.

He was standing outside a small café, talking to a plump woman in a flowered overall. They seemed to be enjoying a joke. She gave him a playful push on the chest and then they both disappeared into the café. Barney glanced in as he went by. The German was leaning against the bar and the woman was serving him with a drink. There were painted metal tables and chairs outside, but they were empty. The German had left his bicycle propped against the wall beyond these tables. It must be out of his sight as he stood at the bar inside. Barney glanced over his shoulder. There was no one behind him. There were no houses on the other side of the road. He was not, as far as he could see, being watched at all. It was too good an opportunity to miss. Scarcely faltering in his stride, he put his hand on the bicycle, wheeled it a few yards down the road, mounted and rode away.

Because he was uncertain of the reception he would get in any village or town he spent a second night in the open, but the next day he knew that this could not go on. He was running short of food, because there was no water he had not been able to shave and he felt he was beginning to look alarmingly disreputable. What worried him more than anything was that he still had nothing but German money and he had no way of telling whether it would be acceptable in France. Would it have been wiser to attempt to exchange it while he was still in German-occupied Alsace? He still believed that it would have drawn unnecessary attention to him, but the next time he came to the outskirts of a small town on his tortuous progress through the French countryside he looked for a bank.

He was far from sure of his whereabouts, but he seemed to have left the German-speaking people behind and although his heart had been in his mouth more than once as a car driven by a German passed him on the road, the area did not seem to be heavily occupied. He propped his bicycle against the wall of the bank he had chosen and went inside.

It was a small branch of a national bank, with just one man and a girl typist behind the counter. Barney waited until the only other customer had been dealt with and then asked, 'I have some German money. Is it possible to change it into francs?'

The man behind the counter gave him an unnervingly piercing look. 'It can be done,' he said.

Barney felt for the money he had seized from Frau Berblinger's hoard and handed it over. He had thought there would be some formalities to complete, but the bank clerk merely stowed the German money away in a drawer and began counting out French francs. Before handing them over he gave Barney another searching look.

'You are not German, monsieur?' he asked politely.

'No, I am French,' Barney said. He hoped it sounded convincing. After his long months hearing and speaking nothing but French he thought that his accent would pass without question.

Still the bank clerk did not pass the French money across the counter to him.

'Are you staying long in our town?' he asked.

'No, I'm merely passing through,' Barney said.

He reached out and secured the money which the clerk had kept under his hand. At least he had got that. He was afraid that his action had looked suspicious and so he took his time about stowing it away, as if he had all the time in the world to spare. The typist was covering up her machine and seemed to be getting ready to leave. She disappeared somewhere out of sight. The clerk was still watching him, but he looked thoughtful and not unfriendly. He was an elderly man, with a lined face and scanty grey hair.

Barney said abruptly: 'I have a bicycle and I'm making for Dijon. Can you give me any directions as to the best route?'

'By the main road?' the man asked quietly.

Barney met his eye and said with equal deliberation, 'I prefer the quieter lanes.'

The other man nodded as if he understood. He glanced at the clock. 'I shall be closing the bank in five minutes. If you will wait for me I will give you the directions you require. Sit down.'

He nodded towards a chair and Barney sat down. It was almost too good to be true, but he believed he had found a friend. The man he had taken for a clerk was the manager of this small branch.

When the typist had left and the main door was locked, the man said, 'I shall not ask you many questions and, in particular, I do not wish to know your identity, but tell me one thing: am I right in thinking that you are an escaped prisoner-of-war?'

There seemed little point in denying it. 'Yes,' Barney said.

The bank manager nodded, satisfied. 'I thought so. That was why I changed your money without question or formality.'

'I'm glad no one else has spotted me as easily,' Barney said with feeling.

'I presume you didn't offer your German marks to anyone else,' the bank manager said drily. 'Is your home in Dijon?'

'No, but I have friends there. I think they will help me if I can reach the town safely.' He was still not sure whether the man had realized that he was British. 'I am a native of Lyons,' he said. He was surprised and elated when this was accepted without question.

'I understand. No doubt you intend to pass into the Unoccupied Zone?'

'Can it be done?'

'Oh, certainly, provided your friends in Dijon are prepared to pay. I believe there is a thriving trade in assisting people to pass *en fraude* between the Occupied and the Unoccupied Zone.'

'Then I must certainly get to Dijon,' Barney said. He stood

up. 'You were going to give me directions,' he hinted.

'I think I may be able to do more for you than that, if you will trust me. Are you looking for somewhere to stay the night?'

'I'm not sure that I can afford it. I've spent two nights in the open and managed all right. I might do the same again.'

'I was going to suggest that you came home with me.'

'Wouldn't that be risky—for you?' Barney asked.

'I'm prepared to accept that,' his new friend replied. 'I live alone. My wife is dead and my son escaped to join the Free French forces in England. There is little I can do. I would be glad of the chance to help you.'

He spoke very quietly, but with evident sincerity, and Barney felt obliged to accept his offer, though not without an inward qualm of conscience. Poor devil, it would go hard with him if the Germans ever discovered that he had harboured a British officer, however unwittingly.

As they walked down the street together, Barney pushing his bicycle, the bank manager said, 'I'm not going to tell you my name, but you may call me Henri.'

'Then I will be "Jean," 'Barney said.

It was strange to sleep in a house again. Barney tried to remember when he had last slept upstairs in a proper bed with sheets and pillows, except when he had been in hospital. It was unfortunate that, in spite of his exercise, he found it difficult to sleep, but it was bliss to be clean. He valued the hot bath almost more than the omelette and tomato salad *Henri-le-banquier*, as he called his new friend in his mind, had prepared for them that evening.

'I've found someone who can help you on your way,' Henri said over breakfast the next morning. 'My next-door neighbour is a doctor and is allowed a little petrol to get him round his patients and to visit the hospital. By great good fortune, he has business in Nancy today and he is prepared to take you with him. From there you should be able to get to Dijon without difficulty.'

It was like being given the keys to the gates of heaven.

Barney became quite incoherent as he tried to thank his bene-factor. Henri smiled and held up his hand.

'Say no more,' he said. 'Perhaps one day you will be able to let me know whether you reached your home safely.'

The doctor was terse and business-like, but he was more inquisitive than Henri had been and asked some pertinent ques-tions. Barney parried them as best he could. It was fortunate that he really had been in a French prisoner-of-war camp and could mostly give truthful replies.

After a couple of miles the doctor drew into the side of the road and stopped the car.

'There's a zonal check-point just down the road and I don't choose to take you through that,' he said. 'They know me and I shall probably be waved on without any difficulty. You can by-pass it by walking across the fields and I'll pick you up about half a mile farther on, at a point where there's a clump of trees and the road bends sharply to the right. Go along now. I shall sit here for ten minutes or so to give you a start, but don't linger on the way because I shan't wait long for you at the picking-up point.'

There was no path and little cover in the fields. Barney walked as fast as he could, but the ground was rough and he had to watch his step. To his horror there were three women working in the next field, fortunately at some distance from him. They were tossing the newly-cut hay and he saw them look up curiously as he passed by. He waved his hand, shouted *'Bonjour!'* and hurried on before they could stop him and ask his business. He could see the checkpoint the doctor had warned him about, nothing much, just a rough kind of sentry box by the side of the road and a couple of German soldiers with rifles slung over their shoulders.

The field nearest to them was full of ripening maize with tall rustling leaves. Barney felt his way through it. He felt as obvious as a herd of elephants, but he heard the doctor's car approaching along the road and trusted that this would divert attention from his passage through the crops. The doctor kept his engine running; he heard the sound of voices and then, before he was out of the field, the car started up again and passed him. He pushed on desperately. How long would the doctor wait for him?

He was clear of the maize and the check-point was behind him. There was a short clear space of grass without cover and then the group of trees the doctor had described. He broke into a run. He was among the trees when he heard voices. He slowed to a walk and approached the road cautiously. The car was there, drawn up by the side of the road, but the doctor was outside talking to a German soldier. Barney froze into stillness in the cover of the trees.

The two men appeared to be examining the car. The doctor gave one of the wheels a disparaging kick, shrugged his shoulders and then climbed back in. The German soldier had a motor cycle. He got on it, but he appeared to be waiting for the car to leave first. The doctor started his engine and drove away. The soldier kicked his machine into life and zoomed down the road in the other direction, towards the check-point.

It was a sickening disappointment. For a minute or two Barney stayed where he was, trying to decide what to do. It hardly seemed safe to walk along the road, and yet it looked as if he had no other choice. He set out, resisting the impulse to look over his shoulder to see if there were any German soldiers coming along behind him. It occurred to him that the doctor might have given him away, but he did not really think this was the case. He had merely been caught out waiting by the side of the road and had had to improvise a reason for stopping.

Barney hurried on. The relief when he rounded another bend and found the doctor had stopped for him was as profound as his dismay had been when he had seen him drive away.

He opened the door and got in without a word. The doctor started to drive away before he had had time to close the door.

'You saw what happened?' he asked.

'Yes. I guessed that the German stopped to ask you if anything was wrong.'

'He did. I had to pretend I'd heard a strange noise at the back after leaving the check-point. We decided I'd picked up a stone in the tread of my tyre.'

'I hardly dared hope you would stop again.'

'I'm a fool. A sane man would have driven off and left you.'

In spite of these words, when they arrived at Nancy the doctor said, 'Have you got the money for a train ticket to Dijon?'

'Yes, I'm not too badly off for money.'

'Then I'll take you to the station and buy the ticket for you.'

He cut short Barney's thanks. 'I just want to be sure of getting rid of you,' he said, but Barney had begun to realize that this brusque manner concealed more practical concern for his safety than the doctor was prepared to admit.

He bought the ticket and handed it over without arousing suspicion. 'You've got an hour and a half to wait before there's a train to Dijon,' he said. 'Don't hang about the station. Go to a café where you can pass the time. There's not much you can get in the way of food without coupons, but you could have a bowl of soup and a glass of wine.'

Again Barney tried to thank him, but he would not stop to listen. 'I'll just wish you *bon voyage* and say goodbye,' he said, and was gone before Barney could reply.

The train journey was uneventful. There were German soldiers on the train, but there were French civilians too and no one questioned his right to travel from one town to another. He began to believe that his escape really would succeed. The long run of successes, the heady sense of freedom, and the excitement of his dangerous situation buoyed him up to a point where he felt light-headed.

He was disturbed by his reactions to the women he encountered; even the least attractive seemed to have some redeeming feature. Sitting opposite to him in the train for much of the way was a young woman wearing a short black skirt and a thin white blouse, with a small gold locket on a chain round her neck. He caught himself watching the gilded trinket as it swung between her breasts and hurriedly turned his head to look out of the window. This was hardly the time to get himself arrested for molesting young women in railway carriages. He smothered an involuntary grin at the thought. At least he could still laugh at himself and perhaps Yvette would be kind to him for old times' sake. He fell into a pleasant dream about the welcome she would extend to him when her long-lost boy turned up on her doorstep.

There were more soldiers at the station when they arrived. He dreaded being stopped and asked for his papers, but he got free of the station without being challenged. He passed the restaurant where he had dined with Yvette on the leave he had spent with her. It appeared to be doing a thriving business, but most of the clientele wore grey uniforms.

He hurried along the streets towards her flat. Unfortunately it was an apartment building with an outer door that required a key to open it. Unless you had a key you had to ring for the *concierge*. Barney rang the bell, trusting devoutly that she would not remember him from his last visit. She was a stout, red-faced woman, with sharp black eyes, and he felt uncomfortable at the way she looked at him when he asked for Madame Gallimard.

'Madame is not at home,' she said. She sounded pleased at having disappointed him.

'Is she away?' Barney inquired.

'No. Madame is out—I don't know what time she will return. Do you want to leave a message?'

Barney shook his head. It was a set-back, but not a disaster. There was a café across the road. He could go and have another bowl of soup and another glass of wine and keep watch on the apartment.

He had a long wait. He spun out his frugal meal as long as he dared, but when it grew dark he felt obliged to leave. He found a niche between Yvette's apartment building and the next-door block and concealed himself in it to continue his wait.

It was nearly ten o'clock before Yvette came home. A car drew up outside the building, a stubby grey car, driven by a soldier. He got out and opened the car door and Yvette got out. She was wearing black, with a silver fox stole round her shoulders, there was a clip at her throat which caught the light as she felt for her key. Her fellow passenger alighted from the other side of the car and walked round the back of it to join her. He was a German officer.

Chapter 9

Barney had a long wait. The car and the driver were waiting for the officer to reappear, which gave him hope that the German would come back quickly, but he stayed with Yvette for two hours. Barney, lodged in a narrow gap between two houses which he shared with a smelly dustbin and from time to time a curious cat, saw no hope but to remain where he was. The streets were almost deserted. He was not sure whether there was a curfew, but he dared not leave his hiding place and risk being challenged by the bored driver.

He flexed his leg muscles from time to time and shifted his feet cautiously. When Yvette's visitor eventually emerged he braced himself and prepared for a quick dash towards the door. It was a large, heavy door on a self-closing spring, which started slowly and then clanged to with a rush. The German opened the door widely with an expansive gesture and stepped out. His driver started to get out, but was apparently told not to bother. The officer opened the car door himself and the engine was already running. The door of the apartment building was slowly closing as the car left the curbside and drove down the road away from Barney. Barney darted forward and caught the door just as it touched the lock. He pushed with all his might and it gave way. He was inside.

The *concierge*'s flat was in darkness. He passed it on tiptoe and made for the stairs, ignoring the lift. Yvette's flat was on the second floor. He was breathless when he reached it. He rang the doorbell and there was a pause before she came to the door.

She had obviously got out of bed. She was wearing a pale oyster-coloured robe beneath which she seemed to be naked. She looked tired and slightly cross. "Did you forget . . .' she asked, and then stopped as Barney moved into the light and she saw who it was.

She stepped back without a word and he entered the flat.

'God almighty, what are you doing here?' she said. She sounded aghast.

Barney went into the living-room before he answered her. There was a bottle of brandy and a couple of used glasses on the table.

'I'm glad to see you're still able to live in the manner to which you are accustomed,' he said. 'I've escaped from prison camp and I'm here to ask for your help. It never occurred to me that you might have a German lover. Is he the reason why you didn't want me to write to you?'

He found a clean glass and poured himself some brandy. Yvette went past him and sat down on the sofa. Her robe fell open and showed a long line of white leg. She smelt of sex. Barney looked away and swallowed some brandy.

'I don't propose to justify myself to you, *mon gars,*' Yvette said. 'It's a disaster for me that you are here and, yes, Wilhelm is the reason why I didn't want to be in communication with a British officer in a French work camp.'

'Are you going to turn me out?'

'No, that would be too dangerous. Did anyone see you come in?'

'No.'

'You're sure?'

'Completely sure. But I did call earlier and ask for you at the *conciergerie.*'

'No doubt I shall hear about that tomorrow from Madame Robert. We shall have to take great care to conceal your presence from her. She would be delighted to betray me. You can stay the night. In the morning I must make arrangements to get you out of here. Have you any plans?'

'I thought perhaps I could get into the Unoccupied Zone and from there into Spain.'

She considered this for a long, frowning minute. 'It's possible,' she said at last. 'It will cost money.'

She saw his doubtful look and added, 'More than you are likely to have about you at the moment, I imagine?'

'I was hoping for a loan, repayable after the war.'

For the first time a slight, ironic smile appeared on her face. 'I admire your sublime faith! You are sure you will survive —and that the British will win the war?'

'I'm sure we will win, yes,' Barney said steadily. 'If I don't make a successful escape all you will have to do is apply to my brother. He will repay you.'

'On nothing but my word?'

'Yes.'

Again she smiled, but this time with a touch of sadness. 'I think, *ma mie,* that you are very fortunate in your brother,' she said. 'Very well, I will arrange funds for you. Repayment will not be necessary. The money comes from your government.'

Barney's head jerked up as light dawned on him. 'Yvette, are you in the Resistance?'

She put a hand over his mouth. 'Don't say it, not out loud,

not even within these four walls. You must know nothing—nothing.'

She gave him some food and made him up a bed on the sofa. He made no comment, but on his way to the bathroom he saw into her bedroom with the big, tumbled, familiar bed and a spasm of anger gripped him. She guessed what he was thinking, but said nothing, merely looking at him with a cynical, mocking expression on her face, until he burst out, 'Yvette, how can you? Doesn't he disgust you?'

'Surprisingly, no. He is kind and somewhat stupid. A hog, but not a bad hog. What was it you said in a joke once about the advice given by a Victorian mother to a bride—"Close your eyes and think of England"? I close my eyes and think of France.'

He was shamed by the sudden flame in her eyes. 'Is it worth it?' he asked.

'From time to time, yes. I am useful. Barney, I have told you, you must know *nothing.*'

'I'm sorry, I won't ask any more questions.'

He was comfortable enough on the wide, well-cushioned sofa, but for the second night he could not sleep. He wanted Yvette. At one point in the night he almost got up and went to her. He wanted to drive out the memory of her German lover by the force of his own body, but the realization that she would probably reject him kept him where he was. He tossed and turned and when he slept his dreams were disquietingly erotic.

He was still asleep when Yvette came out of her bedroom in the morning, his long brown limbs sprawled among the bedclothes which he had thrown off as he twisted about in the night. Something about his complete abandonment to sleep aroused a brooding tenderness in her. She studied his unconscious face and considered its strengths and weaknesses: the strong, determined chin, the mouth with its full lower lip which could give him a sulky look when he pushed it out in displeasure, the beautiful planes of his cheek bones, the heavy eyebrows, the unexpected new streak of white in his hair. He looked very young, but there were lines on his face which had not been there a year ago. Yvette sighed for the bad, carefree boy who had gone forever as she bent over to waken him.

She was brisk and business-like with him over breakfast.

'I must go out,' she said. 'While I am out you must be very quiet. Move around as little as possible; if you use the toilet don't flush it; answer the door to no one.'

'Does your German have a key?'

'No.'

He spent a long, lonely, boring day. Yvette did not return until early evening.

'Everything is arranged,' she said. 'You are to leave here and go to the Café Roland. You are to wear a yellow handkerchief, which I will give you, tucked in the breast pocket of your jacket. You will order a carafe of white wine and a man will come and sit at your table and say: "White wine is best . . . when the day is hot." The pause is important, and you must reply in the same manner: "I only drink red wine . . . after October." '

'Very cloak and dagger,' Barney commented.

'Don't mock. These precautions are necessary. Now, go into the bedroom and remain hidden there while I divert Madame Robert. I am going to ask her to help me take a small table I no longer require down to the *cave* in the basement. While she is safely out of the way you must run down the stairs and out of the front door. Is that understood?'

Barney nodded. 'Does this mean I shan't see you again?' he asked.

'Yes, it is better so.'

'Yvette, are you under suspicion?'

She smiled, with an element of pity for his innocence. 'The French mistress of a high-ranking German officer is inevitably under suspicion,' she said. 'There is no continued surveillance kept on me, but I believe that more than once my flat has been searched in my absence.'

'If they had come here today . . . !' Barney exclaimed.

'Life would have been very uncomfortable for both of us,' Yvette said. 'Now, hide yourself and as soon as Madame Robert and I have carried the little table out and gone down in the lift, get down the stairs and away. You remember the Café Roland?'

'I went there with you, didn't I? Left at the bottom of this road and then the second turning on the right?'

'Good. So now I must say goodbye to you, my Barney, and I can only hope we shall meet again in better times.'

He touched her arm and would have kissed her, but she stepped back, away from him, and shook her head. 'No, I don't want to remember . . . anything that has gone before. Here is the handkerchief. Remember what you have to say—and good luck.'

He waited in the bedroom until he heard her and the *concierge* leave the flat, then he moved quietly out. The front door of the flat had been left open. He heard the crash of the lift doors and the rumble as it went down, then he ran lightly and swiftly down the stairs and out into the street.

The Café Roland was disquietingly full of Germans. Barney sat down in an inconspicuous corner. He pulled the yellow handkerchief into a prominent position, caught the waitress's eye and ordered a carafe of *vin blanc*.

He was still waiting to be served when a group of three German officers came in. They looked round, conferred together and then sat down at Barney's table, the only one with vacant seats. His wine came, but before he had time to pour it out a hand smote him on the shoulder.

'*Bonsoir, Jean,*' a voice behind him said. 'Marc, Philipe and I have been saving a place for you at our table. What are you drinking? Oh, white wine! White wine is best . . . when the day is hot.'

He looked round. The boy who was speaking to him could not have been more than eighteen. He had a thin, lively face and the grin he gave Barney was full of mischief.

'I only drink red wine . . . after September,' Barney said. It sounded stilted in the extreme.

'So early?' the boy said with an exaggerated lift of his eyebrows. Too late, Barney remembered that the month should have been October. He felt perspiration breaking out on his forehead. The boy laughed and clapped him on the shoulder again. 'Bring your wine over and join us,' he suggested.

As he joined the Frenchmen the young boy said, 'It was unfortunate that they should have sat down with you, but amusing, don't you think? I am Alain, this is Marc and Philippe has gone to the telephone to report that we have located you.'

'I was afraid you wouldn't spot me,' Barney said.

'I was given an excellent description of you, and that white tuft of hair is very distinctive.'

'A damned sight too distinctive,' Marc put in. He was an older man, with the thickset body and hardened hands of a labourer. 'We shall have to get rid of it, dye it out.'

'I agree. As soon as you have finished your wine, Jean, we will leave and I will take you to the place where you are to spend the night. Tomorrow you will move on, but I have to warn you that it may be several days before we can get you across the demarcation line.'

Barney glanced round. Surely it was the height of folly to be discussing such things in a crowded bar? Then he saw that the noise and the crowd were as good a cover as any other. There was something about Alain's carefree approach that was infectious, or perhaps it was the wine. His situation began to seem less desperate, more of an adventure.

They took him away shortly after that and installed him in a room in a sleazy flat where he had to sleep on the floor. The hardness of it seemed to suit him, or perhaps he was worn out after his previous restless nights, and he slept like a log.

Alain called for him the next day. 'First we must paint out that white *mèche* of yours,' he said. 'I have the bottle here.' He worked busily and soon Barney had lost the white hair which had grown over his wound.

'It's been decided that you should keep your identity as Jean-Luc Ferrier, since he is, most fortunately, a citizen of

Lyons. Your *pièce d'identité* is being forged and will be ready for you by this afternoon when we leave, also your *carte d'alimentation,* so that you will be able to eat.'

'It sound as though you expect me to spent some time in Lyons,' Barney said in dismay. 'I was hoping to pass through quickly on my way to the Spanish border.'

Alain held up his hand. 'You mustn't tell me anything about your plans after I pass you on. That will be for someone else to manage, but you must realize that these things can't always be arranged at a moment's notice and it will cause far less trouble if you seem to be a legal occupant of the Free Zone with your papers in order.'

'I suppose so,' Barney said. He felt he sounded grudging, but he was conscious of sharp disappointment at the possibility of delay.

'We want you to do something for us in return for our help —take some money through to Lyons.'

'Won't that be risky?'

'For you, yes. It will make the Germans quite sure you are a spy if you're caught. You mustn't be caught, *mon vieux.*'

Alain treated it as a joke, but Barney did not like it, even though some of the money was to pay for his own escape.

The following day he was passed on to a taciturn farmer with land near Châlons-sur-Saône and discovered that he might have to wait days for the opportunity to cross over the line which was now so near. He was lodged in a hot little attic and had to stay there during the daytime.

'We're taking a risk by having you here at all,' the farmer said when he asked if he could go out. 'If you don't like it, you can go.'

On the third day, when he was beginning to think he would go crazy from sitting around doing nothing, he heard an unusual stir of activity in the yard down below. Usually it was deserted during the day, with everyone, including the women, out working in the fields. There was a skylight in the sloping roof of the attic. Barney stood on his rough camp bed and

/213

looked out. There were German soldiers in the yard, two men and an N.C.O., and two dogs.

Barney's hand went to the wound on his arm, still tender from the bite the Berblinger's dog had given him. It had been damnably painful, and that had been nothing but an undernourished little cur. These dogs were Alsatians, heavy, powerful animals, trained to bring a man down.

He looked round. If it came to it, his only chance of escape was through the skylight and over the roof, and there was no real hope that he would get away.

He tried to watch what the Germans were doing, but the amount he could see was limited. They seemed to be searching the barns and outhouses. The dogs were held on a leash, sniffing at the hay. One shed seemed to interest them particularly. They pawed at the door, barking excitedly. It looked as if the farmer was trying to stop the soldiers from opening it, but in the end he shrugged his shoulders and spread his hands in a hopeless gesture.

The door was pulled open, a small black animal darted out and the dogs went mad. One soldier was holding both leashes while the other one opened the door. The combined strength of the two dogs was too much for him. He was pulled off his feet, let go of the leashes, and the dogs were free.

Barney could not make out what was happening. He heard a lot of noise, barking and yelping, squawking from frightened hens, shouts. Then there was a long silence. He sat and waited. A car engine started up. Were the Germans leaving? He looked out, but could see nothing, only a dusty yard settling back into its usual daytime emptiness.

The farmer explained that evening. 'The Huns come round and do a routine inspection every so often. They know people get over the line from around here. I borrowed a bitch on heat from one of my neighbours to keep here while you were in the house.' A very slight smile showed for a moment on his dour face. 'I told them not to open that shed.'

'Weren't they suspicious?'

'I hope not—we're moving you out tonight.'

It was a dark, moonless night. Everything appeared quiet as the farmer took Barney across the fields towards the river, but the man seemed on edge and Barney shared his uneasiness. He guessed the same thought was in both their minds—that the Germans had allowed themselves to be diverted too easily.

They reached the river bank and crouched down.

'There's a barge coming down the river whose skipper will take you all the way to Lyons,' the farmer explained. He shifted uneasily. 'If he doesn't show up in two minutes I'll have to leave you.'

A pin-point of light showed from the darkness on the water.

'That's him! Come on!'

The haste with which he pushed Barney down the bank and into the tiny rowing boat which had come out from the barge betrayed how anxious he was to get rid of him. Barney muttered a word of thanks, but he did not stay to listen.

The little boat moved over the water towards a larger shape in mid-stream. The man rowing it spoke in a whisper.

'Get under the tarpaulin and stay there until I tell you it's O.K. to move.'

The barge was carrying some particularly foul-smelling chemical fertilizer. Barney crawled into the space which had been made for him under one of the tarpaulins and hoped that the sacks surrounding him were not as noxious as they smelt.

They moved off at first light and about half an hour later the bargee gave a thump on the tarpaulin.

'Keep very quiet,' he said. 'We're just coming up to the German check-point.'

The engine slowed, then stopped. He heard feet on the deck and then voices. One of the tarpaulins near him was thrown back and he saw a gleam of light, then the footsteps moved away again. The steady 'pukka-pukka-pukka' of the engine started up again, he felt the dull throb of its beat all through his body. They were under way. He had done it. The

French might intern him if they saw through his disguise, but he was no longer in danger of being thrown into a German prison camp.

Even so, he found it difficult to relax during the long, slow journey and it was a relief when the river at last wound its way into Lyons, even though this meant that he was once again on his own in a strange town.

He went to the café where he had been told someone would contact him, but this time something seemed to have gone wrong. He sat, very slowly drinking his way through the small amount of wine he allowed himself, and no one approached him. Late in the evening he made what he hoped sounded like a casual inquiry about a room for the night.

'Everywhere's packed to the doors,' the waitress said. 'But we might have a room free because I know someone left today. I'll send Charlot over to you. Charlot!'

The proprietor came over to Barney's table. 'You want a room? For how long?'

'Probably two nights,' Barney said. It would be prudent, he thought, to allow for somewhere to stay the following night if no one had contacted him. After that he would have to move on and make his own arrangements.

He used his ration card and was relieved to find that it was received without question. He had to give up food coupons for everything he ate at the café and he realized that the food he had been enjoying on his trip down the river must have been obtained on the black market, since the meat alone far exceeded the ration which never legally rose above a hundred and twenty grammes a week.

His first nervousness had subsided and he sat with fatalistic calm on his second evening, waiting to see what would happen. This time he was rewarded, but not in the way he had expected. He was glancing idly through a newspaper when a voice said doubtfully, 'Monsieur Ferrier?'

He looked up quickly. Standing in front of him was an elderly man, on the short side, with grey hair and an anxious look on his face. He was dressed in a black suit, very shabby, and he twisted a cloth cap between his hands as he stood in front of Barney's chair.

'Yes,' Barney said. 'I am Jean-Luc Ferrier.'

A look of puzzlement came over the other man's face. 'It is perhaps no more than a coincidence,' he said. 'I am Alphonse Ferrier. My son . . . he is also called Jean-Luc. Forgive me, monsieur . . . I had hoped . . . we have had no news of him for months.'

Barney was too taken aback to speak and he could only gaze helplessly at this sad, apologetic little man.

Out of all the thousands of inhabitants of Lyons how the devil had he managed to become known to the father of the real Jean-Luc?

'Monique Lejeune, who works here, brought her shoes to me for mending,' Alphonse Ferrier explained. 'She told me that there was someone staying at the café who bore the same name as my son. She said, too, that he seemed not quite at ease, not quite sure of himself . . . I thought . . . it was foolish of me . . . perhaps a loss of memory . . ."

His voice tailed away and Barney pulled himself together.

'I think perhaps it would be as well if we went up to my room to talk,' he said.

He led the little man up to his sparsely-furnished room on the second floor.

'I can give you news of your son,' he said abruptly. He saw the hope dawning on the older man's face and added quickly, 'Not good news. I very much regret to have to tell you, Monsieur Ferrier, that your son was killed in an air raid while we were being transferred from the hospital in France to a work camp in Germany.'

Alphonse Ferrier sat down heavily on the one hard chair the room contained. 'It was what we feared,' he said. 'You are quite sure . . . ?'

'I was with him when he died,' Barney said. 'He lived for only a few minutes after the bomb had fallen.'

He waited for the next inevitable question, but for the moment the father of the man whose identity he had stolen was taken up by his private grief. Barney used the pause to make up his mind what to do. Was there anything to be lost by speaking the truth? Alphonse Ferrier already knew that his identity was false, but somehow Barney did not think he was likely to denounce him.

'I have some things that belong to you,' he said. He fetched out the black leather wallet he had carried ever since he had taken it from Jean-Luc's pocket. It contained little enough: a couple of photographs—and now that he looked at them again he could see Alphonse Ferrier in one of them, looking somewhat younger—a letter from home, a religious medallion.

'I made the wallet for him and his mother gave him the St Christopher on the day he joined up,' Alphonse Ferrier said, taking the medallion in his hand. 'She'll be glad to know he had it with him . . . ' He looked up. 'She would like to see you, I think, monsieur. Anything you can tell her, anything at all . . . we have waited so long for news.'

Barney hesitated. 'I'll come to see you, if I may, tomorrow,' he said. 'This evening . . . it is necessary for me to be here in the café.'

Monsieur Ferrier looked at him with puzzled eyes, but he did not ask any questions. 'I'll give you my address,' he said.

'I have it,' Barney pointed out gently. 'Unless you have moved?'

'No, we are still at the same place.'

'It would be a great help to me if you would not talk about me to anyone except your wife until we meet again,' Barney said.

For the first time something like an understanding of his situation seemed to penetrate. Alphonse Ferrier nodded. 'I'll keep quiet,' he said.

Barney went back to his seat at the café table, but nothing more happened. No one attempted to speak to him. Something had gone wrong with the arrangements which had been made for him in Dijon. He spent hours turning it over in his mind that night and in the morning he decided to tell his 'father' the truth.

It was a difficult interview. He was shamed by the dignified grief of the two middle-aged people as he described, as kindly as possible, the fate of their son. When he had finished, Madame Ferrier wiped her eyes on the edge of her flowered apron.

'He is with God,' she said with simple conviction. 'He was a good boy. He was born to us rather late, our only child. It is hard, hard, to lose a son, monsieur.'

'My own son has also been killed in an air raid,' Barney said. He could not think why he chose to confide in this simple couple. He scarcely ever thought now of his baby's death. The little life had never become real to him and with all he had been through since, he had almost forgotten his first anger. 'He was only six weeks old.'

Madame Ferrier exclaimed in horror, her own troubles momentarily forgotten.

'Was that in France, monsieur?' Alphonse Ferrier asked quietly.

'No, it was in England,' Barney said. 'I am a British Army officer, trying to get home. I took your son's identity and it has served me well until now. It's because of me that you were not notified sooner of his death; you must forgive me.'

'It matters very little. We had a few more months of hope, but always in our hearts we knew he must be dead. What are your plans, monsieur?'

'I was to have been contacted here in Lyons and taken to the Spanish border, but the arrangements seem to have broken down. I think I shall have to make my own way.'

'I've heard of such things being done,' Alphonse Ferrier said. 'It's possible I may be able to help you. I'll make some inquiries. Will you be staying on at the café?'

'I think not, particularly since I've already made your friend Monique suspicious of me.'

'Monique is a good girl, she'll keep a still tongue in her head,' Madame Ferrier said. She exchanged a quick look with her husband. 'It would be best perhaps if you came here, monsieur.'

'I don't want to bring the police down on you,' Barney said.

'We'll say you are a nephew, with the same name as our dead son.' Monsieur Ferrier spoke with a sudden gleam in his eye. 'I'd like to put something over these German swine. We haven't got them quartered on us here, but they've swallowed up the rest of France and it'll only be a matter of time before they move south. I know them! I fought them in the last war.'

It was a relief to Barney to leave the café, even though it meant severing his only link with the Dijon organization. He settled in with 'Tante Marie' and 'Oncle Alphonse' and was relieved when they allowed him to pay a small amount towards the cost of his board and lodging since he could see that times were not easy for them. It was a bad time, he discovered, to be a shoemaker. Not that there was any lack of work; Alphonse could have made his fortune if he had been able to get the materials he needed.

'There is no meat, therefore there are no hides to provide the leather to make shoes or repair them,' he explained. 'I ask myself where they have all gone, these animals we no longer slaughter? And I will tell you the answer—they have gone to Germany! I am a skilled craftsman and here I am whittling clogs so that my old customers can have something to put on their feet. A year or two more and I'll have forgotten how to make a decent pair of shoes!'

It was several days before he was able to tell Barney, 'I think I've found someone who might help you on your way. His name is Louis Lamartine.'

Madame Ferrier made a disparaging noise and Alphonse hurried on, 'Yes, yes, I know; he's a scoundrel, but it's known that he travels south quite frequently—on business, he says.'

'Black market,' Madame Ferrier supplied.

'Very possibly. But me, I mend his shoes, and I can tell you they don't get the sort of wear I see in them from walking city pavements. He has been in the mountains, and more than once. I believe he's in touch with the smugglers of Andorra.'

'Just the sort of person I need,' Barney said. 'Do you think he'll take the risk of helping me?'

'For money, Louis will do anything,' Alphonse said.

Barney found that he was right about this. A meeting took place between Barney and Louis Lamartine and a bargain was struck. Louis would take Barney to the frontier, to L'Hospitalet, and introduce him to some 'friends.' The status of these 'friends' was delicately left in doubt, but since he was confident that they knew all the mountain paths and could put him into Spain without touching the Spanish customs post it seemed that Alphonse was probably right and they were engaged in Andorra's principal industry of smuggling.

Barney was rather taken with Louis, a cheerful rogue who did not pretend to any motive but greed for helping an escaped prisoner. He bounced through life like a rubber ball, verbose and unworried by the possible hazards of his occupation.

'Everything can be bought, if the price is right, *mon vieux,*' he confided to Barney. 'Patriotism? Very fine, for those who can afford it. Charity? I leave that to the religious; it's their price for getting into heaven. I'm doing you a service, right? I expect to be paid for it.'

'How much?'

'Fifteen thousand francs.'

'You can't be serious!'

'Consider the risks, consider the outgoings! I could lose my livelihood if I got caught. So pay up and look cheerful, *mon vieux*—or stay where you are.'

'What do I get for this huge sum of money?'

'My company to the border, an introduction to a guide who will accompany you through the mountains of Andorra, and—most important of all—someone to meet you in Spain and take you to Barcelona.'

After some hard bargaining Barney eventually beat him down to twelve thousand francs. 'For one man alone it is hardly a paying proposition,' Louis said reproachfully. 'If you were one of a party . . . however, for once I will allow my heart to rule my head. Twelve thousand it is, and believe me, you are the first to have got the better of Louis Lamartine.'

Since he still managed to look remarkably cheerful, Barney deduced that he was still sure of a profit and, once the bargain was struck, Louis lost no time in putting his arrangements in hand. Ten days after his arrival in Lyons Barney said an affectionate farewell to his 'aunt' and 'uncle.' Madame Ferrier insisted on embracing him and he bent his tall head down and kissed her warmly, but when she tried to give him her dead son's religious medallion he wanted to refuse it. Only when he saw her hurt look did he allow her to hang it round his neck.

He clasped Alphonse Ferrier warmly by the hand. Alphonse smote him on the shoulder and cleared his throat. *'Bon chance, bon voyage,'* he said gruffly.

'After the war I'll come back,' Barney promised.

'You English—you still think you are going to win?' Louis asked.

'Certainly. And so do you or you wouldn't be helping me.'

'I believe in hedging my bets,' Louis said with total seriousness.

The Ferriers' anxiety to find out what had happened to their son reminded him more forcibly than ever of his own family at home and the distress his long silence must be causing them. He asked Louis about sending a message to them.

'Certainly,' Louis said. 'You can send a telegram.'

'A *telegram?* To England?'

'Oh, yes! From the Free Zone I assure you it is possible. Keep it short and do not give an address or sign your full name. I will see that it is sent from another town. It will be more discreet not to attempt to send it from Lyons.'

Barney wrote: 'Safe and well. Hope to be home soon. Start fattening up a suitable calf,' and addressed his message to Dan.

The journey to L'Hospitalet was by no means as straightforward as Louis had made it sound, although he was able to provide transport in the shape of a battered car which ran, as did most of the vehicles on the roads, on gazogene from a charcoal-fired burner housed in a trailer at the back. The power it provided was not always sufficient and more than once Barney had to get out and push the car up a hill. It also seemed to him that Louis was going by a very roundabout route, but since he said it was for the sake of safety Barney did not quarrel with this. He was less patient when Louis made one or two 'business calls' on the way and he was far from pleased when he discovered that he was to be parked for a couple of days in a flea-ridden little inn where Louis appeared to be well-known, while Louis went on alone to make arrangements for the next stage of his journey.

It was the third day after they left Lyons before they arrived at L'Hospitalet-près-l'Andorre.

'From here you have to walk. That's your route,' Louis said, indicating a track which led away from the side of the road where they were standing. He looked round him with a slightly anxious air which began to affect Barney.

'Are your friends late for the rendezvous?' he asked.

'No, we are a little early, I think.' He pointed triumphantly down the rough track. 'There they are!'

Two men were coming towards them with the steady, loping stride of the mountaineer, both tall and thin, both carrying heavy packs on their backs. The one in front raised a hand in greeting.

'That's Miguel and behind him is his brother, Ramon,' Louis said.

He greeted the two men in a patois Barney was unable to follow. They seemed to be as silent as he was talkative. They merely nodded and slipped the heavy packs off their backs. Louis opened the back of his car and the contents of the packs were transferred, then he took out his wallet and began counting money. He paused as if he thought he had paid enough, but the elder of the two men, the one called Miguel, uttered one laconic phrase and Louis reluctantly added another thousand francs to the wad of notes he had handed over.

He waved a hand at Barney and Miguel and Ramon looked at him closely. 'You can walk?' Miguel enquired in good French.

Barney nodded. 'As far as is necessary.'

'Tonight it won't be far. You will go with us to Les Bons, where we live. Tomorrow will be harder, over the mountains and into Spain. You must be prepared to keep going.'

'So now we must say good-bye,' Louis Lamartine said, holding out his hand. 'Good luck, *mon vieux!*'

He seemed anxious to get away with his load of contraband and, after a quick word with the two brothers from Andorra, he climbed into his cumbersome car and drove off.

'So, now we start,' Miguel said.

They set off in single file, Miguel leading the way, Barney in the middle and Ramon in the rear. They walked fast and Barney soon began to find the pace difficult to keep up on a track which became steadily steeper. He had to stop at one point to get his breath back. 'Are we actually in Andorra yet?' he asked.

'We are following the line of the border,' Ramon said. 'But soon, at the point where the river runs south, we turn away from it and go over the Solana d'Andorra, then we follow the Riu San Josep until we reach the path which leads down into Soldeu. After that you will be safe.'

'Am I not safe now?'

'By no means. The French police could quite easily challenge us at this point. However, we are not usually unlucky.'

He had said enough to reconcile Barney to their forced march. He became as anxious as the two brothers to hurry. It was not pleasant walking; the path, such as it was, was of a kind of loose shale, of granite hardness; it slid beneath the feet and cut into Uncle Jakob's boots, which Barney was still wearing. He felt his feet growing sore and his ankles ached from the effort of keeping his balance on the loose stones. Miguel and Ramon, he noticed enviously, might have been walking across a grassy meadow. He stumbled and slid behind them, especially as the path began to lead downwards towards Soldeu. They had been walking for about two hours.

The two brothers did not pause at the village, but led Barney straight on, along the valley close to the river. He was beginning to feel very tired, but at least this was a little easier than the mountain track had been. He looked with misgiving towards the southern mountains.

Les Bons was a small group of grey houses, built into the hillside out of the same rough stone which had been giving him so much trouble on the mountain paths. They gave him a meal and a rough bed, but it seemed to Barney that he had no sooner stretched himself out and laid his head down than he was being shaken awake again. Miguel threw back the shutters. A glimmer of grey light was just beginning to show in the east.

Before he put on his boots Barney examined with some misgivings a blister which had been raised the previous day on the side of his left heel. It seemed to have grown bigger during the night, a pocket of liquid under stretched blue skin. He teased some wool out of the paillasse of fleeces on which he had been lying and used it to pad the boot in the hope of easing the friction.

Miguel's wife gave them a thick omelette and strong, hot coffee before they left.

'Real coffee,' Barney said appreciatively. It was the first he had had since before Dunkirk. A taste of freedom, he thought fancifully; though presumably there was little coffee to be had in England at the present time.

It occurred to him as they set out that he had given very little thought in recent weeks to what he was likely to find when he arrived in England. He had been able to obtain some Swiss newspapers while he was in Lyons, which at least gave him some idea of the present situation of the war, but he was still quite ignorant of how it had affected ordinary life at home. The situation seemed to be about as bad as it could be. The Russians had been at war with Germany since June and it was obvious that things were going badly for them. Nothing, it seemed, could stop the advance of the army of the Reich, but at least Hitler's ambitions in the east had diverted his mind from the invasion of the British Isles.

Had Dan received his message? Had he passed it on to Rilla? It was a long time since Barney had thought about Rilla, but now he allowed himself the luxury of conjuring her up in his mind. The picture was not very clear, but he remembered her beautiful eyes, her silky hair, the endearing way she had of catching her lip between her teeth and, above all, the exquisite texture of her skin, like white satin. There was one thing about being married; once he got home he would not have to go out hunting for a woman; he had one ready and waiting for him and, as he stumbled along in the semi-darkness behind Miguel and Ramon, he felt that he could hardly wait to get home and get his arms round her. The plain truth was it did not much matter whether it was Rilla, or Yvette, or Candida—he had almost forgotten about Candida, but she had been damned good value in the past—or anyone. He was starving for the sight and sound and feel of a woman and he would make do with whatever came his way.

An hour later all thoughts of sex had faded from his mind. He could think of nothing but the agony of putting one foot in front of the other and keeping up with Miguel and Ramon. They strode along, apparently unworried by the ruggedness of the trail, and they both had packs on their backs which he estimated weighed about a hundred pounds each. He had believed himself to be reasonably fit, but as the day wore on he realized the vast difference between the walking he had done earlier and the demands of the Pyrenees. The sun got up and blazed down unrelentingly on the three tiny figures toiling up the mountainside. Thirst was a torture, but there seemed to be no water in this barren, rocky landscape.

They stopped at midday for a brief snack. The sun was directly overhead, but Barney managed to find a patch of shade in the shelter of a great rock and sank down thankfully. They gave him a slab of cheese between two pieces of dry bread and a swig from a bottle of rough local wine which only temporarily quenched his thirst. He undid his left boot and examined the blister on his heel. It had broken and the liquid inside had soaked through his sock, sticking it to his flesh. The skin tore as he pulled the fabric away and underneath the place was raw. He spilt a few drops of red wine on it with the vague idea that it had antiseptic properties. The sting of the acidic wine on the open wound set his teeth on edge. He put his sock and boot back on, wincing as the rough wool grated against the bare flesh. No matter what it felt like he had no choice but to keep on walking.

The brothers watched him in silence. They were wearing rope-soled canvas shoes. It hardly seemed possible that they would survive the roughness of the ground, but they did grip the surface and Miguel and Ramon had no difficulty walking in them.

They toiled on, mostly upwards, but sometimes they were forced to descend, and then they had the added labour of climbing back up again. The rock was darker in colour, the boulders were bigger; there was no visible path and yet the brothers seemed to have no hesitation about the route they were following. The heat had a sultry intensity now and black clouds were massing over the peaks ahead of them.

'There will be a storm,' Miguel said.

'We get a lot of thunderstorms at this time of the year,' Ramon added.

It did not appear to concern them. They just kept on walking. The muscles of Barney's calves and thighs ached to the point where he was afraid to ask for a rest in case he was unable to get started again, and the raw place on his left heel throbbed with pain at every step.

The storm hit them at about four o'clock in the afternoon. The air darkened and heavy drops of rain began to fall on the dry rocks. The temperature dropped dramatically and yet the air did not seem any fresher. Thunder reverberated through the mountains, echoing and re-echoing from one peak to the next.

The lightning shot across the sky in great jagged darts. A little wind sprang up and then the rain came down in torrents.

They stopped when the rain came down too heavily for them to see where they were going, huddling against an overhanging rock, but it was made plain to Barney that it was more important that the great packs should not become sodden than that mere human beings should keep dry. The rain soaked through his shirt and trousers and, whereas he had been overheated before, he now began to feel chilled to the bone.

The wine bottle was circulated and it did put a little heart into him.

'How much further?' he asked.

'Another hour, perhaps two, then we will take a little rest,' Miguel said. 'The worst part is still to come.'

It was not a very encouraging answer. Barney bit back his dismayed exclamation and concentrated on easing his tired limbs while he still had the chance. The worst of the storm was over in half an hour, but the thunder still rumbled round the hills and the lightning still flashed across the sky as they set off again. Worst of all the rain was still falling in a thin, persistent drizzle making the rocky path treacherously slippery.

As Barney had feared, the rest and the change in temperature had stiffened his legs and the first few hundred yards were agony. He stumbled along, shivering with cold where before he had been drenched in perspiration; his preoccupation with his aches and pains made him careless. They were going downhill when his foot slipped on a flat slab of rock. He fell full length and when he was able to get up he felt a sharp pain in his knee. One of his hands, where he had flung it out to save himself, was bleeding and pitted with sharp pieces of grit.

He told Miguel and Ramon that he was not hurt, but he saw them look at one another and Miguel said something in a low voice which he did not understand. Going up the next slope the pain from his knee was almost unbearable. The brothers were well ahead of him. They waited for him to catch up, but when he reached them they were talking again in the patois he did not understand.

His legs gave way and he fell to the ground in front of them.

'You're slowing us up too much,' Miguel said. 'If you can't keep up, we'll go on without you. Get on your feet.'

Barney tried to get up. He got to his knees and put his injured knee down on a piece of broken rock. Pain ran up into his groin. He stood up and staggered off the path to a rough boulder and leaned against it, retching. The sour wine he had drunk came up into his mouth and he spat it out.

Ramon came up behind him. He pointed to the mountain ahead of them. 'We've got to cross that coll before nightfall, otherwise we'll be late for the rendezvous in Spain tomorrow. You wouldn't want to miss that, would you?'

At that moment Barney felt that he would just as soon die on the mountainside, but he managed to shake his head and when they began climbing again he followed them.

It felt as if they were scaling a precipice. More than once Ramon turned back to help him over some particularly difficult stretch and without that help he knew he could not have survived. The rain had stopped, but the wind persisted, whistling eerily through fissures in the rock. The sun was going down and the air was chilly, but Barney was once again bathed in sweat. The breath tore through his lungs in great gasps as he fought his way up the last, almost vertical face. He heard Ramon's voice saying, 'You've done well. Look round you. We're at the top.'

Barney straightened himself up and looked round. The sun had disappeared, but the sky was still red and gold. The black thunder-clouds were edged with light. He was surrounded by mountain peaks, grey upon grey, catching the last of the evening light and fading away into a hazy pink-flushed distance. He turned his back on the two brothers, leaning forward with his hands on his thighs as if to get his breath back, but the sobs that shook him were forced out of him by fatigue and pain.

'Another few kilometres,' Miguel said. 'We must go down into the valley before it grows dark.'

'Can't we stop here?'

'No, it's too high. You'll be more comfortable lower down.'

Darkness crept in on them as they began to descend. Barney found that in some ways it was even harder going downhill than up, certainly it threw more of a strain on his damaged knee. The valley they were making for was merely a dip between two mountains, but it was sheltered and there was a little sparse grass to soften the ground. They had some more food and settled down for the night.

Barney found it impossible to sleep. He was too tired; he was cramped and cold and every muscle in his body ached abominably. When he moved his knee was agony. He dared not take off his boots because he knew that his feet were so swollen that he might not get them on again. He lay as quietly as he could between Ramon and Miguel, who slept as effortlessly as they walked, and was glad when the first pale light began to show in the sky. He wondered whether he should wake Miguel, but it was not necessary. These, apparently, were the hours to which he was accustomed and he woke up of his own accord before the first rays of sunshine penetrated their shadowy hollow.

They resumed the interminable trek. To Barney's relief his knee seemed a little less painful than it had been the night before, but the first few steps were difficult as he tried to shake off his stiffness. He stumbled awkwardly and Miguel looked round with a frown as a stone went clattering down the hillside.

'We must be very careful now that we are in Spain,' Ramon explained in a low voice.

'We're in Spain!' Barney exclaimed.

'Sh—voices carry in the mountains. Yes, we've been in Spain since last night. Didn't you realize?'

Barney shook his head. He gave Ramon a wide, triumphant grin.

230/

'Don't smile too soon,' Ramon said. 'Our way still lies through the mountains and it's not easy.'

They settled down again into the same steady rhythm. With Ramon following him Barney tried not to show that he was soon reduced to limping once more. The light was still too dim to see anything more than the ground in front of him, with Miguel's feet usually just ahead on a level with his own head. They kept it up for another two hours and then the ground began a steady descent, until they reached an open space which contained one or two wooden huts. Leading up to the huts was a more obvious track than the faint path they had been following and beyond it were wide green slopes.

'The shepherds bring their flocks up here,' Ramon explained.

A man came out of one of the huts. 'Wait here,' Miguel said to Barney.

He and Ramon went on. They shook hands with the waiting man, slipped the heavy packs from their shoulders and laid them on the ground. He indicated the interior of the hut and they disappeared inside. When they emerged ten minutes later they had fresh packs on their backs. They brought the third man over to Barney.

'This is Juan, who will take you on from here,' Miguel said. He held out his hand. 'Good luck.'

Barney shook hands with both of them and then, without wasting any more time, they turned back the way they had come. As far as he could see, they were as fresh as they had been when they set out the day before.

The new guide spoke very little French, but he managed to make Barney understand that he had a companion who had returned to the valley.

'To fetch a car—for you,' Juan said.

The going was easier now, but the grass made his leather-soled boots slippery and the need to brace himself on the slope sent constant stabs of pain through his knee. They reached some bushes and then a belt of trees. Juan touched Barney on

/231

the arm and pointed. The road was in sight.

They saw the car a long way off, climbing up the twisting road. Like the Andorran brothers, Juan wasted no time in handing Barney over. He scrambled down the bank by the side of the road and opened the car door as soon as it stopped.

"Pedro—Barcelona," he said.

The car started, a little reluctantly. It was an ancient vehicle, but after the hardships he had experienced it seemed as good as a Rolls Royce to Barney. He stretched out his legs luxuriously. He was within touching distance of hot baths, decent food, friends. He could go home to Appleyard and see his mother and Dan and dear old Fluke. Rilla could come and join him, though he wondered in his sudden rush of exhilaration whether he was going to be able to hold out until then before he found himself a woman. How long would they keep him hanging around before they repatriated him, and what were the Spanish girls like?

The car gave them trouble all the way, the engine coughing and spluttering in a way that would have alarmed Barney if he had not been floating along on his wave of euphoria. It finally ground to a halt on the outskirts of Barcelona. Pedro got out and raised the bonnet. He grimaced and scratched his head, then he came back and poked his head through the window. His French was poor, though more extensive than Juan's had been.

"We'll have to push," he said. "There's a garage only a kilometre down the road, but I'd like to get the car into a side street before I leave it."

Fortunately they were on a slope. Pedro got back into the car and Barney went to the back and started pushing. This final exertion when he had thought it was all over was almost too much for him. He felt the sweat breaking out on his forehead as he put his back into it and got the car moving. He was too taken up with his effort to see the two Guardias Civiles coming towards them. It was only when they spoke that he looked up and realized they were telling him to stop.

He straightened up, a sickening dread in his heart. Pedro

got out and broke into voluble explanations. The policemen were asking questions. Desperately, Barney tried to understand what was being said. They wanted to see Pedro's papers. That was not unreasonable, the merest routine. Any policeman would have done the same. He forced himself to lounge carelessly against the side of the car. One of the policemen glanced at him as he handed back Pedro's documentation and obviously asked who he was. For the first time it occurred to Barney that he must look a complete ruffian: unwashed, unshaven, his clothes sweat-soaked and dirty. Pedro hesitated and then did the only thing that was likely to save his skin if Barney's true identity became known. Barney's few words of Spanish were not sufficient to follow what he said, but the way he shook his head and shrugged his shoulders was eloquent. He was protesting that he did not know this man he had picked up by the side of the road.

The interest of the Guardias quickened. They turned to Barney. One of them was holding out his hand. They must be asking for some form of identification.

He looked at them helplessly. He had no papers. He looked up and down the long, empty road. There was no escape.

'I am British,' he said in English. 'An escaped prisoner-of-war.'

They took him into custody, and Pedro too, although Barney backed up his story that they were complete strangers. At the local police station they chattered excitedly over the telephone with superior officers, and then they locked him up. After all his long exertions, his trek through Germany and France, the grinding fatigue of his climb over the Pyrenees, he had reached, not freedom, but a Spanish prison.

Chapter 10

At the end of June 1941, only a few weeks after her holiday with Ann in Weymouth, all Rilla's letters to Barney since the previous November were returned to her. Ann, darting into her room with a breathless request for the loan of some lecture notes, found her collapsed across the bed in floods of tears.

'Rilla, honey, what's happened?' she asked.

'All my letters,' Rilla whispered. 'All my letters, Ann! I wrote and wrote, week after week after week, and he never had any of them! He's dead, I know he is! He must be!'

Ann looked helplessly at the tumbled pile of unopened envelopes. Poor Rilla. Poor, dear, sweet Rilla. She put her arms round her friend and comforted her as best she could, but there was little she could say.

Despairing of her own ability to help Rilla, she put through a telephone call to Dan. She told him, a little diffi-